MEL...
SOPHIA

MELINDA
AND SOPHIA

Susanna Hughes

This book is a work of fiction.
In real life, make sure you practise safe sex.

First published in 1995 by
Nexus
332 Ladbroke Grove
London W10 5AH

Typeset by TW Typesetting, Plymouth, Devon
Printed and bound by
BPC Paperbacks Ltd, Aylesbury

ISBN 0 352 33045 7

One

The soft leather fitted her like a second skin. The hood had been laced so tightly at the back of her head it followed every contour of her face. Her hair had been threaded through a gap in the top of the lacing to form a short pigtail, its flaxen blonde colour a stark contrast to the black leather from which it protruded. There were only two openings in the hood; an oval for the mouth and a small circle at the base of the nose. The eyes were covered, the leather over them padded on the inside to ensure the darkness the hood imposed was total.

Her wrists were bound behind her back, two leather cuffs strapped around them. The cuffs were joined by a single metal link. She was naked apart from the rather old-fashioned full cut black nylon panties all the slaves wore while in transit.

A hand guided her forward down a short, stone-flagged corridor. The corridor, like the cell she had been in, was cool and her nipples were so stiff and puckered they seemed to pull on the surrounding flesh of her breasts, stretching it taut. A door opened in front of her and she felt carpet under her feet as she was led through into another room. She heard footsteps leaving the room and the door close with a loud clunk but she knew she was not alone.

1

'Take your panties off.' The voice was male, its authority absolute.

Melinda managed to wrestle the waistband of the panties down over her hips at the back. She squirmed her hands around to her sides, straining against her bondage, and pulled the black nylon down a little more, alternating between left and right, stretching out her fingers and wriggling her legs until, after a great effort, the panties fell from her thighs and she could step out of them.

'Kneel,' the voice said.

The command thrilled Melinda to the core. It was part of the litany of submission, a symbol of obedience, and the prelude to the pleasure she took in her role as a perfect slave. The knot of excitement the constriction of the bondage had already caused cinched tighter.

She sank to her knees a little awkwardly without the use of her hands for balance. In the darkness behind her blindfold she saw an image of herself kneeling in front of her unknown master, the hood making her anonymous – an object not a person.

'Open your legs,' the voice ordered. Though the English was perfect the man's accent was Italian.

Melinda squirmed her knees apart. The carpet was coarse and scratched her flesh.

'Forehead to the floor,' was the next command.

Gingerly Melinda leant forward, unable to judge precisely how far forward she would have to go. She managed to rest her forehead against the floor without banging her head. The position thrust her buttocks up into the air, her labia almost vertical, framed between her pert buttocks, her bound hands sitting on top of the base of her spine.

'Very pretty.' The tone of the voice had changed.

Melinda heard a rustle of material and felt a draught of air against her flank as the man moved around her.

'Have you been shaved?' He was looking at her almost hairless sex.

'Yes, master,' Melinda replied quickly. It was the only time she was allowed to speak, in response to a direct question.

'I like that,' the man said.

'She needs shaving again.' This came from a female voice with an American accent. It surprised Melinda. For some reason she'd assumed she was alone with the man.

'When were you last shaved?' the man asked.

'Some days, master,' Melinda replied, her voice muffled by her position. Her naturally sparse pubic hair had nevertheless grown a light stubble.

'A lot of *maîtres* insist on it,' the man explained.

'And this is what she wants?' the woman asked.

'Is it, child?' the man asked.

'Yes, master,' Melinda replied with absolute sincerity. Her firm, round breasts were pressed against her knees, the flesh ballooning out at the sides. She felt her nipples, as hard as glass beads, trapped in a sandwich between the two. She was sure they would be able to see evidence of her willingness if they looked at her sex. She knew it was wet.

'The little bitch,' the American said with an expression of disbelief.

'You must not judge her, Mrs Chapman. You do not understand how the *Organisation Internationale des Maîtres* works.'

'I understand only too well.'

'You understand here,' he said tapping his forehead, 'but not here.' He put his hand on his heart. 'If

3

you do not share the desire for submission you cannot possibly understand what she feels.'

'They're really turned on by it?'

'What you see with your own eyes cannot, I think, be faked. And no force is used. The *maîtres* take advantage of –' he searched for the right word '– a natural inclination.'

'Fascinating. And there are places like this all over the world?'

'Not like this. Most are larger with very tight security. We are extremely small by the standard of most establishments and have little in the way of security.'

'The slaves try to escape?'

'The security is to keep the outside world at bay, not to keep the slaves in. We are quite isolated up here fortunately.'

'And where do they come from?'

'The slaves? All over the world. They are usually brought into the organisation by one man, their first master, but after three months they have to be moved. There is an auction. The *maîtres* bid against each other.'

'I see.'

'Would you like to see more?'

'Sophia told you to give me the whole enchilada. She is trying to persuade my husband to become a *maître* . . .'

'And you must give your approval?'

'Oh sure, Harry ain't going to make a move without my say so. Not if he knows what's good for him.'

'You have the necessary premises?'

'We've got this great big house up in Vermont. Nothing for miles. It's already got electronic security better than Fort Knox.'

'Then we will continue.' The man turned to Melinda again. 'Head up,' he commanded.

4

Melinda raised her head. Immediately she felt a hand move to her breast and push it up towards her chin, exposing the flesh normally hidden under its curves.

'This is how they are all marked,' the man said.

'Marked!' The woman's voice rose sharply. Melinda felt the woman's dress brush her arm as she came round to look at what the man was showing her. 'Jesus,' she said under her breath.

Neatly centred under the crescent-shaped crease where the meat of her breast tucked into her chest was a small square containing the letter 'M', etched in purple indelible ink, like a tattoo.

'M for *maître*,' the man explained, dropping Melinda's left breast and pulling up the right where another square M was sited, 'and M for the slave's name, in this case Melinda.'

'And they agree to this?' Melinda could hear the woman was breathless, her voice not properly modulated.

'Oh yes. All the girls must agree to this. And much more.'

'More?'

'They must agree not to speak unless they are spoken to and to obey without question. They are the rules.'

'And if they don't obey?'

'They must agree to be punished.'

'Punished?' Mrs Chapman's voice went up in pitch.

The man laughed softly. 'The relationship between a *maître* and his slave is a matter of mutual duty and obligation. Part of the *maître*'s duty is to design punishments that fit the crime.'

'But you said there was no force.'

'There is not.'

'So if they refuse to be punished?'

5

'They are sent home. They are cut off from the O.I.M. completely.'

'As simple as that?'

'Yes, as simple as that.' He laughed again. 'I can assure you that since the O.I.M. provides them with everything for which they crave, punishment is rarely refused, however intricate. Besides . . .'

'Besides what?'

'Punishment is part of the process; part of their inclination.'

'They like it?'

'Let us put it this way. Their tolerance for punishment is greater than you might expect.'

'Fascinating. And what is your role?'

'Most of the *maîtres*' establishments have someone like me, a major-domo; an overseer. I am responsible for maintaining discipline, for seeing that the slaves do as they are told and carry out their duties to the letter. Some establishments are so large it is necessary to have several overseers to keep good order.'

'All men?'

'No. A lot are women. The slaves fear the women most I am told. They are . . . less forgiving.'

'I can imagine. Does your job entitle you to certain privileges?'

'Only the *maître* and his guests are allowed full knowledge of a slave. I may do anything I choose short of that.'

'How many slaves do you have here?'

'I think we are the smallest of all the houses. Only three. Some houses have sixty to eighty. Is there anything else you would like to see?'

'Yes. Most definitely.' Melinda sensed the woman walking around behind her again. She felt a hand stroke her neck. 'I can touch her, can't I?'

'Of course. The *maître*'s guests are treated as surrogates for the *maître*. There is no distinction.'

Melinda felt the woman's fingers closing on her nipple. In the darkness imposed by the leather hood her sense of touch was exaggerated and her body trembled.

'She's very sensitive,' Mrs Chapman commented. 'I'd like you to continue your demonstration.'

'Demonstration?'

'Of the girl's obedience.'

'You may test her yourself if you wish.'

'Really?' The woman's voice crackled with excitement. 'What would you normally do with a new arrival? She is new, isn't she?'

'Fresh in this morning.'

'So?'

The man hesitated. 'Normally I would . . . I would see if she had been properly trained.'

Mrs Chapman laughed. 'How delicately put.'

Melinda felt her sex throb. Cloaked in darkness and her naked body so openly displayed, the conversation between the two strangers aroused her. They talked about her as an object, not as a person. Her identity, and her ability to make even the smallest choice for herself, had been completely excised. Her wishes and desires were irrelevant though they coincided perfectly with her situation. What she wanted at the most profound level was what she had got. The man had spoken the truth. Fear of being cut off from the *maîtres* was enough to ensure total obedience.

'What is your name?'

'Aldo.'

'Stand in front of her then, Aldo.' The tone of the woman's voice had changed again. It had become deeper and huskier. Melinda could feel her presence

7

immediately behind her, the hem of what felt like a silk skirt brushing the back of her arms. 'Is it true what he says about you, girl?' Mrs Chapman asked. 'Will you obey?'

'Yes, mistress,' Melinda said.

'And that is what you want?'

'Oh yes, mistress,' Melinda replied fervently. She could still feel the impression of the woman's finger on her nipple.

'Well, we'll have to see, won't we? I want to see for myself how well trained you are. Take his cock in your mouth. You understand?'

'Yes, mistress.'

'Do it then,' the woman said irritably.

Melinda heard a zip being undone. She leant forward and her mouth made contact with a hairy, muscled thigh. Groping upward with her lips she came across the shaft of his cock. She could feel it beginning to swell. Opening her mouth wide she anchored her lips around it and sucked it in.

'Well, just look at that,' Mrs Chapman said.

Melinda sucked her cheeks in and felt the cock swell dramatically, the blood pumping into it.

'Is she good at it?' Mrs Chapman asked.

'Yes, I think she is.'

'And all the slaves are trained like this?'

'Oh yes. They must obey without question.'

Melinda was licking the ridge at the bottom of Aldo's glans. In the darkness imposed by the leather hood her sense of touch had increased and she seemed to be able to feel every contour of the man's phallus. It had grown so rapidly it now filled her mouth. She pulled back slightly and began bobbing her head to and fro, hoping to imitate the feeling he would get if his cock was ploughing her sex.

8

'She's very good,' he said, his hand stroking the top of the leather hood. 'Why don't you see for yourself?'

'What do you mean?'

'They're trained to serve both sexes.'

'Really? I didn't . . . my God.'

'Lie down over there,' the man suggested.

'I'd like to see her face. Is that allowed?' the woman asked tentatively.

'Of course.'

Melinda felt the man's hands circle her head. He pushed her forward, so his cock was filling her mouth, its glans deep in her throat, and began loosening the laces of the hood. As light permeated under the leather Melinda screwed up her eyes to protect them. Suddenly the man pulled his phallus out of her mouth, and, taking hold of the top of the leather hood, whipped it off Melinda's head.

'Why, she's just so pretty,' the woman said. She pulled off the band that held Melinda's hair in the pigtail and combed it out with her fingers. 'There now,' she said.

Gingerly, Melinda opened her eyes. The first thing she saw was Aldo's erection, glistening with her saliva. It was quite an ugly object, excessively bent like a bow and gnarled with a network of prominent blue veins. It grew from a forest of wiry pubic hair so profuse it covered most of his belly. Hanging down under the phallus was an equally hairy scrotum, its balls large and heavy.

The man's voice did not match his appearance. His voice had appeared cultured and urbane, but his body was squat, muscular and coarse. He had a barrel chest and short legs, with incredibly broad thighs. He was naked – the denim shorts he had been wearing now around his ankles – and his body was matted with black hair. His head, on the other hand, had been completely shaved. He had a bull-neck, a thickly-boned forehead and small dark brown eyes.

Mrs Chapman was blonde, her hair tied rather severely into a chignon on the back of her head. She had big blue eyes and her features were very symmetrical, with a straight nose and sharp cheekbones. Her mouth was fleshy and wide. She was at least a foot taller than the man and her legs were very long.

She was wearing a cream silk shift that left her shoulders and arms bare. Like the rest of her body they were slender and bony. The skirt was cut above the knee and Melinda could see her bare legs were as well proportioned as the rest of her. Her skin was evenly tanned to a deep bronze.

Her eyes had wandered from Melinda's face to Aldo's erection.

'You know, you're quite a man,' she said. She came to stand in front of him and ran her hand over his thickly-haired chest, then squeezed the well-defined muscles of his bulging biceps. She snaked her hand down to his cock and circled it with her fist. Melinda saw it throb. 'Suck it again, girl,' she ordered.

Melinda leant forward. Only the glans projected from Mrs Chapman's fingers but she wrapped her lips around it and sucked it hard. The man groaned.

'Will she really do it to me?' the blonde whispered to Aldo.

'Anything you want,' he confirmed.

She let go of his erection and walked across the room. They were in a cellar, with no window, the light coming from two opaque glass lamps screwed to the wall. The walls were painted white and the carpet was grey. There was a small table and chair, a comfortable armchair, and an antique wardrobe and chest of drawers of the same type. At the far wall was a single bed. The mattress was covered with a single white sheet and had a wooden frame. Attached to each corner of the frame Melinda could see leather cuffs secured to it by short thick chains.

'Do you want to know the truth?' the woman asked as she sat on the edge of the bed. 'I've never done this before.'

'Do you want me to leave? It's quite permissible.'

'No,' the woman said quickly. 'I definitely want you to stay.'

'Then just tell her what you want.'

'Got it.' The blonde looked at Melinda. 'I think you'd better come over here, girl,' she said, the husky tone returning to her voice.

Melinda crawled forward on her knees. She could see the woman watching as she inched awkwardly towards her, her breasts bobbing up and down. As soon as she was kneeling in front of her the woman got to her feet, the silk of the dress brushing against Melinda's face.

'This is very exciting,' Mrs Chapman said, almost to herself. Reaching behind her back she unzipped the dress, then pushed the shoulder straps down and let it fall to the floor. It bunched around Melinda's knees, the material feeling soft and warm. Mrs Chapman was wearing a lacy white bra to support her firm, quite meaty breasts. Her hips were sheathed in silky white French knickers with panels of lace cut into a V-shape across her belly, partially exposing the tanned flesh underneath. Melinda could see a mass of long curly pubic hair escaping from the loose-fitting gusset of the garment. The woman's belly was flat, almost concave, and her spectacularly long legs finely shaped. She stepped out of the dress, stooped to pick

11

it up and threw it on the nearby armchair. Then she hooked her hand around Melinda's head and pulled her face on to her silk-covered navel.

'Take my knickers down,' she whispered, the passion in her voice only too evident.

With her hands secured behind her back there was only one way Melinda could obey. She moved her lips up to the waistband of the knickers and sucked it into her mouth until she could get a firm grip with her teeth. Then she tugged it down. Fortunately the knickers were not tight and after three or four sharp jerks Melinda had managed to pull them down to the woman's thighs, exposing a rich forest of blonde pubic hair. She began to pull them lower but the woman, impatience asserting itself, wrenched the material from her lips and skimmed them down the rest of the way herself. As they fell to her ankles she sat on the bed again. Her eyes were almost level with Melinda's. She stared into them, Melinda's irises the colour of jade.

'This excites you, doesn't it?' she asked. An electricity had been generated between the two women that made the air seem to crackle.

'Yes, mistress.'

'How long have you served the *maîtres*?'

The question was impossible to answer. Melinda had lost all concept of time. It was of no importance to her since it was not something she could control. Time, like everything else in her life, was determined by her master.

'I don't know, mistress.'

'How many masters have you had, child?' Aldo prompted.

'Four.' It was not strictly true. Her last master had not been part of the O.I.M. but that was too complicated to explain.

'And you are experienced with women?' Mrs Chapman asked.

'Yes, mistress.'

'Her third *maître* was a woman,' Aldo explained. He was staring at both of them intently, his erection showing no sign of waning.

'There are women *maîtres*?'

'There are some, yes.'

The blonde stretched her hands up behind her back to the clasp of her bra. She freed it then let the thin shoulder straps fall over her arms. Leaning forward she allowed the cups of the bra to fall away from her breasts.

'Do you like my tits?' she asked the man. They were pear-shaped and hung low like ripe fruit and were as tanned as the rest of her body. Her nipples were already puckered, each surrounded by a dark brown band of areola.

'You're a very beautiful woman, Mrs Chapman,' Aldo said with obvious sincerity. Once again Melinda was struck with the contrast between his voice and his outward appearance.

The blonde pushed her left breast against Melinda's face. 'Suck my nipple,' she ordered, the words giving her a frisson of pleasure which made her quiver.

Melinda manoeuvred the little bud of flesh between her lips then sucked on it hard.

'With your teeth, pinch it,' came the next order.

Melinda obeyed, feeling the woman's body shudder as the tender flesh was trapped between her teeth.

'Now the other one.' The woman shook her shoulders, making her breasts slap into Melinda's face, then centred the right nipple on Melinda's mouth. 'So obedient,' she commented as she felt Melinda's teeth pinch with exactly the right amount of pressure, the borderline between pain and pleasure perfectly judged.

The blonde took Melinda's head in both her hands and pushed it down to her belly as she sank back on to the bed. She opened her legs and hooked them over Melinda's shoulders and around her back. She felt Melinda's hot mouth pressing against her mons.

'I've never done this before,' she said, turning her head to look at Aldo.

'Never had a woman?' He came closer to the bed, his misshapen erection sticking out from his loins.

'No,'

'You don't have to,' he told her.

'No, no . . . I want to. Can't you see that?'

Looking at him, she pushed Melinda's head down and angled her sex up towards her mouth. Her labia were large and plump and hairy. With no hesitation Melinda used her tongue to delve between them, right at the top of her sex, to find her clitoris. She felt it pulse strongly at the first contact and her own, pressed between her thighs, throbbed in sympathy. She heard the woman gasp as the tip of her tongue circled the lozenge-shaped promontory, forcing it back against the underlying bone.

'Do you want her whipped?' Aldo suggested, taking his erection in his hand and stroking it up and down.

Mrs Chapman's eyes had been closed due to the rush of feelings from her sex. The man's suggestion made them spring open.

'Whipped?' she echoed. Melinda could feel the blonde's whole body tremble at the mention of the word.

'Yes,' the man said. He opened the top drawer of

14

the chest of drawers and took out a long, thin, stiff strip of leather, about an inch wide, with one end braided into a leather handle. The other end was split into three strips. 'You have to learn how to deal with the slaves if you are going to have your own. They need discipline.'

'Yes,' the woman said, beginning to lose control. The artfulness of Melinda's relentless tongue and the softness of her mouth against her sex gave her feelings she had never experienced before and sent ever-increasing waves of passion pulsing through her body. But she still had enough control to know the idea of seeing the girl whipped would excite her further. 'Yes,' she repeated. 'Whip her for me.'

'You're not doing that very well, are you child?' the man asked Melinda, to create an excuse for punishment.

Melinda tried to shake her head without losing contact with the swollen clitoris under her tongue.

'Don't argue with me.'

He moved slightly to stand to one side of Melinda's kneeling body. Raising his arm he swung the leather tawse. It made an odd whistling sound then thwacked down on the meat of Melinda's buttocks just below where her hands were bound by the leather cuffs.

Melinda's yelp of pain was gagged on the woman's sex. The heat of the air she expelled involuntarily was enough to take Mrs Chapman over the edge. Her thighs clasped around Melinda's head like a vice as a climax as sudden and intense as any she could remember seized her like the hand of a giant and shook her about, tossing her from side to side until every last drop of feeling was squeezed out of her.

'Jesus ...' she said finally, opening her eyes, the muscles in her thighs relaxing. She saw the man's arm

15

was raised again. 'No,' she cried but it was too late. The tawse fell precisely on the red weal it had already left on Melinda's bottom and another exclamation was forced from her mouth by a bolt of pain. Instantly Mrs Chapman felt the blast of air enveloping her clitoris and she was launched again into a second bout of orgasm as intense as the first.

This time, as the climax passed, she unwound her legs from Melinda's back and pulled away, her sex too tender to be assailed again. Instead she watched as the man raised the whip for a third blow, his other hand pushing Melinda's head down on to the mattress so her buttocks were more fully raised.

Thwack. It was the hardest stroke of all. Melinda felt the pain explode through her nerves. Then, as always, the pain turned to pleasure; a sticky, hot, squirming pleasure. She squeezed her thighs together to put pressure on her throbbing clitoris and wriggled her buttocks from side to side, wallowing in the flood of feelings that overcame her. She was tantalisingly close to orgasm. One more stroke would bring her off but she knew it would never come. The overseer was too experienced to make that mistake.

'Take it in your mouth again, child,' the overseer said, pointing his cock towards her.

'No,' the blonde said at once. She had other ideas. The softness of another woman's mouth against her sex, the idea of using another woman in this way and the impact of the whip on Melinda's body and on her own mind had given her two explosive orgasms. But it had also left her with an overwhelming need. 'No. I thought you'd like to . . . You're not allowed to fuck the slaves, is that what you said?'

'Yes.'

'Then fuck me, Aldo. Come here and fuck me.'

16

As she said the words she twisted round on the bed until she was lying along its length. She opened her arms and her legs. She had never wanted a man more in her life. And there was something about this man, his short muscled body and hard, gnarled cock, that turned her on as much as the extraordinary situation. She had already decided she would do everything in her power to see that her husband became a *maître*. There was no question about that now.

'Come on,' she urged as Aldo hesitated.

'I'm not ... I don't know whether ...'

'I'm not a slave, Aldo.'

'I know, but ...'

The sight of her puffy, fat labia and the opening of her vagina between them overcame his scruples. In one stride he jumped on the bed, fell on top of her and plunged his cock into her sex, pounding it up and down with startling power.

'Say my name. I want to hear it. Cherry, call me Cherry.'

'I want to fuck you, Cherry,' he said.

'Yes, tell me.'

'I want to spunk you, Cherry.'

'I love it. Harder. Do it harder.'

He was already pumping into her at incredible speed. He raised himself on his hands and arched his body like a bow, pushing his cock deeper. The blonde gasped.

'Like that?' he asked.

'Oh yes.'

Melinda watched helplessly as the woman's body stretched out under the man, every nerve and sinew taut. Her own body was trembling with need too, a need she had felt so often since she had become part of the O.I.M., a need she knew she would be unable

17

to satisfy. It was no longer for her to decide when she ate or slept or bathed; it was not her decision what she wore, or when her hair was cut. She had no dominion over her body anymore and like everything else, her orgasms were in the hands of her master – to be granted or denied at his discretion.

She watched as the blonde was pleasured, and listened as she screamed obscenities, obviously enjoying the overseer's power and virility. She could see his buttocks, hard and dimpled with muscles, driving his phallus into the centre of the woman, where only minutes before her mouth had been.

Melinda's shoulders ached from the bondage and her calves and thighs were cramped from being so long on her knees. The three whip strokes she had suffered had left red weals across the rich curves of her buttocks and her sex ached with a dull throb of frustration. But Melinda had no regrets. She knew, despite the discomfort, this is where she belonged.

The woman's screams subsided and she came, moaning and gasping for air. The man slowed his efforts and let her orgasm run its course, the contractions of the woman's sex over his cock taking him closer to his own completion. Satisfied that she was finished with him he suddenly pulled his erection from her body and rested it, glossy with her juices, on her hairy mons. She raised her head to look down between their two bodies just in time to catch the first spasm of his cock as it spat white semen out, splattering her tanned flesh right up to her breasts. His spending was so hot it made her gasp.

Melinda watched too, wondering if her new master would use her in this way, and hoping against hope that he would.

Two

'Please, please . . . I'll do anything, anything, please mistress . . . You've got to let me explain. You don't understand what the master's doing . . .' The naked girl was young and slim with a narrow waist and long fair hair. Her breasts were firm and supple and needed no support and her mons was completely shaved.

'Don't make things worse for yourself. I told you to be quiet.'

'All right, I take it all back. It was a mistake. It was all a mistake. Please don't do this to me.'

'I should gag her,' Aldo said. 'The master said she should be gagged.'

'Do it.'

That was not difficult. The girl was bound hand and foot, tight leather thongs wound around her wrists and ankles. Her arms were stretched out above her head where the bondage had been attached to a metal ring jutting from the wall. Her feet barely touched the floor. Though she shook her head from side to side, Aldo merely had to catch her cheeks in his hand and, before she could say another word, force a large rubber ball gag between her lips. It was attached to an oval of black leather which he strapped around her head and which covered most of the lower part of her face.

She still tried to speak, her eyes bulging and her face contorted with the effort, though the sound she produced was mumbled and indistinct.

They were in a long wooden-framed room, a wall of windows on one side looking out on to a neatly-tended garden. It looked as though it had once been a gymnasium but now its walls were not fitted with exercise equipment but were festooned with harnesses in leather and steel, whips of every sort, gags, leather and rubber helmets and hoods and chains and ropes and leather straps of every description. The wooden floor was strewn with equally sinister-looking bondage contraptions. Running down the centre of the room was a thick beam hanging down from which were two steel cables attached to pulleys and an electric winch.

Melinda had spent the night in the cellar which had turned out to be immediately under this room. Now she stood with two other girls, side by side against the windows, the sun streaming in through the glass and warming their naked bodies. She assumed the other two girls and the one strung up against the wall were the three slaves Aldo had referred to last night.

'This has to be a lesson to you all,' Sophia said, walking up to the three women. Melinda recognised her perfume immediately, a heavy musky scent she had first inhaled what seemed like months ago, but was in fact only weeks. Sophia had come to inspect her at halfway houses provided by the O.I.M. for slaves in transit between masters. Unfortunately, Melinda's arrival at her establishment had been delayed by a rogue element in the O.I.M. who had kidnapped her before she could be delivered to Sophia.

But despite everything in between, Melinda had not forgotten her first encounter with Sophia. She felt again the same mélange of fear and excitement the woman inspired.

Sophia was undoubtedly a stunningly beautiful woman. This morning she was dressed in a tight black suit, the jacket shaped by a little peplum on the hips, its skirt skin-tight and short enough to show most of her thighs. She was tall and her finely-contoured legs were sheathed in light tan tights with a glossy, lustrous finish. Her black high-heeled shoes shaped the muscles of her calves and increased the pout of her firm buttocks at the back of her thighs. Her haughty elegance and the way she held her body with her back straight and her head high, suggested an aristocratic pedigree as did the sharply-chiselled features of her face. She had a thin straight nose and high cheekbones. Her eyes were large and dark brown and her hair as black as ebony. Before, when Melinda had seen her, it had been plaited and pinned to her head but now it was brushed out and was so long it almost reached to her waist, its strands seeming to reflect the light.

She wore no blouse under the jacket and Melinda could see the swell of her breasts at the neckline.

The dark brown eyes were looking at Melinda, as though remembering what had happened between them at the halfway house.

'You know the rules, don't you?' she said to Melinda eventually. For a moment she rested her hand on Melinda's shoulder. The touch made Melinda shudder. Unlike the two girls at her side, her hands were bound behind her back in the tight leather cuffs.

'Yes, mistress Sophia,' Melinda said, reminding herself that was how Sophia had told her she preferred to be addressed.

21

'Penelope here decided she wished to obey no longer.'

This statement produced a further outburst from the bound slave. She writhed against her bonds and shook her head. She tried to speak but made little impact on the gag. Sophia ignored her.

'Aldo, I think we shall begin,' Sophia said, indicating a small table that had been placed alongside the captive girl.

The overseer, unlike some of his peers in other establishments, was dressed normally in a white shirt and dark slacks. He took a roll of elastoplast from the table, tore off a strip about ten inches long and stood in front of Penelope. He lifted her left breast up towards her chin and stuck the tape vertically to hold it in that position. The purple square containing the letter M was exposed. Quickly Aldo repeated the process with her right breast, this time revealing a purple square and the letter P.

Penelope struggled harder, wriggling against the leather thongs that bit into her flesh, twisting to and fro and trying to shake her breasts to dislodge the tape. Sweat ran down her face and her body.

Sophia walked up to the table. Next to the roll of elastoplast was a small rectangular tin in dark blue, very like an old-fashioned ink pad for rubber stamps. There was also a pair of stainless steel tweezers. Sophia picked up the tin and tweezers and stood in front of the struggling girl.

'It is useless to struggle. The master has ordered your punishment. You must accept it,' Sophia said quietly, almost sympathetically.

The girl shook her head furiously.

Sophia extended her hands and touched her cheek. 'Accept it,' she repeated soothingly. 'It's over for you.'

22

Penelope looked into her mistress's eyes. Melinda could see she was desperately trying to communicate something to her but getting not the slightest response from Sophia she had decided that her struggle was useless. There was nothing she could do to stop what was going to happen to her and she allowed her body to go limp, the fire in her eyes dulled.

'That's better,' Sophia said. 'You must be very still.'

She flipped open the lid of the tin and with the tweezers extracted a small square of what looked like gauze, being careful not to touch the material with her skin. It corresponded in size to the purple squares marked in Penelope's flesh and was the same purple colour. Melinda could see it was wet, soaked in some chemical from the tin.

Sophia moved closer to the hapless girl and very carefully positioned the square exactly over the purple square under her left breast, not actually touching the skin until she was completely satisfied it was correctly aligned. Then she pressed it home.

Immediately the girl's body tensed. She moaned but managed to hold her body perfectly still.

Meticulously Sophia took out a second square with the tweezers. It was exactly the same as the first. She positioned it just as precisely over the square P and pressed it down. Again the girl tensed and moaned. Every muscle in her body was rigid but she remained still.

Sophia looked at her watch, a Cartier Santos encrusted with tiny diamonds around the square face. She stroked Penelope's face as if to reward her for not struggling. Penelope pressed her cheek against the fingers, her eyes pleading for the mercy that would never come.

The room was silent. The three slaves watched, a chill of fear in the heart of each of them. It was the worst punishment they could imagine and Melinda felt her body shiver involuntarily.

Three minutes passed. Looking at her watch again, Sophia took the tweezers and pulled the left square away. She waited ten seconds then peeled off the right. Somehow, though Melinda had no idea how, the purple squares had drawn out the dye from the epidermis. As Sophia wiped the residue away with a cotton pad, Melinda saw that under each breast, instead of the neat squared letters, was a patch of angry red skin, perfectly square but with no sign of the letter that had once marked the girl.

'The scar fades to almost nothing with time,' Sophia said. The marks under Melinda's own breasts seemed to be tingling. She wanted to finger them but would not have dared even if her hands had been free. It was the ultimate punishment – what they all feared most. The girl was being cast out of the O.I.M. She would no longer be allowed to serve the *maîtres*.

'Cut her down,' Sophia ordered.

Aldo took a large knife and cut through the leather thongs, their knots, tightened by Penelope's struggles, now too knitted together to ever be undone. Her arms dropped to her sides like lead weights. He sliced through the bonds at her ankles.

'Leave your breasts as they are for at least two hours. There may be some chemical left and it will mark anything it touches. You can take the gag out, Aldo.'

'I think the master would prefer her gagged, mistress. She was supposed to be gagged before she came up here.'

'Very well.' There was a pair of rather old-fashioned full cut black panties on the small table. Sophia picked them up and handed them to Penelope. 'Put these on.'

If there was any doubt about the meaning of what they had seen this confirmed to all the slaves that Penelope was being sent away. The panties were only worn by slaves in transit. She was being sent home, never to be involved with the O.I.M. again.

The girl's resistance had disappeared. She stepped into the panties and pulled them up over her hips, covering her hairless pubis and her sex. It would never be used by a *maître* again.

Sophia nodded and Aldo quickly bound the girl's arms behind her back in leather cuffs. He led her out of the room as Sophia came back to the three remaining slaves, looking at each in turn. There was no need for her to say anything; no need to point up the lesson of what they had just seen. It had struck ice into the heart of each one.

Somewhere in the distance they heard an engine being started. Melinda knew it would be a van, a plain windowless van, and Penelope would be crouching in the back of it on the beginning of her journey home. Tears, Melinda suspected, would be welling in her eyes.

The villa was large and impressive. It was beautifully sited on the top of a hill overlooking a lush green valley, the only building for some miles. It was typical of nineteenth-century Italian architecture, with none of the foibles of English Victorian buildings of the same period; a solidly-built square building with large casement windows symmetrically arranged on either side of the panelled double front doors. The exterior walls were plastered and painted in an orange colour that the sun had bleached to a delicate shade of amber. A red brick wall, again bleached by sunlight, surrounded the house on all sides, enclosing a collection of outbuildings at the back; a large swimming pool constructed in blue mosaics to one side and a formal garden at the front. There was a wrought iron gate set in the wall on the opposite side from the pool and a gravel drive which swept around in an elegant curve to the front door.

The punishment room was in one of the outbuildings, all of which had been built with a system of interconnecting cellars, where Melinda had been kept on her arrival and where she had entertained Mrs Chapman. A covered walkway, trellis intertwined with a mature vine, led through to the back door of the main house.

Melinda had hardly dared glance at the two slaves by her side. Now, as Aldo returned, they were led away through the walkway into the house, and Melinda was left alone with Sophia.

'Well,' Sophia said, roaming the room, her high heels clacking on the wooden floor, occasionally stopping by some piece of bondage equipment and fingering it almost lovingly. 'Our liaison was unavoidably delayed.'

Melinda said nothing. She had not been asked a question.

'But I do remember you. I remember you well.' She turned to look at Melinda intently, then walked up behind her. 'Show me your marks.' Sophia released the metal catch that held the two leather cuffs together, then stood in front of her.

Melinda lifted her breasts, one by one, revealing the two letters that identified her.

'You are a beautiful one. I can see why my husband wanted you. Clasp your hands behind your back again.'

Melinda obeyed at once, her breasts pushed forward.

'Tell me what you feel?'

'Frightened, mistress,' she replied truthfully.

'Mistress Sophia,' Sophia corrected. 'You are frightened at the thought of what happened to Penelope?' She turned and walked away, looking out of the window at the gardens outside.

'Yes, mistress Sophia.'

'And you are not excited? Not excited by me, by the prospect of being with me? Or does that frighten you too?'

'No, mistress Sophia.' Melinda did not know what to say. Of course her body was tense with excitement. The very fact of being in this room naked and exposed thrilled her, but at the same time it was hard to forget what had happened to Penelope. That was the worst nightmare of any slave and Melinda had never seen it done before.

Sophia approached Melinda again, her high heels echoing on the wooden floor. She came so close for a minute that Melinda thought she meant to kiss her. Her powerful perfume waffled through the room, redolent, it seemed to Melinda, of the musky aroma of sex.

'My husband went away this morning. He will be back in a matter of days. Meantime, you will be brought to my room tonight. I've had to wait a long time for you, haven't I?' The material of the black jacket brushed Melinda's naked breasts.

'Yes, mistress Sophia.'

It was extraordinary for a slave to be given this sort of information. Melinda had never been told what was going to happen to her from one minute to the next. But she remembered being astonished before, at

27

the halfway house, when Sophia had told her how she was going to be brought here, to her villa outside Rome, and how she would be shared between husband and wife. Apparently the way Sophia did things was very different from the other members of the O.I.M.

'Do you find me attractive?' Sophia asked.

'Yes, mistress Sophia,' Melinda replied earnestly. In her time with the masters she had learnt to desire and serve women as much as she desired and served men. Women had been more cruel to her, it was true, but at their hands and in their beds she had learnt that sex with a woman could be as explosively enjoyable as sex with a man. She had never exhibited any penchant for women before the châtelaines of her first master had used her, but now found the thought of what she knew Sophia would demand of her totally enthralling.

'After all, we are not strangers, are we?' Sophia's hand strayed to Melinda's breast. She pinched her nipple lightly.

'No, mistress Sophia.'

'You do remember, don't you?'

Melinda remembered. She had been made to use a whip on Sophia but not in the conventional way; Sophia had insisted she use the handle of the whip like a dildo and insert it in her sex. Melinda shivered involuntarily at the memory.

'I see you do,' Sophia said, spotting her reaction.

The overseer had returned and stood by the door awaiting instructions. Melinda had the feeling that Sophia would have been tempted not to wait until tonight if he had not come back.

'Was she beaten last night?' Sophia asked him, taking Melinda by the arm and turning her so she could see her pert apple-shaped arse. The red weals that had been inflicted while she lapped at Mrs Chapman's sex were barely visible now.

'Yes. Three strokes,' Aldo replied.

'She needs freshening up. Perhaps I will do that to-night.' Sophia's hand caressed Melinda's rump. 'Take her to her quarters, then have her brought to my room at nine. She's to be alone until then.'

With that, Sophia turned on her heels and strode from the room purposefully, the clack of her high heels echoing back from the walls.

'Well, child,' Aldo said, his face contorted into a smile and his eyes staring straight at Melinda, 'it seems you have made quite an impression on the mistress, doesn't it?'

'Yes, master.'

'Things here are a little different from what you have come to expect. We are more relaxed and there is less security. That does not mean punishment for transgression is any less severe as you have seen for yourself. Do you understand?'

'Yes, master.'

'There are only two other slaves beside yourself. You are permitted to talk to them when you are alone, but only when you are alone. The rule of silence must be obeyed at all other times unless you are asked a question. Do you understand that?'

'I may talk to the other slaves, master?' That had never been allowed at any of the other establishments Melinda had been to.

'Only in private. If you say a word in front of me or the *maître* or any guest you will be punished. You are not permitted to touch the other slaves at any time; that rule is unchanged. Do you understand?'

'Yes, master.'

'And naturally, you must obey every order at once.'

Melinda nodded.

'Follow me then.'

They walked out of the punishment room, through the vine-covered walkway and into the house. It was pleasantly warm and Melinda felt no chill on her naked body. The overseer led the way along a short corridor and up what was obviously a back staircase. It was narrow and poorly lit. Melinda caught glimpses of the opulent furnishings of the house. The furniture in the hall was mostly antique with small side tables, display cabinets for a collection of Italian plates and a Chippendale chair upholstered in striped green and white silk. The carpets were expensive and the curtains elaborate, with flounced edges and massive tie-backs. She was taken along a first-floor landing and up a second staircase to the top floor.

Aldo took her down a long corridor that led to the front of the house. Here the view from the windows was beathtaking, the sun lighting one side of the valley while the other was shaded by tall broad-leafed trees, rolling hills and greenery as far as the eye could see.

There was a whole line of doors along the corridor and Aldo opened one at the far end, indicating that Melinda should go in ahead of him. The room was quite small with a single window overlooking the front of the house and an interior door which was ajar and through which Melinda could see a plain white tiled bathroom. The bedroom itself had a double bed and was decorated in a pretty flower-patterned wallpaper, tiny primroses in a diagonal design. The same print was repeated on the curtains at the window and on the counterpane. There was no bedside table and no bedside lamps and no light switch, Melinda noticed, except for the overhead light, its bulb covered by a yellow shade. There was a large bow-fronted mahogany chest of drawers standing next to the window.

The impression of normality the bedroom conveyed was dispelled by the fixture on the far side of the room opposite the foot of the bed. It was a black tubular steel X-shaped cross bolted to the floor and ceiling about a foot out from the wall. At the intersection of the two bars a thick leather belt was attached and there were leather cuffs at the foot of each bar and overhead, clearly enabling a victim to be spread-eagled against it.

'Over here,' Aldo said, standing by the frame.

It was only when Melinda got closer that she realised that the leather cuffs and central leather belt were duplicated on the other side of the tubular metal facing the wall, presumably so two people could be accommodated at the same time.

The overseer pushed Melinda against the frame facing out and quickly wrapped the central belt around her waist, cinching it tight. As he pulled her arms up and out above her head and strapped them tightly into the leather cuffs an involuntary gasp escaped her lips as she felt the jolt of excitement bondage never failed to provoke in her body.

As soon as her limbs were secured Aldo went to the chest of drawers and opened the bottom drawer. He took out one of the strangest objects Melinda had seen. It looked like a boot tree that had been turned inside out; two plastic semi-circular tubes were attached to two metal braces. The curved hollows of the tubes were wider than they would have been on a boot tree however and their hollows not so deep.

Before Melinda had time to puzzle over what the

device might be, the overseer had dropped on his knees in front of her and slid the hollows of plastic against her inner thighs where they conformed perfectly to the contours of her flesh. He pulled the metal braces tight, so the hollows were pushed outward, thus opening Melinda's thighs further and holding them apart. The purpose of the device was obvious. Though the ankle cuffs held her legs open it was still possible for her to bring pressure to bear on her sex by squeezing the top of her thighs together. This device prevented that completely, not only making it impossible for Melinda to rub the top of her thighs against her labia, but actually opening her labia themselves, depriving her clitoris of even this faint pressure.

Getting to his feet, Aldo smiled at her. He ran his hand over her belly and down her almost hairless pubis. His middle finger butted up against her now exposed clitoris. It was already engorged. He pushed it gently from side to side. Melinda moaned. Her body sent a surge of feeling through nerves already sensitised by her bondage. He took his finger away immediately.

'Not too much,' he said. 'Just enough to keep you wanting.'

Delicately he picked up her left nipple between his thumb and forefinger, lifting her breast by it, until he could see the purple mark underneath. He pinched the nipple hard enough to leave a crescent-shaped indentation where his nail had been. Again Melinda groaned. Moving his hand to her right breast he took the whole meat of it in his hand and squashed the pliant, spongy flesh against her chest. Melinda could see a bulge distending the front of his trousers. His fingers released her breast and centred on her nipple

32

again. This time he rolled it between his thumb and forefinger, the friction generating heat.

'It will be my turn with you next,' he said.

He went back to the chest of drawers and took a long strip of black silk from the top drawer. He positioned it over Melinda's eyes and wound it around her head, knotting it at the back so tightly the silk pressed against her eyeballs and excluded even the faintest light.

That was the worst. Melinda knew what the overseer had wanted to do and he had succeeded perfectly. He had worked her body into a state of need and left an unforgettable impression on her nipples and her clitoris, like fingers pressed into putty. He had created a desire and at the same time made sure every means to satisfy it was taken away from her. But the blindfold was the worst torture of all. Without it, standing in the sunny room, she could at least distract herself by looking out of the window or counting the flowers on the wallpaper to take her mind off what her body felt. In the blackness the strip of silk imposed, she had no such option. It was impossible to think of anything but her body, her hard nipples and throbbing clitoris and the bondage that held her so tightly. It was impossible not to conjure up images, on the blank screen of her mind, of what had been done to her or of the numerous ways her masters had chosen to tease and torture, and ultimately, to pleasure her.

She felt the overseer's hand on her cheek, patting it gently, then heard the door open and close, and he was gone.

For all Melinda's desire to obey she immediately struggled fiercely against her bonds, writhing this way and that to find some way to put pressure on her throbbing clitoris. She only succeeded in making matters worse. Her breasts slapped against each other, arousing her nipples further and sending waves of sensation down to her sex, reinforcing what it already felt but bringing her no closer to what her body craved. The feeling of constriction which her struggles produced and the unyielding grip of the leather also increased her sexual temperature and her need.

Determinedly she tried to calm herself. She stopped struggling and tried to relax. But in the blackness her clitoris immediately claimed centre stage. It seemed to have a life of its own, living and breathing as a thing apart.

'No,' Melinda said aloud, hoping it would understand that it must stop. But it did not. Pulses of feeling and need radiated out from it.

In her mind she saw Aldo's gnarled cock sinking into Mrs Chapman's ripe, hairy, wet sex. The image made her body shudder. It was as though she could feel his phallus inside her, thrusting up into the recesses of her body, hard and hot and twitching.

'No,' she cried louder, shaking her head from side to side to rid herself of the image. But it was a vicious circle. The more her clever bondage prevented her from plunging herself into orgasm, the more she was reminded of her situation and of the total submission she had commissioned for herself. And the more she thought of *that*, the more she contemplated how completely she had been deprived of will and even the ability to touch her own body, the more excited she became and the worse was the craving for an orgasm she knew would never come.

It had happened in all her masters' houses. In all the other establishments she served she had been left like this, provoked and needy, waiting for her master to decide when, if ever, she would be granted sexual relief. This was different however. In all the other houses she had never known how long the torture would last, how long it would be before she was called to attend her master. But today she knew. Sophia had told her. Though she had no way of telling the time, no way even of knowing when it had got dark, she did know the time span was limited and at the end of it the beautiful, black-haired Sophia would put an end to her misery.

The thought of Sophia made her body lurch into another surge of pleasure. She fought to control it, pulling against the leather cuffs at her wrists in an effort to cause a stab of pain that would act as a cold shower to her overheated emotions, but the cuffs were too well padded to cause discomfort. Squeezing her thighs against the plastic plates braced between her legs didn't help either – the curves were too well fitted to pinch against her flesh.

For hours Melinda suffered, her body like a piece of flotsam on a stormy sea, tossed here and there, from the crest of a wave to the bottom of a trough, unable to resist the powerful currents of feeling her mind engendered, unable to reach the shore and the relief of orgasm. The room was hot and getting hotter and streams of sweat ran down her body, her inability to wipe them away only adding to her sense of helplessness.

Eventually, her body found the solution in sleep. Whether for a matter of minutes or hours she did not know. She was only aware that she had been asleep at all when she was started awake by the noise of the bedroom door opening then closing sharply again.

Melinda listened intently but whoever had come into the room remained perfectly still.

Then she heard footsteps going into the bathroom and the noise of water running. The bedroom door opened again.

'Haven't you started yet?' It was Aldo's voice.

Melinda heard footsteps coming back into the room. She could feel the heat of a body next to her own.

'Get on with it,' Aldo barked.

Melinda heard the noise of water. Suddenly she felt the soft bristles of a shaving brush against her labia. The touch made her gasp, the tension in her clitoris instantly renewed. The brush applied a thick coat of lather across the whole area, up on to her belly and down on to the tops of her thighs. Then Melinda felt the familiar coldness of a razor as the lather was carefully scraped away, fingers pulling at Melinda's flesh to stretch it out this way and that, allowing the razor to get into even the most inaccessible of places.

When the job was finished the overseer ran his hand brusquely over Melinda's sex.

'Good enough,' he said.

The procedure had left Melinda's body tingling again but her frustration was lessened by the fact that this could only be a prelude to being taken to Sophia.

Her bonds were released and the blindfold removed. As her eyes adjusted to the light she saw it was dark outside. An old woman in a black dress was carrying a bowl of water back into the bathroom. A tray of food – cheese, salad and fruit – and a jug of water had been set on the foot of the bed.

'Eat, then use the bathroom,' Aldo ordered as the old woman left the room.

Melinda did as she was told. She consumed the food hungrily, glad that it afforded her a distraction from her sexual appetites. When she had finished she used the bathroom. Aldo followed her inside, watching her while she peed, then ordered her to take a shower. In common with all the quarters she had occupied under the masters, the bathroom had no mirror. Her appearance was not her concern anymore. Her make-up, hair and clothes were done to suit the whim of others.

As if to confirm this, the old woman had come back to the bedroom with a small bag of make-up and a hairbrush. As Melinda sat on the edge of the bed the woman brushed out her hair and applied eyeliner, eye-shadow, blusher and red lipstick, which she painted on with a brush.

She waited to see if the overseer approved then left when he nodded his assent. Aldo pulled out a short black satin slip from the middle drawer of the mahogany chest. It had a scoop neck and spaghetti straps.

'Put this on,' he ordered.

Melinda slipped the cool satin over her head. It barely covered her buttocks and fitted so loosely it seemed to float away from her body.

'Very pretty,' Aldo said. 'Very elegant. Now these.'

She hadn't noticed the black high heels standing by the bed. The old woman must have brought them in when she returned with the make-up. The heels were spiky and very high and there was an ankle strap attached to the back of the shoe. Melinda slipped her feet into them and knelt to buckle each strap. The buckle was finished in gold.

Aldo looked her up and down critically. 'Follow me,' he said, obviously satisfied that she was ready.

He led the way into the corridor. After so long without shoes Melinda found it hard to keep up, the leather biting into her feet and the heels making her totter. From the windows of the corridor she could see the moon. It was almost full, just a bite-sized chunk missing from the full disc, and lit the valley in shades of grey, the shadows of the trees pitch black. As far as she could see there wasn't a single artificial light in evidence anywhere in the landscape.

They walked down the back staircase then turned left along a much broader hallway, its ancient oak floorboards covered with Persian rugs. The hall ended in a pair of tall double doors. The overseer did not knock. He opened the right-hand door and shepherded Melinda inside.

The room beyond was lavishly decorated. The walls were lined in a thick woolly material that was the deepest shade of burgundy red, and the deep pile carpet was the same colour. The bed, facing two large casement windows overlooking the front of the house, was a four-poster, its oak uprights elaborately carved to look as though they were encrusted with ivy. There was a small sofa to one side of the bed and burr-walnut bedside chests supporting cylindrical lamps. The lampshades, the counterpane and the upholstery of the small sofa were all an oatmeal cream, as were the heavy curtains that were still tied back at the side of the window frames.

There was a door to one side of the bed and a square alcove at the back of the room where Melinda could see rows of built-in wardrobes.

Aldo took Melinda by her arm and led her over to the bed. Lying on the counterpane was a length of neatly-coiled white rope. It was thick and its corded strains were made from silk. The overseer positioned Melinda in front of the left-hand post at the foot of the bed then pulled her arms around it, crossing her wrists and binding them together securely with the rope. From the top drawer of the bedside chest on the right-hand side he extracted what looked like a perfect replica of a snake, fashioned in cylindrical silver scales that were jointed to move flexibly and about eighteen inches long. But as he brought it closer Melinda saw that the snake had heads at each end, both very realistic, with a large jaw and small emeralds inlaid in the silver to form the eyes. Aldo brought one of the heads up to Melinda's left nipple and she watched as he pressed it between his thumb and forefinger and its jaws opened. Feeding her nipple into the snake's maw he released what must have been a spring-loaded hinge and Melinda felt a familiar thrill as the cold metal sank deeply into her tender flesh. Looping the metal body of the snake around the post the overseer clipped the jaws at the other end into Melinda's right nipple. He dropped the tubular body. It fell on to Melinda's bound wrists, sending a surge of pain racing through her as the weight dragged on the nipple clips. The pain, inevitably it seemed, turned to hot, almost sickly pleasure. She closed her eyes as a reaction to it and when she opened them again the overseer had gone.

Somewhere in the house Melinda could hear music, the faint echoes of what sounded like a Haydn symphony. When it had finished silence descended. Minutes passed slowly, Melinda's body taut with excitement. She listened intently for any sign that Sophia was on her way. None came.

It occurred to her quite suddenly that this might all be a cruel game; that Sophia had no intention of coming to her tonight. The other masters had often built up her hopes only to dash them cruelly. It was a technique they used often to increase the dependency of the slaves and to make them truly grateful for even the slightest favour. A slave who was not serving a master, who was neglected and deserted by him, had no reason to exist. She was in a sort of limbo and would do anything to regain a place in his attention. It was quite possible Sophia was adopting the same approach – deceiving Melinda into thinking she would be used immediately – as a means of reinforcing the idea that her needs and desires as a slave meant nothing and that she was not worthy of the slightest consideration. If that were the case Melinda's disappointment would be a torture more hurtful than any physical pain.

After what Melinda estimated to be more than an hour, the idea had taken root and she was certain she was right. This was all a game. Her excitement began to drain from her body. The feeling from the jaws of the snake's head clamped over her nipples turned from a mélange of pleasure and pain to a dull, persistent ache. The white silk bound so tightly around her wrists, which had been another provocation, also began to hurt.

The odd thing was she didn't hear her enter the room. She didn't hear her cross to the bed either and jumped when her hand touched the pert curves of her naked buttocks.

'You must be very uncomfortable.' The hand stroked the camber of Melinda's bottom brushing against the hem of the satin slip. Sophia was wearing a white silk nightgown, her large breasts almost escaping its loose, plunging neckline. Melinda felt the rich, sensuous material swish against her flesh. Her excitement returned in a rush, flooding through her body in a crimson tide, the strong scent of Sophia's perfume enveloping her in its heady aroma.

'Mistress . . .' she dared to whisper, throwing her head back.

'Oh, so needy,' Sophia mocked. Her hand picked up the metal cylinder of the snake, and lifted it until Melinda's breasts were lifted too and the snake's heads bit deeper into the impressible buds of flesh. Melinda moaned.

Sophia's other hand pushed down between the clefts of Melinda's buttocks until her fingers could pry open her soft, newly-shaven labia. One, then two, slipped into Melinda's vagina. The rush of feelings had stimulated a flood of juices and Melinda's sex was soaking wet.

'So needy,' Sophia repeated, driving her fingers up into her slave's vagina then twisting them around as she pulled on the metal snake so Melinda's breasts were stretched taut.

The fingers withdrew. Sophia dropped the snake, causing a sharp sting of pain in Melinda's nipples. She came around to the side of the bed. Her dark brown eyes looked into Melinda's as she slid the straps of the nightgown off her shoulders and let it cascade to the floor. She did not pick it up. Her naked body was magnificent, lithe and supple, and her large breasts defied gravity, their nipples tipped upward. Like her slave, her labia had been meticulously shaven of all its dark black pubic hair.

Quickly she stripped the counterpane and the top sheet off the bed. The bottom sheet was the same burgundy red as the carpet and walls.

Sophia's hair had been tied in a plait that hung down her back. She reached behind her to free it, then shook her head to produce a mantle of black hair across her shoulders. She lay on the bed and opened her long, finely contoured legs, bending them at the knee. Her labia was completely hairless. Reaching over to the top drawer of the bedside chest she

41

took out a small white jar. She unscrewed the cap of the jar and dipped her fingers into the gelatinous cream it contained, transferring a large dollop to her mons, before putting the jar back in the drawer.

She raised her hips off the bed, angling her sex towards Melinda. Her left hand, its fingers still coated with cream from the jar, massaged the residue into her breasts, one after the other, until the meaty cushions of flesh were shiny with it. Her right hand, meantime, spread the unction over her pubis and down between her legs, spreading it into her labia and the bud of her anus, making that also glossy and gleaming with oil.

Melinda watched as Sophia's long, slender fingers, their nails varnished a deep red, stroked the plane of her own sex, following the long crease down to the puckered fistula of her anus, then moving up again to part the furrow of her labia. Her left hand soon joined the right. One held the labia open, to allow free access to her clitoris. Melinda could see it exposed, a pink lozenge of flesh, poking out from the fingers that stretched the labia away on either side.

'You've made me so hot,' Sophia said. She was teasing herself, the tip of her finger poised above her clitoris but not on it. 'Can you see it? Can you see my cunt?' Melinda remembered Sophia had used the same crude language before at the halfway house. It seemed incongruous from such a cultured woman. It obviously excited her.

'Yes, mistress Sophia,' Melinda said, glad of the opportunity to say something. She could see the scarlet maw of Sophia's vagina. It seemed to be contracting regularly.

Sophia gasped as she allowed her finger to drop on to her clit. It moved over it from side to side, so fast her hand was a blur of movement. Sophia's body trembled. 'Oh yes,' she hissed. 'Yes.'

She came almost instantly. Melinda saw her body arch off the bed and her eyes close, the outline of all the muscles in her body rigid. Her hand stopped moving, gripping her sex tightly instead, as if trying to prevent her orgasm from seeping away.

In that, however, she was unsuccessful and as her climax passed she opened her eyes. Slowly she sat up, combing her long hair with her fingers. She got to her knees and crawled forward until she could reach Melinda's wrists. She untied the knot of the white silk rope and let it fall to the bed, then took one of the heads of the snakes in her fingers.

'It'll hurt,' she said.

As she opened the jaws the nerves that had been numbed by the metal sprang back to life, reasserting themselves with a sting of pain that made Melinda shudder. The removal of the second clip produced the same result.

'Take the slip off,' Sophia ordered. 'And the shoes.'

Melinda pushed the spaghetti straps off her shoulders and let the loose garment float to the floor. Her excitement was intense. Sophia could have brought her here just to watch. But it appeared she had something more intimate in mind.

'You were shaved?' Sophia asked.

'Yes, mistress Sophia.' Melinda said, bending down to unbuckle the ankle straps of the shoes before kicking them off.

'Not a heavy growth I think,' she said, scanning Melinda's mons minutely. 'Lie here.' She patted the bed beside her.

Almost before Melinda had time to obey, Sophia's mouth was sucking at her breasts, her tongue licking at the tortured nipples and soothing it with her saliva, while her hands kneaded the spongy flesh.

'Oh mistress ...' Melinda gasped, knowing she should not speak but the tenderness of Sophia's ministrations forcing the words from her.

Sophia's mouth trailed up to Melinda's neck, kissing and nibbling all the way. She raised her head and looked into Melinda's green eyes before plunging her mouth down to envelop Melinda's lips and squirming it against them as her tongue penetrated between. She unfurled her body and lay on top of her slave, pressing the whole length of it into her and moving sensuously against her.

Sophia's thigh pushed between Melinda's, squashing up against her labia. Melinda could feel the juices of her body anointing it, making it wet. Melinda's pulse was racing. She hadn't expected this at all. Other masters had teased and tortured her mercilessly, used and abused her by every means and allowed her to come – if indeed they had – only as an afterthought. The pleasure Sophia was giving her was much more unequivocal.

Sophia broke the kiss. With no hesitation she turned herself around and plunged her mouth down between Melinda's legs, using her hands to spread her legs as she, at the same moment, swung her thighs over Melinda's head. As she pressed her lips to Melinda's sex, she pushed her nether lips down against her slave's mouth.

No orders were given; no commands. There was no need. The mistress and the slave were joined, locked together in a perfect circle, everything else subordinated to their indivisible needs.

Melinda felt Sophia's tongue on her clitoris and her hands working under her thighs until her fingers could slip into her vagina again. Eagerly Melinda did the same, looping her arms around Sophia's buttocks so she could delve between her oiled labia to find the opening to her vagina as her tongue lighted on her swollen clitoris.

Desperately Melinda tried to concentrate on serving her mistress, working the tiny bud of flesh to and fro as her fingers sawed in and out of the tight wet cavern of Sophia's sex. But her own need was impossible to ignore. The unexpectedness of this treatment, the tenderness with which Sophia had soothed her nipples, the way she had lain on top of her and pressed the whole length of her body into Melinda's had already kick-started the motor of her orgasm. Now Sophia's tongue and fingers relentlessly working on her sex were accelerating it and taking away all semblance of control.

'Mistress, mistress, mistress,' she gasped, her lips moving against the lips of Sophia's sex as her orgasm exploded in her body, the caged-up frustration of last night and the seemingly endless day released at last. Her body went from soft pliancy to total rigidity, locking itself around Sophia's tongue and the fingers that moved at the core of her being. It felt like an infinity of time before the tendrils of orgasm freed her from their tenacious grip.

Melinda immediately renewed her assault on Sophia's sex. She sucked the top of her labia into her mouth and pressed them together with her lips so the clitoris was trapped between. At the same time she drove two fingers, then three, into her vagina, as deep as they would go, straining the tendons of her hand to push them forward. She felt Sophia's sex throb and contract. She knew she was coming too.

Opening her mouth she allowed the labia out, only

to find the clitoris with the very tip of her tongue. She flicked it against the most sensitive part, every tiny movement producing a shockwave of feeling in Sophia's body.

'Yes, yes,' Sophia cried, raising her head from Melinda's thighs. 'Yes!'

The last word was almost screamed out. It echoed around the room as her orgasm echoed through her body, buffeting her with sensation, vibrating every nerve and reaching into every corner of her mind, the echoes gradually getting fainter but taking a long time to die away completely.

Sophia rolled off her slave. They lay side by side, the little trills and tremors of orgasm still playing in their bodies, larger stabs of pleasure still capable of taking them by surprise.

'You're very good,' Sophia said. 'I look forward to sharing you with my husband. We'll take you together. He'll spunk you, then I can suck it out of your cunt.' The crude words seemed to excite Sophia anew. She sat up and looked down at Melinda, her eyes sparkling and her long black hair dishevelled. 'He'll want to have you whipped, of course. I'd like to see that. I'd like to see you whipped.'

She reached over to the top drawer of the bedside chest and extracted a black rubber ball about the size of a small melon. The whole surface of the rubber was indented with tiny dimples, a little like a golf ball.

'I was going to whip you tonight,' she continued. 'That's why I had Aldo tie you to the bed. I was going to stripe that pretty behind of yours. Still, there's plenty of time for that. Do you know what this is?' She held up the black rubber ball.

'No, mistress Sophia.'

'Well . . .' She placed the ball at the bottom of her

navel. 'Roll on your side facing me,' she ordered. The affection and tenderness she had displayed earlier seemed to have disappeared, her tone now cold and uncaring, much more the style Melinda had come to expect from her masters. Melinda did as she was told as Sophia shifted on to her side too and pushed forward so the rubber ball was sandwiched between the base of their navels.

Sophia looked down at their bodies. She moved her big breasts so their nipples were touching Melinda's.

'Push your belly against mine, girl,' she ordered.

Melinda used the muscles in her buttocks to push her pelvis forward. Almost instantly she felt the soft rubber ball mould itself to her shape, pushing down between her legs. As Sophia pushed from the other side the ball began to vibrate and Melinda felt a surge of pleasure from her clitoris as the vibration spread through her labia.

'Oh mistress . . .' she gasped, unable to stop herself, feeling once again the whole length of Sophia's supple body pressed against hers.

'Yes,' Sophia said, the vibrations of the ball obviously having exactly the same effect on her, its surface moulding itself to her body like clay. 'Harder,' she said. 'Press harder.' She kissed Melinda on the mouth and wrapped her arms around her body, hugging her tightly. 'Come on, come on,' she said, the words forced out against Melinda's lips. 'Fuck me with it.'

As she said it, she pulled Melinda over on top of her, her hands grabbing Melinda's hips and pulling them to and fro as if to indicate exactly what she wanted. Melinda caught on at once. She realised it was what she wanted too. She bucked her hips and felt the vibration of the ball increase as she drove it against Sophia's sex and lessen slightly as she pulled back.

'Yes, like that,' Sophia encouraged as Melinda's hips took up a regular rhythm, like a man, using the ball in place of a cock.

Melinda pumped harder, her own feelings as strong as the feelings she knew were coursing through Sophia. The vibrations of the ball seemed to surround her clitoris, defining its shape and separating it from the rest of her body until it was like a thing apart; a living thing, huge and distended. As she bucked her hips it almost felt as though her clitoris was a cock and she was using it to fuck her mistress.

'Mistress, mistress,' Melinda breathed, using all her strength to drive her hips faster and more powerfully.

She felt Sophia come, her fingers clawing at Melinda's buttocks, her body trembling and out of control. But Sophia's orgasm was fed back through the ball into Melinda's clitoris and set her off too, the extra stimulation causing her already overwrought feelings to explode.

But it was not enough. Whereas before their orgasms had been complete, the feelings that roared through both their bodies now were not an ending in themselves but a beginning. Sophia hugged Melinda's body tighter and rolled it over on to her back, taking her position on top and using her hips and her clitoris in imitation of a man. There were no barriers anymore, and no need to be told what to do. Their fingers groped at their breasts and nipples. They smoothed and caressed the acres of flesh that surrounded them. Their mouths kissed hungrily, tongues and lips squirming together as the ball trapped between their bodies sent its relentless reverberations deep into their sexes. They were lost, lost in each other; the point at which one body ended and the other began blurred and irrelevant. The only thing that mattered were the peaks and troughs of feeling as orgasm after orgasm overwhelmed them.

'I will never enjoy you again like this,' Sophia's voice said.

Did Melinda dream those words or was that really what Sophia had said as their bodies could take no more and the last orgasm faded away before they rolled apart, breathless and finally replete?

Three

'Tomorrow it's my turn,' Aldo reminded her, his fingers like a vice on her arm. Melinda was sure they would bruise her. 'You've had it easy so far.'

He had collected her from Sophia's bedroom and was leading her, naked again, along the corridor on the second floor. Melinda was still in a daze, the multiple orgasms she had experienced slow to release her body, let alone her mind, from their grasp.

'Inside,' he said brusquely when they reached the door to the bedroom where she had spent the day.

He opened the door, thrust her inside and closed it again without another word. The bedroom was dark but as Melinda's eyes adjusted to the moonlight that streamed in through the gaps in the curtains, she could make out two figures lying in the bed.

'Hi,' one said in an American accent. 'We're not asleep.'

'Don't be surprised,' the other said. 'We all share. You have been with Sophia, yes?' The second girl had an accent too but it was more difficult to decipher.

Melinda was so used to the rule of silence she found it hard to reply.

'I was like this too. Difficult to speak, yes? I am Leilah and this is Amber. You know it is allowed to speak when we are alone? You have been told this?'

'Yes,' Melinda managed to say.

'We share the same bed,' Amber said. 'They kept us away all day while you were waiting for Sophia.'

'Share?' Melinda was finding it hard to comprehend and even harder to speak. Apart from the briefest of interludes, when she had escaped from the ex-member of the O.I.M. who had kidnapped her, Melinda had had no reason to form her own ideas let alone express them. She had been treated as an object whose opinions and desires were not of the slightest interest, so the need to communicate had simply been irrelevant.

'Come and sit down,' Amber said gently, having experienced what Melinda was going through herself. 'You'll need to sleep.'

'Yes,' Melinda agreed.

'We talk in the morning,' Leilah said, throwing aside the top sheet. Both women made room for Melinda in the bed and, like her, were naked. Questions began to well up in her mind as she climbed between the sheets but, when she rested her head against the pillow and felt the warmth of the mattress where Leilah had been, her eyes closed and almost instantly she was fast asleep.

'Shh . . .' was the next thing she heard. 'You'll wake her.'

She opened her eyes to bright sunlight flooding through the gaps in the curtains. She saw Amber tiptoeing to the bathroom.

'It's all right,' she said with an effort. 'I'm awake.'

'Sorry, I had to pee,' Amber said, going into the bathroom.

Melinda sat up.

'You sleep well I think,' Leilah said, getting out of bed to pull the curtains back from the window.

Melinda watched her in fascination, completely un-
used to seeing a slave having the freedom to perform
even this simple action without being commanded
to.

'Leilah?' she asked, remembering the name.

'Yes?'

She had seen both girls in the punishment room
but she had not dared to look at them closely. Leilah
was clearly an Arab. She had long black hair which
was shiny, thick and completely straight, and an olive-
skinned complexion. Her eyes were so dark a brown
they were almost black and she had incredibly white
and regular teeth. Though her body was not fat there
was a plumpness about her hips and shoulders and
buttocks and her breasts were large and pendant,
hanging down from her chest, unable to support their
own weight. What had obviously been a thick bush
of pubic hair had been shaved away though the black
stubble was quite apparent.

'I'm Melinda,' she said. The sound of her name on
her own lips sounded particularly strange.

'And I'm Amber, remember?' the American said,
coming out of the bathroom. Amber was tall and
slim. She had long straight blonde hair parted down
the middle and blue, almost turquoise, eyes. Her
breasts were small and flat, as were her buttocks
which seemed hardly to rise at all from the top of her
thighs. Her waist was narrow and her belly so flat it
was almost concave. Her hip bones stuck out prominently on each side. Her best feature was definitely
her legs. They were long and lithe and supple, her
thighs dimpled just below the crease of her sex and
her calves shapely and firm. The Achilles' tendon at
her ankles was thin and pinched. 'You were really
whacked last night.'

'I was . . . I . . .'

'You can't get used to talking, right? It was the same for all of us, don't worry.'

'But remember it is not allowed unless we are alone,' Leilah said.

'You share this room all the time?' Melinda asked.

'Yes.'

'And the girl . . . the girl we saw punished?'

'She was one of us until yesterday.'

'What did she do?'

'We're not sure. It wasn't Sophia. It was the master. She did something crazy with him,' Amber said.

'We were not allowed to see her after that,' Amber added.

'Must have been very bad, very bad,' Leilah added.

'Must have been.' Melinda could not suppress a shudder at the thought of what had happened to the hapless girl.

'You've met Aldo,' Amber said. 'He's a bastard.'

'Yes.'

'He'll be in for you today. Sure as eggs. He'll want a piece of you while you're still fresh meat.'

'And we must help, I think,' Leilah said.

'Help?'

'He likes to have it all,' Amber explained.

'He never takes any of us alone.'

'Oh, he's not allowed to fuck us. That's one rule that's not been changed. But he gets so near it, it makes no difference, if you ask me.'

Melinda remembered what he had done to Mrs Chapman.

'Does the master know?'

'We are sure that he does. Only Sophia does not. The master and Aldo are very close. Too close. Closer than I have known.'

'How many masters have you had?' Melinda asked, the words coming more easily now.

Leilah sat down on the foot of the bed. 'Only one before this. My first master, in Cairo.'

'I'm from Boston. I've had three before this.'

Just as Melinda was about to tell them of her history the bedroom door opened and the old woman in the black dress who had attended Melinda the day before pushed a small trolley into the room. On the trolley was fruit, bread and a jug of water.

'Breakfast,' Amber said. The old woman left without a word.

They ate as Melinda related her story, and were astonished when she got to her kidnapping from the halfway house. Several O.I.M. slaves had undergone the same ordeal as prisoners in the rogue master's Roman villa and they were both glad they had not been among them.

Before she had finished telling them of her escape, the bedroom door opened again. Aldo stood in the doorway, the doorknob still in his hand, his mouth twisted in a crooked grin.

'I want you all in the punishment room as soon as you've showered,' he said, before slamming the door shut again.

'I thought so,' Amber said. 'He can't wait to get a piece of you.'

'It's his entitlement,' Leilah said.

Quickly they used the bathroom, showering and drying themselves and brushing out their hair as best they could with no mirror.

Leilah led the way out of the bedroom and down the stairs. Melinda had only just got used to the idea of being able to talk relatively freely – at all the other houses to be caught talking to another slave was one of the worst crimes and punished severely. Now it appeared they were allowed to walk about the house unsupervised and without their bodies being subjected to bondage. That was also going to take some getting used to. With all her other masters she had been led everywhere by an overseer and often in some complex bondage harness or bizarre costume.

They reached the covered walkway that led to the punishment room. The sun was still low in a cloudless blue sky but heat had already built up and the outside air was warm. The vines covering the trellis work were intertwined with jasmine and the scent of its flowers filled the air.

'This is going to be bad for you, I think,' Leilah said.

'We have to obey orders,' Amber added. 'Whatever he wants.'

'It's all right,' Melinda said. She knew she would have to do the same if she was in their position. She felt a knot of anticipation form in her stomach. The customary mixture of fear and excitement cinched it tighter.

Leilah opened the door to the punishment room and they filed in one by one. Aldo was standing in the middle of the room, his hands hooked around the beam that ran down its centre. He lifted himself off the floor until his chin was level with the beam, then raised his legs so they were at right angles to his body, his abdominal muscles rigid. He was stripped down to a pair of black Lycra briefs that clung to his hard buttocks and sweat glistened on his bulging biceps. Ten times he performed the exercise, the movements completed with almost balletic precision. Then he dropped to the wooden floor, lay out flat, laced his fingers together behind his head, and did a series of sit-ups, his body twisted around to point his left elbow at his right foot and vice versa on alternate efforts.

The three naked girls stood watching, waiting for their instructions.

Aldo stopped and got to his feet. Though sweat plastered down the hair of his body he was not in the least bit breathless. He smiled at Melinda with menace. 'I've been thinking what I would do with you,' he said. His teeth were irregular with two or three chipped and he had a gold filling on the right-hand side. 'A pleasant prospect,' he said in his cultural manner, so at odds with his appearance. 'The master is going to be enamoured of you, my child,' he continued. 'And so are his friends.' The idea made him laugh. 'You weren't whipped last night, were you?'

'No, master,' Melinda replied.

'The woman is too soft. She has no idea what is best for the slaves.' He turned to the other two girls. 'Put her on the frame.' He indicated a metal structure standing on the floor at the far end of the room.

Taking her by the arms Leilah and Amber led Melinda over to it. The frame was a simple metal rectangle about the size of a single bed. Attached to it were numerous leather straps, obviously intended to secure its victim in place, and hanging above it towards one end was a metal bar secured to a pulley on the overhead beam, exactly like a trapeze.

'On your back,' Amber whispered.

Melinda lay on the frame. Its base was made from a single sheet of metal, perforated with inch-wide holes. The metal was cold and uncomfortable. Melinda felt her nipples stiffen.

Leilah and Amber each pulled one of her arms above her head and secured them by the wrists to the corner of the frame. Aldo walked over and stood looking down at her.

'It is necessary to tie her down tightly,' he said, a cruel smile flickering on his lips.

There were thin leather straps that fitted through the metal perforations to secure her elbows and the top of her arms to the frame. Two thicker straps were buckled around the top of her chest and under her breasts.

Amber passed a wide belt across Melinda's navel, Leilah buckling it tight on the other side of the frame.

The overseer had gone to the cleat on the wall where the rope from the overhead pulley was tied off. He unwound the rope and let it out until the metal bar was just above Melinda's legs. The bar was at least three feet wide and fitted with the familiar leather cuffs at each end. Quickly the two girls strapped Melinda's ankles into the cuffs, spreading her legs apart. The moment the cuffs were buckled the overseer pulled on the rope, hoisting up the metal bar until Melinda's legs were stretched out straight, at right angles to her body, and her buttocks were raised off the frame too. The belt around her waist held the rest of her body down, the leather biting into her flesh.

Melinda felt a rush of panic. She was completely helpless, her sex open and suspended in mid-air, the close shave it had been given exposing every crevice and crease of her labia. It was her first master who had said that every slave reached a point when, however committed they were to their vows of submission, something – some act, some demand, some bondage device – made them rebel. Melinda had been bound in many ways, her body twisted and abused, and had reached that point only once before. She had no idea why but this position was causing her the same anxiety, her vulnerability and helplessness creating a fear and dread she could barely control. She desperately fought her bonds, trying to squeeze her thighs together to close her sex, struggling against the metal bar to pull her legs down. It was useless. The leather straps were perfectly secure. She succeeded only in chafing her skin.

She only needed to say one word, of course. She knew that. All the slaves knew that. She only had to tell him to stop and it would be over. She would be bound, as Penelope had been bound in this very room, and the gauze pads applied to her marks. In hours she would be on her way home, her contact with the O.I.M. broken for ever. The thought brought her back under control like a slap in the face. She didn't want *that*. She had faced worse than this, she told herself. She stopped struggling and took a deep breath.

Leilah was looking down at her with concern, reading the emotions she was feeling accurately. She stroked her forehead gently to calm her but Aldo spotted the gesture.

'Stop that,' he barked. He had seen her crisis too and knew what her struggles meant. 'If she does not wish to continue she only has to say the word. Is it that you wish to be released?'

'No, master,' Melinda said determinedly.

'Good. Get the whips then. We will continue.'

Strangely, Melinda felt relief at that. She had been whipped before. It was something she knew she could take.

She saw the girls move away across the room while the overseer went back to the foot of the frame. He extended his hand and ran it down the V formed by her suspended thighs, then pressed his hand against her sex, his palm covering the entrance to her vagina, his fingers curled around the top of the labia, his middle finger butting against her clitoris.

'No,' she said, before she could stop herself. She tried to squirm away from him. Why she was so deeply affected by being bound like this she could not understand, but she desperately did not want him to touch her like this. She felt as though a layer had been peeled away from her defences and new, raw nerves had been exposed; nerves he was touching.

'I told you, child, no is very serious,' he said, grinning. 'Do you really mean no?' His hand ground down on her. She could feel her vagina sucking at his palm and greasing it with her juices. His finger was pressing her clitoris hard against her pubic bone. Was this how it would all end? She only had to say one word and it would be over.

'Answer me,' he barked. He withdrew his hand and looked down at her sex. It was glistening wet, scarlet and angry where he had trapped her veins.

Melinda saw Amber and Leilah come back. They held short leather riding crops. Instead of the usual leather loops at the ends they were tipped with a thin tapering nylon line. Melinda tried to concentrate on the whips.

'Answer me,' Aldo repeated.

'Punish me, master,' Melinda intoned, trying not to look at the way his eyes were examining her sex and hoping he would not put his hand there again.

'That's more sensible. I will have the greatest pleasure in carrying out your request.' He looked up at the girls. 'Do it,' he ordered.

To Melinda's relief he moved to the side of the frame. She could see the tight Lycra briefs were distended by his erection, the ridge of his glans clearly defined under the clinging, tight material.

Amber stood at the bottom of the frame to the left, and Leilah to the right. They obviously had no need to be told what to do. Amber raised the whip and slashed it down across the top of Melinda's right thigh. Almost before the stripe of searing heat the stroke produced in Melinda's body had registered, Leilah cut her whip down across the top of Melinda's left thigh. Again, with no pause, Amber's whip stroked down, this time lower on Melinda's suspended buttocks. Leilah followed her example and also aimed lower.

The searing pain turned to exquisite, mind-bending pleasure. Melinda felt each stroke burn into her but though each produced a wave of stinging pain, its aftermath was that unique mélange of sensation, a pleasure striated with pain. The longer the whipping went on the deeper the sensation seemed to skewer into Melinda's psyche, touching the hidden secrets that lay there and satisfying the deepest needs. The crisis was over. The relief that she had not succumbed to her panic added to the incredible feelings that flooded her body.

The tail of the whip flicked at her sex. It was not deliberate but inevitable given Melinda's position. Her sex reacted with a throbbing pulse and a spate of juices that Melinda could feel running into the cleft of her upturned buttocks.

She was coming. She pulled at the leather that held her so securely, not because she wanted to escape but because she wanted to thrill herself with the feeling of her restraint. An orgasm roared through her, the gap between its conception and completion no more than the time it took for two more swinging strokes of the whip.

'Stop,' Aldo ordered as he saw the unmistakable signs of Melinda's condition.

The girls stopped immediately.

'You know what to do,' he said.

They did. It was the usual procedure, the one they had experienced themselves many times. They dropped to their knees and each began kissing and licking the red weals they had so carefully marked her with.

'Oh, master,' Melinda gasped, unable to believe what she was feeling, their mouths incredibly cool against the burning hot flesh. The weals were so sensitive it was as though each stroke of the whip had created a clitoris which their tongues could probe and provoke. Instantly Melinda's first orgasm gave way to a second, spurred on by the sudden intrusion of fingers – whose she did not know – deep into her soaking wet vagina. The fingers went deep, filling her as she felt her sex contract around them, clinging to them, using them to concentrate and shape the climax that ripped through her nerves. Every muscle in her body pulled against the bondage, the fact of her constriction acting like a vice to hold her orgasm in. It went on so long and so hard it blanked out everything but the feeling it caused.

How long it was before Melinda realised the girls had stopped she did not know. Her eyes had been closed by the force of her passion and, when she opened them again, Aldo was standing over her. He had pulled down the Lycra briefs and his gnarled and crooked erection was sticking up from his loins.

'Now it's my turn,' he said, circling his cock with his fist, and squeezing it hard. 'You're going to lick it for me.' As he said it he knelt on the frame and swung one leg over Melinda's body so he was astride her, her firm breasts resting against his thighs. He pushed forward until his erection was at her chin. 'Make it good,' he said.

Melinda raised her head and gobbled the misshapen cock into her mouth, glad of the distraction from the feelings that plagued her own body. The weals on her buttocks and thighs continued to sting and now that her climax had passed the prickles of pain were not so easily turned to pleasure. She moved her tongue against the ridge of his glans and felt his cock pulse instantly.

As she began to work it in and out between her lips she felt her legs being lowered, the iron bar descending until it rested on the foot of the frame. Leilah moved into Melinda's line of sight. She was holding a long thin tube that sprouted from a small, cylindrical block. The tube was made from rubber and flexible. Melinda saw it disappear behind the overseer's back then felt it being dipped into the molten lake her sex had become. It did not dwell there for long. Leilah was using it as a source of lubrication. Satisfied the tube was well greased with Melinda's juices she planted its tip at the base of the overseer's anus. She pressed her big breasts into his back and waited for instructions.

Amber had also come into view. As Melinda sucked and licked at the overseer's phallus, Amber sat on the edge of the frame and extended one hand to the base of his cock. She circled her fingers around it and squeezed it hard. Melinda felt it surge in her mouth. Then Amber snaked her other hand down between his buttocks to reel in the sac of his balls. Again this produced a surge in his erection.

'Now,' he ordered, looking over his shoulder at Leilah.

Leilah pushed the tube forward, overcame the initial resistance of the little ring of muscles, and plunged it home. She operated a small switch on the cylindrical base and the probe began to vibrate strongly.

'Yes,' he said.

Amber juggled his balls in her left hand while her right squeezed rhythmically at the base of his shaft, butting against Melinda's lips when she thrust her mouth forward. Melinda could feel the vibrations spreading through his body and up into his cock. It was pulsing and jerking in her mouth and she knew he was going to come. With the attention of three beautiful slaves it would have been impossible for him not to.

As she felt his cock turn from pulsing to a jerking, uncontrollable spasm, he pulled it out of her mouth. The circle of Amber's fingers slid up to the ridge of his glans and, as her other hand gripped his balls and Leilah pressed her breasts against his back and the long vibrating tube into his anus, spunk jetted out from the little slit of his urethra. It splashed down on Melinda's face and into her hair.

'That's only the first time, child,' he said, when his ejaculation finally ceased.

'Put these things on.'

For once Melinda knew what to expect. In the houses of the other masters she had never had the slightest idea what was going to happen but alone with the other two girls in the small bedroom and allowed, for once, to talk to them, they had told her precisely the normal routine and the duties she would have to perform. In this household the slaves were used to doing light domestic chores during the day but mostly they were there to serve the master – who, of course, Melinda was yet to meet – and Sophia, and the various guests they chose to invite to the house.

Sometimes, Amber and Leilah explained, the master brought home a single man or a couple who had been allowed to select one or more of the slaves, while on other occasions a dinner party had been arranged and the slaves had been used as a form of entertainment, usually ending up by accompanying one of the guests to his or her room.

Tonight they guessed there was to be a dinner party. The girls had spotted Camille arriving, her presence always a precursor to some such event. The girls had told Melinda about this woman. She was not an overseer in the formal sense, but she was a close friend of Sophia's. She came to the house frequently and always helped Sophia supervise the slaves, seeing to their make-up and costume for the parties. She was, Amber said, a dedicated lesbian without the slightest interest in men and had been allowed free run of the slaves, her preference in choosing a partner only second to the master himself.

Sure enough, as it began to get dark Camille opened the bedroom door. She was a smart, elegant woman with short strawberry blonde hair and a hard face, her features giving the impression they had been chiselled from stone. Her eyes were blue and contained a glint of steel. She was not a woman to be crossed, that much was clear.

Camille had ordered Melinda to follow her downstairs. On the first floor she had gone into one of the large luxurious bedrooms where the guests were accommodated. Laid out on the double bed was a red lace basque with long ruched satin suspenders. There was a pair of red suede high heels on the floor and a cellophane packet of stockings.

'Come on, do as I say,' Camille prompted as Melinda hesitated.

'You know you must obey me?'

'Yes, mistress.'

'Get on with it then.'

Melinda picked up the basque and wrapped it around her body. She started to try to fasten the catches at the back.

'I'll do that,' Camille said. Her accent was French.

Camille's fingers were long and bony. She pulled the edges of the garment together and began fastening it up, starting at the top and working down. It was tight and boned at the waist to produce an hourglass figure. The corset had no bra; two crescent shapes at the front fitting under each breast but leaving them bare.

'Put the stockings on yourself.'

Melinda sat on the edge of the bed. She opened the cellophane packet and unfurled the black stockings. They were ultra sheer with a glossy sheen that made them shiny. She rolled one into a pouch around the toe and inserted her foot into it, then unrolled the nylon up her calf and on to her thigh. It seemed a long time since she had seen her legs sheathed in stockings and the sight made her sex pulse, remembering how her very first master had liked to have her dressed in this way. Carefully she clipped the darker broad welt of the stocking into the suspender at the front, its metal clip discreetly covered with a diagonal sash of silk satin. She reached around to the side, adjusted the suspender to make it longer, then clipped it into the welt. The suspenders pulled the nylon into two triangular peaks of jet black which contrasted dramatically both in colour and texture to the creamy smoothness of the flesh above them. As she pulled on the second stocking in the same way she was conscious of Camille's eyes locked on her hairless labia.

'Very good,' Camille said. She was not tall but she was slender and curvaceous, her breasts jutting firmly from her white silk blouse. Her hips were plump and her legs, under a tight-fitting pencil skirt, shapely. 'Stand.'

She took Melinda over to a dressing-table and sat her in front of its mirror. For the first time in days Melinda glimpsed her own face. It had become so unfamiliar she almost found it hard to recognise herself. She stared into her own eyes to try to see if the experiences of the last weeks had registered there, but the eyes that stared back at her gave nothing away. They were the eyes of a stranger.

Camille quickly made her up. She used dark eyeshadow and a thick mascara and painted on an equally dark red lipstick. She brushed her hair and played with it until she appeared satisfied with its shape.

'Now the shoes.'

When Melinda got to her feet she discovered she was breathless. It had been a long time since she had worn anything as tight as this basque and she was finding it difficult to breathe. She went back to the bed and slipped her feet into the red high heels. Their height tilted her forward, tightening the muscles in her buttocks and calves.

Camille looked her up and down. 'I should have come earlier,' she said. 'I would have liked to have time with you. Sophia said you were special. You are certainly that.' Her hand stroked Melinda's buttocks. 'Wait here. Practise with the shoes,' she added, obviously making a conscious effort to pull herself away.

It was totally dark outside as Melinda was left on her own. She saw the glare of headlights briefly illuminate the windows and heard the crunch of gravel under a car's tyres as it pulled up to the front door. She thought she heard a door in the corridor outside being opened and closed. The hostess, she imagined, was going to meet her guests.

Doing as she was told, she paced up and down the large bedroom trying to get used to wearing high heels again. As she had noticed when she had been taken to Sophia, the long period without wearing high heels had left her tottering around on them, especially with the precipitous heights her new mistress seemed to favour. Ignoring the cramp in her calves and the bite of the leather around her feet she practised walking up and down the bedroom.

Oddly, she thought, considering there was a time when she had ached for a chance to see herself, she did not want to face the mirror in the dressing-table again. She glimpsed herself briefly as she walked by, the red basque obscenely exposing her very round, fleshy breasts, the suspenders neatly framing the shaven pubis at the apex of her thighs and the top of her labia squeezed between them, but she did not look again. She looked like a whore, and though that idea excited her she had no desire to stare at herself more intently. Consciously, she picked a route across the bedroom that avoided the mirror.

She heard noise from downstairs, the sound of footsteps and the buzz of conversation and laughter. It soon subsided as the voices moved away, perhaps into the dining-room. She could hear the occasional clatter of crockery. Time passed slowly.

'Come on.' The overseer had opened the bedroom door after what must have been two hours. He waited in the hall for her, then took her by the arm and guided her along the main hallway to a wide wooden staircase she had never seen before. At the bottom they faced the double doors at the front of the house, a large chandelier, with droplets in sparkling crystal, hanging from the high ceiling above the vestibule.

They turned down along the side of the stairs and into a short corridor hung with antique tapestries. They came to an imposing double doorway, its oak door carved in relief with hunting scenes.

'Wait here,' Aldo commanded, walking back the way he had come.

The noise of the dinner party seeped through the doors. It was obviously not a large-scale affair as the voices were muted and indistinct. As Melinda stood waiting to be presented to the guests, she remembered her first master, Walter Hammerton. It was Walter who had recognised her secret needs, needs that, until he had faced her with them, she had barely acknowledged herself. He had introduced her to the *Organisation Internationale de Maîtres*. He had presented her to his guests at a dinner party too, but on that occasion she had been in bondage and under strict supervision. It was a measure of the distance she had travelled in her acceptance of her own nature that now, though free to run away, to get into one of the cars outside and flee everything around her, she stood calmly awaiting her fate.

She wondered if, beyond the doors, the master would be sitting at the head of the table. Sophia was a challenging substitute but like every slave she longed to meet her new master. It was him, after all, who would ultimately determine the course of the next three months of her life. She was convinced, however, that he was not inside. Over the months she had developed a sixth sense when it came to her masters. Their presence in the house was like a change of temperature and one she could detect easily.

She was right.

'Take this in,' the old woman in the black dress said. She had appeared from a door on the other side of the corridor carrying a silver tray on which stood a Georgian silver coffee pot. 'Serve the coffee.' She opened one of the double doors and closed it again as soon as Melinda was inside.

The dining-room was impressive, its walls decorated with original eighteenth-century frescoes, a marble and granite floor and an oak dining-table and chairs from the Empire period that could have seated thirty. Only one end of it was laid out with white napery, silver cutlery and crystal glasses and only four chairs were occupied.

Sophia was wearing a tight black silk body with a neckline that plunged to her waist, her large unsupported breasts billowing against the material. Over the body she wore a short figure-hugging skirt, a tube of white Lycra covered in tiny white sequins like fish scales. The skirt was so short it left most of her long nylon-sheathed legs on display.

Camille, on the other side of the table, sat in an equally clinging red dress, its strapless bodice of tight satin like a corset, its skirt only marginally longer than Sophia's.

'Good evening, Melinda,' Sophia said. 'Pour the coffee for us, please.' She indicated the small white coffee cups that had been placed to the side of each place setting. The dessert, a confection of chocolate and cream, was still being consumed. Melinda moved to the table and poured the steaming hot liquid into Sophia's cup first.

The other two guests were a couple; the man in an evening suit and black bow-tie, the woman a brunette in a dress of dark rich mauve. The man was balding with a horseshoe of brown hair around his shining pate. He was deeply suntanned and more than a little over-weight and had a small-featured, chubby little face with a dimple in his chin. His eyes were a light brown and set very deep so that they appeared smaller than they were.

As Melinda poured her coffee the brunette got to her feet. She said something to the man in a language Melinda did not understand. Her eyes were looking at Melinda's naked breasts. Melinda walked around the table and filled the other cups.

'Put it down over there,' Sophia said, pointing at a small table on the other side of the room. Melinda tottered over to it, only too aware of the eyes staring at her buttocks.

The man spoke in the same language the brunette had used and his wife, if that was who she was, laughed. The mauve dress had a halter neck which fastened around the woman's throat and left her back com-pletely bare. Its long skirt dipped to her ankles but was split on one side right up to the top of her thigh. Her legs were encased in sheer grey tights with a dia-mond motif printed into the nylon.

'Now back here,' Camille said.

Melinda returned to the table. The man pulled his chair out and turned to get a better view.

'She is the new one?' the brunette asked.

'Yes, Alessi, brand new.'

'I haven't even had her yet,' Camille said.

The attention of the whole table was focused on Melinda now.

'I like the Arab girl,' the man said.

'Oh, I like the American,' Camille commented. 'Those long legs.'

'The American's got no tits,' the man said, his ac-cent heavy with some middle-European dialect.

'Oh,' Alessi told him, 'the Arab's definitely got the sort of tits you like.' Her voice had the same accent.

'Where's Giorgio incidentally?' the man asked. 'Shouldn't he have droit de seigneur?'

'He's in Bologna on business.'

'Funny,' the man said, 'I thought I saw him at Sabattini's.'

'No,' Sophia said. 'He's away.'

Alessi put her hand out and stroked Melinda's shoulder. 'So, is she available or isn't she?'

'You know the rules,' Camille said.

Alessi's hand moved to Melinda's breast. 'Lovely tits. Well, Boris, what do you think?' she said to her husband.

'We can wait.'

'Oh, Boris, and now I've got myself in the mood.' Her hand squashed Melinda's breast back against her chest.

'You can have either of the others,' Sophia suggested.

'Come on, Boris, you'll have a good time.'

'If that's what you want,' he agreed.

'Take her to the red room then.'

'I should have her first,' Camille said petulantly.

'I thought you were spending the night with me,' Sophia said sharply.

'And Amber?' Camille asked, brightening at the idea.

'Of course.' Sophia patted Camille's hand on the table.

'Take her to the red room then,' Sophia said. 'Just remember the rules, Boris. Giorgio has to take her first.'

'Don't worry, I'll see he's good.' Alessi said. 'I'm sure I can find something else for him to do.' She smiled wickedly.

71

'I'm sure you can.'

Alessi took Melinda by the arm and guided her out through the double doors, with Boris following in their wake. They walked down the corridor back to the front hall then turned left into what was obviously the main sitting-room, a large salon dotted with a big modern sofa and leather wing chairs. At the far side of this room Alessi led them through into a small square room decorated in red. It was furnished with an antique desk and a swivel chair, a small red leather Chesterfield and a large leather footstool with buttoned upholstery that matched the sofa. There was a marble fireplace, the grate of which was filled with a huge display of colourful dried flowers.

The room was lit by a table lamp perched on the corner of the antique desk. Apparently not satisfied with this, Alessi went to a switch by the door and turned on the overhead lights, a bar of rather incongruous spotlights. The room was flooded in bright light.

Coming back into the centre of the room where she had left Melinda standing, Alessi cupped her cheeks in her hands and kissed the semi-naked girl full on the lips, plumbing the depths of her mouth with her tongue. Boris stood behind them, pushing his body against Melinda's back and stretching his arms around both women, making Melinda the filling in a sandwich of bodies.

'Is it on?' he asked.

'She'll turn it on,' Alessi said. Melinda had no idea what they were talking about.

Boris said something in the language they had used in the dining-room.

'You must speak English,' Alessi chided. 'You know that.'

Alessi dropped to her knees. As Boris's hand fondled Melinda's breasts, tweaking her nipples and kneading the flesh like bread dough, his wife's tongue snaked into the furrow of Melinda's smooth hairless sex, her hands pulling her thighs apart. Instantly Melinda felt a shock of pleasure as the stranger's tongue locked on to her clitoris.

'Down,' Boris ordered. He pushed the footstool to the back of Melinda's stockinged legs and forced her to sit on it. As soon as she had, Alessi pushed her back so she was lying flat on the buttoned leather. The stool was not long enough to accommodate her head and it projected over the edge uncomfortably. The brunette picked up her legs and hooked them, one by one, over her shoulders, then renewed her assault on Melinda's now open sex, her tongue moving from her clitoris to the puckered bud of her anus, pushing into it and then into her vagina. Melinda felt her juices flow as the woman's tongue strained to get deeper into her sex.

Almost directly above her head she saw the man unzip his trousers and strip them down to his ankles with his briefs. He was anxious to get in on the act. He knelt behind Melinda's head, his erection fully grown.

'Is she giving you a good time?' he asked, watching his wife's head bobbing between Melinda's legs, the suspenders of the basque strained taut across the top of her thighs, pulling at the black welts of the stockings.

'Yes, master,' Melinda moaned. The feelings Alessi was creating seemed to be intensified by the tightness of the basque.

Boris pushed forward, forcing her head down until it was bent back at right angles to her spine, her hair

73

brushing the carpet. He positioned the tip of his erection against her lips. 'Suck on it,' he said.

Melinda pursed her lips around it and sucked hard as it slid into her mouth. She discovered that in this upside-down position, her throat was more open and in a direct line with her mouth – like a sword swallower – and she could take it deep. He plunged it in until his pubic hair was at her lips and his glans buried against the ribbed walls around her tonsils, so deep she had to fight the gagging reflex. The position was uncomfortable – her neck spasming with cramp, her body arched off the stool to try to relieve the pressure – but at the same time it was exciting. She had never done this before and once she got used to the depth of penetration he could achieve she found her body thrilling as he stroked in and out of her.

Boris's hands reached forward to gather up her tits, his fingers stretching over them like claws, pulling them up, then playing with her nipples and using them to suspend her breasts until they looked like two fleshy pyramids rising from her chest.

The dual assault on Melinda had been so sudden and unexpected that her reaction was purely instinctive. One minute she had been standing in the dining-room, the next she was here, impaled on the erection of one partner and the tongue of the other. Admittedly the eyes of the guests had stirred her body but that was no preparation for this. The suddenness of it and the ease with which the couple had reduced her to a receptacle for their desires had left her reeling and made her response that much more intense.

Instantly, she felt her body begin the customary rhythms of orgasm, a churning motion like the engine of a ship below decks, faint but impossible to escape from. As the man pumped his cock into her mouth,

74

using it exactly as if it was her sex, she found she could hold herself open for him with surprising ease by relaxing all the muscles of her mouth and just using her tongue to flick at his glans on its inward journey. Deep in her throat she felt his erection throb, a feeling that seemed to be communicated to her own sex and made her throb in turn.

Alessi moved up to Melinda's clitoris, feeding on it greedily and nibbling and sucking at it to make her come, wanting Melinda's orgasm as a precursor to her own.

She got what she wanted. As Boris's cock jabbed into the deeper recesses of her throat again and Melinda felt its heat and hardness there, her body lurched into orgasm, her mouth closing involuntarily around the cock it held, wanting to come over it as surely as if it had been buried in her vagina. The feeling of penetration, of being filled and fucked by a cock, had been transferred to her mouth. But, of course, she came on Alessi's artful tongue too, as it nudged the raw nerves of her clitoris to and fro, the two shocks of pleasure arcing together to form one.

As soon as the mists of passion had cleared a new need asserted itself. Melinda brought one hand around to her face and groped around for the man's balls. She wanted to make him come, like this, deep in her throat. She was hungry for it. She needed it. Her excitement was borne of what had happened this evening. What they had done to her was the perfect expression of what she wanted most. The eyes in the dining-room looking at her critically, like an object, then this couple bringing her here, tilting her over the stool so quickly and casually without the slightest hesitation. She had been treated as a thing to be used. That was what excited her more than anything else.

To be done to, not to do. That was the need Walter Hammerton had recognised in her. That was the truth.

She could see Boris's hairy balls hanging down from his phallus like the fruit of some exotic plant. She caught them in her fingers and pulled them out, stretching the skin of his scrotum while at the same time she sucked on his cock, sucking hard to draw him in still deeper, if that was possible.

He kneaded at her breasts.

'She's very good,' he said in a voice that betrayed no passion. But his cock was not so cool. As he said the words Melinda felt it spasm, jerking strongly against the tight prison her sucking mouth had created, and spunk spat out into her throat. Eagerly she swallowed it as each new jet produced another sticky flood. When finally the jerking movement stopped she explored the slit of his urethra with her tongue, her hands squeezing his balls as if to milk him of every last drop.

Alessi raised her head. Melinda's body had transmitted Boris's orgasm to her as if an instrument perfectly tuned for that purpose.

'She's made you come.'

'Jesus has she. Made me come so deep.'

He pulled back, his hands leaving white marks on Melinda's breasts where, in the throes of ecstasy, his fingers had dug into them.

'Now me, I think,' Alessi said, getting to her feet, her lips wet with Melinda's juices.

Melinda raised her head gingerly, feeling her cramped neck muscles tingle with pain. Alessi unfastened the halter neck and pulled down the long zip at the side of the mauve dress. She let it fall to the floor. Her breasts were small but her nipples were the size

76

of cherries. She kicked off her shoes and peeled down her tights. She wore no panties and her pubis was covered with a mass of curly black hair. After getting used to the shaved sexes of the women in the house it looked strange to Melinda. The hair was so thick she couldn't see her labia at all.

'Get up,' she ordered. Melinda got to her feet. Alessi lay on her back on the stool, exactly as Melinda had. She opened her legs, making it quite clear what Melinda was expected to do.

Melinda got to her knees between Alessi's legs. She dipped her head forward and flicked out her tongue, delving into the forest of hair to find Alessi's clit. Out of the corner of her eye she saw Boris coming to sit on the Chesterfield behind her, watching the action intently.

Alessi's sex was wet and her clitoris swollen. Melinda circled it once with her tongue and felt Alessi's body shudder. She licked up and down the hairy labia and produced another tremor.

'Use your fingers,' Alessi commanded.

Melinda caressed the fleshy curves of Alessi's thighs. She was quite plump and her flesh was soft and pliant. Melinda slipped one hand between her legs and manoeuvred two fingers into the wet opening of her vagina. As she pushed them in, the silky wet walls parted and Alessi moaned. She pushed them deep then scissored her fingers apart, exploring the inner contours. At that moment she felt a hand on her back and looked around to see that Boris had stretched forward and was stroking his hand along her spine. As she put her mouth back on Alessi's sex, Boris's fingers slipped into the cleft of her buttocks and down to her labia.

Her orgasm had left her sex throbbing. She tried to

concentrate on Alessi, tonguing her clitoris up and down in a strict tempo as her fingers used the same beat to stroke in and out, but Boris was not content to remain unengaged and drove his fingers into her vagina.

'Imagine it's my cock,' he whispered.

'Oh God,' Melinda cried, the words gagging on Alessi's sex. The tip of one of Boris's fingers had found a particular spot in her vagina that exploded with sensation. Feeling her reaction he caressed it relentlessly, scraping his finger against it. He dropped to his knees beside her and used his other hand to attack her clitoris, one arm around her buttocks, the other under her belly.

Melinda lapped at Alessi's sex, the beginnings of an orgasm the inevitable response to this double assault. Luckily she could feel Alessi's sex pulsing too, her vagina contracting and her clitoris spasming with increasing frequency.

Boris drove his fingers deeper. It was exactly what Melinda wanted. She felt his other hand working rhythmically at her clit, pulling it from side to side, hard and relentlessly. She remembered how his cock had felt buried in her throat and imagined it was in her sex now. She wondered how long it would be before she had a hard throbbing erection buried in her there. That would not happen until she was taken to the master. She yearned for that; to feel him filling her, taking her, completing her again.

'Oh, oh, oh . . .' The words, hot and breathy, were propelled against Alessi's sex as Melinda's orgasm overtook her. It started a chain reaction. Alessi's thighs clamped around Melinda's cheeks, the muscles rigid as her orgasm, in turn, seared into her body. With an enormous effort she raised her head to look

78

at the girl's face between her legs and their eyes met, the expression they both contained the same one of passion. Then Alessi's head dropped back and she lay prone, allowing the waves of pleasure to wash over her.

Eventually Alessi rolled off the stool and on to the floor and Melinda slumped against the red leather. Both were panting for breath, still given to the tiny trills and tremors of sensation that the aftershock of such an intense orgasm had inevitably produced.

But it was not over for Boris. Seeing the two women come together and feeling Melinda's orgasm with his own hands had given him another erection. The sight of Melinda, the tight red basque biting into her flesh, the taut shiny stockings pulled into chevrons on her creamy thighs, and at the centre of it all the scarlet gash of her sex, wet and inviting, was too much for him to bear.

He crawled between Melinda's legs, pulling at her hips to get her to raise her buttocks towards him. She co-operated, looking back to see his erection approaching and finding herself unconsciously wriggling her bottom in anticipation.

'No!' Alessi screamed. She had closed her eyes to enjoy her private pleasures but opened them just in time to register what was happening. 'You fool, have you forgotten?'

She jerked her head up to the ceiling. Boris and Melinda both followed her eyes. There, at either end of the bar that held the spotlights in place, was a small but unmistakable video camera, red lights on the side indicating that they were turned on. The whole episode in the red room had been watched by Sophia and Camille and, perhaps, recorded for the master.

Four

Sleeping in the same bed with the other two girls was not easy. Both of them were beautiful and though the double bed was large the three naked bodies inevitably came into contact with each other. The feeling of soft female flesh, of buttocks and thighs and breasts, was a constant provocation.

The difficulty of restraint grew greater as the days passed. Neither Melinda nor the other two girls had been called to Sophia for seven days. Neither had they been subjected to the none-too-tender attentions of the overseer. And the master had not returned. It was, they all agreed, a familiar pattern – the slaves were neglected deliberately to increase their sense of need. It was something all the girls had experienced under their various masters. But knowing this did not make it any easier at night when every accidental touch and nudge sent shivers of desire through their sexually overwrought bodies.

They took it in turns to lie in the centre of the bed because that was the worst position, assailed on both sides by flesh. Sleep, often after hours of temptation, came as a blessed relief.

Of course, they were not physically restrained from touching each other. Some of the masters had insisted that the slaves were bound at night to prevent them from touching their own bodies, let alone anyone else's, but here there was nothing to stop them from doing whatever they pleased. There was no video camera to watch over them and anyone approaching the room could be heard striding down the corridor long before he or she got to the bedroom door, so there was little danger of being surprised. What prevented them from indulging their incessant desires was their nature. Each of the slaves felt that to disobey a direct instruction was to betray something deep inside themselves. Their submission, their commitment to the masters, could not be breached so flagrantly. That was not to say that they hadn't cheated or allowed themselves minor infractions when they thought they could get away with it, and even when they knew they wouldn't in order to incur punishment – the excitement of which ran deep in them all. But to break this rule, to obtain sexual satisfaction from each other, was no minor matter.

Melinda found Leilah's body particularly alluring. She loved her big, spongy breasts, her long black hair and the shade of her olive-skinned complexion. But despite the enormous need she felt to press herself into Leilah's body, to feel those pliant breasts and suck at her fleshy mouth, to dig her fingers into her vagina and drown in the beauty of the girl, Melinda was in no mood to allow herself such grave disobedience. Her experience with the other masters had already made her break the rules – though through no fault of her own – and she had vowed to be the perfect slave now, as perfect as she had been for her first master, Walter Hammerton.

If she was tempted to run her hands towards Leilah's bosom or kiss her silky flesh, she thought of Hammerton's eyes, those blue steel eyes that had first drawn her into the web of the O.I.M. She would see them frown, the warmth they displayed when she performed to his satisfaction replaced by ice, freezing her in their glare.

That did not stop the desire of course, only prevented her malfeasance, and Melinda lay awake for hours, feeling the softness and sensuality of the bodies lying next to her and dreaming of the time when she had been chained to her bed each night, blindfolded and gagged, temptation unequivocally removed.

By the morning of the eighth day since the dinner party Melinda's body was stretched like piano wire, ready to thrum at the slightest provocation. The sight of Leilah showering in the bathroom, her hands working the soap into her pendant breasts and equally curvaceous buttocks, was enough to make Melinda tremble visibly.

There was worse to come. They had been instructed to shave their sexes every morning and every evening. It was not something they could do effectively for themselves, so the shaving ritual had become another form of torture. To lessen the stimulation it caused they would each use the shaving brush and shaving soap provided on their own bodies. They could shave the triangle of their mons with little difficulty but inevitably the delicate folds of their labia needed assistance. Each girl would lie on a towel on the bathroom floor while the other two helped each other apply the razor, one pulling the deckled nether lips this way and that in order to allow the other to get the blade into the most inaccessible places, the supine victim desperately trying to keep herself under control.

They took it in turns to be the last because that was the hardest to bear. This morning it was Melinda's turn. After smoothing and stroking the razor against Amber's sex, while Leilah held her flesh firm, Melinda then had to stretch and pull at Leilah's sex as Amber used the razor. Of the three girls Leilah's sex needed most attention, her jet-black hair growing profusely between her legs, right down over the bud of her anus and along the top of her thighs. Even in the short time between shavings a thick stubble developed which took a considerable time to eradicate.

Last was worst for this reason. After the fingering and close inspection of both girls Melinda's body was awash with desire. Watching as the white soap was scraped away to reveal the scarlet openings of their vaginas, and feeling the soft – and often pulsing – labia and the inevitably swollen clitorises as she made a flat plane for the blade, left Melinda weak and wet. Tipped on her back in this state, her legs spread open and her sex exposed to probing fingers and the cold steel razor, was almost more than she could stand. It was Leilah's turn with the blade today and as she worked, her eyes studiously locked on Melinda's sex, her big breasts swayed from side to side. As much as she tried to fight the thought off, Melinda found it impossible not to imagine what one of those breasts would feel like dangling over her mouth, how its spongy pliant flesh would press against her face as she hoovered its nipple into her mouth. Equally, as Amber's fingers prepared her intimate flesh for the razor, pulling the very top of her labia first and stretching the clitoris that lay underneath it, Melinda found it impossible not to respond to the spasm of pleasure that leapt through her body.

'We'll be quick,' Amber said, knowing exactly what Melinda was going through. Yesterday she had been last and remembered vividly what torture it had been.

It was comforting but untrue. They could not be quick. It seemed to take for ever, the fingers prodding and pulling at her flesh, then the cold, tantalising touch of the razor. Each stroke sent a rocket of pleasure shooting through her body, the temptation to pull both girls down, to writhe and squirm against their glorious flesh and to allow herself to come in a sea of sensual delight, almost impossible to resist.

But it had to be resisted. Melinda knew that. It was a test as devious and pervasive as any she'd experienced under the masters, and one she was determined to pass.

Every nerve in Melinda's body was clenched and her muscles locked against the possibility of doing anything she would regret, but finally it was over. They helped her to her feet and she dried herself energetically with a towel, harshly rubbing her delicate flesh to avoid the last provocation.

Back in the bedroom they heard steps approaching down the hall. The overseer opened the bedroom door.

'You,' he said to Melinda, 'with me now.'

Melinda felt her heart thump. This was a break in the routine of the last week. Did it mean she was being taken, at last, to meet her master? Or at least to see Sophia again?

Aldo smiled at the other two girls. 'It's time you two were put through your paces,' he said. 'I'll be back.'

He closed the door as Melinda tripped out into the hall.

They walked down to the first floor and along the broad corridor that led to Sophia's bedroom, Melinda's heart pounding in anticipation. But her hopes were soon dashed when the overseer opened the door to a small narrow windowless room some way from the double doors of Sophia's bedroom.

The old woman in black was waiting. She sat at a dressing-table strewn with make-up. Behind her was a wardrobe and a chest of drawers.

'Twenty minutes,' Aldo said, pushing Melinda inside and closing the door after her.

The woman got up from the chair and pulled Melinda over to it. Her fingers were hard and bony and hurt Melinda's arm. The dressing-table had no mirror and Melinda was made to sit facing outwards, the light from an overhead lamp shining right into her face.

The woman began applying make-up. She worked quickly, using an eye-liner and shadow, and a deep red lipstick. She varnished Melinda's fingernails and toenails in the same colour. A heavy, flowery scent was applied to Melinda's breasts, between her legs and behind her ears.

From the wardrobe the woman searched through a rack of dresses and pulled out a red Valentino suit, a short skirt with a beautifully-tailored jacket with two large gold buttons. She then found a very plain white georgette blouse with a scoop neck. She lay them across an old armchair, the upholstery of which was wearing away at the arms. From the top drawer of the chest she extracted a black lace suspender belt and a packet of stockings. Opening the packet she shook out the stockings. They were white with welts made from white lace.

Taking Melinda by the arm again she pulled her to her feet and indicated the clothes.

Melinda picked up the suspender belt and wrapped it around her waist. It was quite wide, with a band of black lace that covered almost half her belly, its long black suspenders hanging down her thighs. She clipped it into place and sat on the chair to pull on the stockings, watching as the tight nylon, woven with Lycra to give it a glossy sheen, encased her long legs.

As she stood up and climbed into the skirt and blouse she saw the woman take a pair of red high heels from the bottom of the wardrobe. Their heels were spiky and covered with a metal shell that had been coloured gold. The woman dropped them to the floor in front of Melinda.

The white blouse was almost transparent and Melinda knew her breasts could be seen through it quite clearly. She zipped up the tight skirt at the back. It was just long enough to cover the white lace welts of the stockings. Melinda pulled the jacket on and stepped into the shoes. The woman indicated that she should sit again and was brushing her hair when the overseer came back into the room.

'She's ready?'

The woman took two polished silver bracelets from the top drawer of the dressing-table. They were identical and hinged so they could be clipped around the wrist, the only difference between them being that under the clip of one was the head of a snake while on the other was its tail. Opening the bracelets the woman fastened them around Melinda's wrists. They fitted snugly, allowing no movement up or down but not biting into the flesh either.

Aldo pulled Melinda to her feet. He brought her hands together in front of her and slipped the silver snake's tail into the open jaws of the snake's head. Melinda heard a sharp metallic click and her wrists were locked together. She could see a small keyhole at the back of the snake's head.

'Come on,' he said.

They set off through the house. Taking the main stairs down to the front door Melinda saw one of the double doors was already open. There was a large black car parked outside with its engine running, a uniformed chauffeur sitting behind the wheel. To the left of the door was a long pier mirror and as Melinda strode past she caught a glimpse of herself in it, the expensive suit, blouse, hosiery and high heels transforming her. She looked like a model; tall, elegant and slender. Only the silver bracelets holding her wrists together were a reminder of her true position.

The overseer held the rear passenger door open and Melinda climbed in, a little awkwardly with her wrists bound together. The interior of the car was spacious, the seats upholstered in grey leather. It was cool too, the air-conditioning left on to cope with the fierce mid-morning sun. The overseer got in beside the driver, who immediately set the car in motion, its big tyres showering up gravel from the drive.

Melinda's heart was thumping again. She had been disappointed that she had not been taken to Sophia but her excitement had doubled now. She guessed that she had been prepared in this way for only one reason: she was going to be taken to meet her new master. She was glad she had seen herself in the mirror. He would see her looking her best.

It took thirty minutes to get to the outskirts of Rome and another forty to weave in and out of the frantic traffic before they arrived at their destination. The driver and the overseer talked in Italian, laughing frequently but making no reference to Melinda as far as she could tell. The driver's eyes were shaded with sunglasses and Melinda could not see whether they lingered on her in the rear-view mirror. She was sure that if they did he would get a view up her skirt to her lace-welted thighs and even, perhaps, glimpse the dark crease of her unclothed sex.

Melinda recognised the Borghese Gardens as the car reached the hill at the top of the Via Veneto. It turned left and came to a halt outside a smart pink awning on a large, imposing and obviously expensive restaurant, a polished brass plate to the left of its revolving door declaring it to be DANTE.

Aldo got out of the car. A doorman in an elaborate uniform, with so much gold braid on the front of his jacket he looked like a hussar, walked towards the car and the overseer took him to one side. Melinda saw a tip change hands before Aldo returned to the car and opened the rear passenger door.

'Out,' he said.

The street was quite busy with people bustling about at the beginning of their lunch hour and businessmen in Armani suits going into the restaurant for lunch. Not one failed to notice the beautiful blonde struggling to get out of the car with her hands manacled together in front of her. Not one pair of eyes didn't dwell on her as the squat shaven-headed man took a small key from his pocket and unlocked the catch behind the snake's head on one of the bracelets, allowing her hands to fall to her side. Indeed, several stopped in their tracks and stared as the doorman tipped his top hat and escorted the red-suited woman inside.

The eyes of the onlookers excited Melinda. She had spent much of her time in private. secluded from the real world. Occasionally, very occasionally, she had been presented with it, and when she had come face to face with the reality of how people saw her, she had felt not humiliation but pride. She was not ashamed to be a chattel, owned as an object by her master. It was her choice and she wore her thraldom like a medal, her head held high.

The interior of the restaurant was plush and elegant. The foyer was large with a dark blue carpet and white walls hung with oil paintings of Roman monuments, a huge crystal bowl of flowers on a circular table in the centre of the room. The doorman removed his hat and said a few words to the black-suited *maître d'* who stood by a brass lectern at the entrance to the restaurant itself. The man nodded his understanding and took two steps towards Melinda.

'Good morning, *signorina*. It is a pleasure to welcome you to my restaurant. The *signor* is waiting.' He bowed slightly. His face was tanned, his thick hair absolutely white. 'Please to follow me, *signorina*.'

He turned on his heels and led her through into the main restaurant, a large room with tables set with pink linen and small bowls of pink carnations. A party of five men, who had witnessed Melinda's arrival, were being seated at a circular table as the *maître d'* walked past. One of them, a small, bespectacled man in a grey suit, tried to catch Melinda's eye, and when she ignored him, stepped directly in her path.

'You for hire?' he asked in an American accent. ''Cause I'd pay a lot for what you've got.'

Melinda tried to side-step the little man but he anticipated her and side-stepped in the same direction, blocking her again.

The *maître d'* had advanced several paces before realising that Melinda was no longer following him.

'Name your price,' the American continued. 'Money no object.'

'*Scusi*, sir,' the *maître d'* intervened. With seemingly no effort he literally picked the man up by his collar, shunted him to his table and pushed him down

89

into a chair one of the waiters was obligingly holding out. Smiling politely, he nodded to the other four men who watched with astonished expressions. 'A little misunderstanding, I think,' he said. 'This way, *bella signorina*,' he said to Melinda, resuming his journey across the dining-room.

At the far side of the room, on a large round table in the corner, a tall man with very rich wavy brown hair and a rugged handsome face, sat alone. His eyes were dark brown and penetrating, their whites completely clear. He wore a dark blue suit, a cream wool waistcoat, a light blue cotton shirt and a dark blue and cream silk tie. He had a gold wedding ring on his finger.

As Melinda approached the table he got to his feet and extended both his hands, picking up her left wrist and pressing her hand to his lips.

'My dear, how nice to see you. Sit please.'

The *maître d'* had already pulled a chair from under the table and Melinda sat down, her pulse racing. Without having to be told she knew instinctively that this man was her master.

'Thank you Angelo,' he said. 'Would you be kind enough to bring the *signorina* a glass of Ferrari spumanti.' There was a glass of sparkling wine on the table in front of him.

'*Si, signor*.' The *maître d'* bowed deeply, his hands on his knees, and hurried away. Obviously the master was a regular and honoured customer.

'Well, my dear,' the master said, his eyes moving slowly from Melinda's face to her body. She had not buttoned the jacket and saw he was examining the outline of her breasts. His eyes dropped to her lap. 'I have to say I was attracted to you the moment I saw you.' He had seen a great deal more of her than this,

writing naked on an examination table for the benefit of a video camera. 'But you are certainly not a disappointment in the flesh.' There was something about
the way he said the word 'flesh' that made Melinda
shudder. He put his hand out and covered her wrist,
which was resting on the table, his fingers stroking
the silver bracelet. 'You feel cold,' he said.

'No, master.'

The restaurant was heavily air-conditioned but that
was not what had sent a chill through Melinda. There
was something about her instinctive response to this
man that had turned her heart to ice. For the first
time, she had not been instantly attracted to her new
master. She tried to analyse what was causing her to
feel like this but there was nothing on a rational level.
It was just a feeling, and an unwelcome one at that.

The *maître d'* arrived with a tall glass of sparkling
white wine on a silver tray. He put it down in front
of Melinda and spoke to the master in Italian.

'English please, Angelo, in front of my guest.'

'Of course, I beg your pardon. Would you like to
see the menus now or shall I come back later, *signor*?'
he asked.

'No, Angelo. Bring us *aragosta griglia* and *insalata
verde*. And a bottle of that delicious Frascati.'

'At once, sir.'

The *maître d'* hurried away. Melinda watched him
go, weaving his way across the now-full restaurant as
waiters with gleaming trays covered by equally
polished cloches began delivering the first orders to
the tables. It was a world away from the cloistered
secret life that had marked the majority of Melinda's
time with the masters.

'As I was saying, my dear, you are a very beautiful
woman. I look forward to getting to know you more

intimately. You may drink your wine.' The master's English was good, with only the slightest hint of an Italian accent.

Melinda brought the glass to her lips. The wine was fruity and delicious.

The master leant forward and put his hand on Melinda's thigh under the table. He worked it up until it was resting on the white lace welt. He squeezed her flesh hard.

'That is very exciting,' he said, looking into her eyes. 'Has my wife had you shaved?'

'Yes, master.'

'Today?'

'Yes, master.'

He edged his hand higher. She felt the warmth of his palm on her naked flesh above the stocking top, then his fingers stretching out to feel for her labia, as if to confirm it was hairless. The tip of one finger made contact. Apparently satisfied, he withdrew his hand, picked up his wine glass and sipped the chilled wine.

Melinda saw that a waiter was staring at their table. He had seen what had happened and stationed himself so he could see more.

'Put your hand under my napkin,' the master ordered. 'Unzip my fly.'

Melinda did as she was told. She slid her hand under the pink linen napkin that matched the pink linen tablecloth and groped around for his zip. An erection already bulged out against the material. The waiter's eyes watched her. The master had either not seen him or did not care about his interest.

'You see how you excite me?'

'Yes, master.'

She pulled the zip down and let her hand fall into his lap. She had not been ordered to do anything else.

'Put your hand inside. Squeeze my cock.'

Melinda's fingers found the shaft of his phallus under his pants and squeezed it. The waiter moved slightly to his right to get a better view.

'Take it out now, *caro*.'

Melinda found her way through the folds of his underpants and the tail of his shirt and extracted his erection from the front of his trousers just as a waiter arrived at the table.

'*Buongiorno, signor*.'

'*Buongiorno, Alberto*,' the master replied, tucking his napkin firmly into the waistband of his trousers.

The waiter added a long thin lobster fork to the array of cutlery on the table, then offered them bread from a basket containing four different types. Melinda shook her head to refuse, her hand still firmly planted in the master's lap.

'Pull the foreskin back,' the master said as the waiter poured sparkling mineral water into the glasses set out in front of them. He obviously spoke no English as he did not react to the master's words.

Melinda, trying to keep her upper body as still as possible to disguise what she was doing with her hand, took the flap of skin covering his glans and jerked it back. The master moaned.

'*Signor*?' the waiter queried.

'*Niente*,' the master said. The waiter completed his duties and moved away. 'Not very subtle,' the master chided. A male diner at the next table had also heard the noise. He looked around to see its cause. His eyes lighted on Melinda and examined the transparent white blouse minutely. 'As you were with the countess you must be very good at taking a cock in your mouth,' the master continued. 'She has special machines, I hear. Is that true?'

'Yes, master.' Melinda gripped his cock tightly but did not move her hand.

'Do you like taking a man in your mouth, *caro*?'

'Yes, master.' She felt his cock pulse as he said the words.

'Feeling him come in your mouth?'

She remembered Boris and how he had come so deep in her throat, with her head bent back over the footstool.

'Oh yes, master.'

Almost unconsciously Melinda began moving her fist up and down the master's erection. It was not easy to keep her arm from making exaggerated movements above the level of the table and she could see the waiter who had been watching them before staring intently. Fortunately, one of his colleagues hurried up to him at that moment and spoke in angry-sounding Italian, obviously asking him why he was standing doing nothing in the middle of a busy restaurant. He walked away with obvious reluctance.

'That's very good,' the master said.

She tried to increase the pace and felt his cock pulse strongly again.

'Have you been in your mistress's bed?'

Sophia had told her they shared all the slaves so Melinda saw no reason to lie. 'Yes, master.'

'How many times?'

'Just one, master.'

'What did she do to you, girl?'

'She had . . . she used a vibrator, master. A big ball of a vibrator. She made us press our bodies together very tightly.'

He said something in Italian under his breath.

'It was very strong.'

'And what else. Did she lick you? Did she?'

94

'Yes, master.'

The words were exciting him, Melinda could feel that. She searched desperately for something to say, wanting to please him. She remembered what had happened at the halfway house.

'At the halfway house . . .'

'Yes?'

'She made me use the whip on her.'

'A whip?' He sounded surprised.

'Not to beat her, master. She wanted me to use the handle, to put the handle in her . . .' She could not think of the right word to use.

'In her vagina?' he prompted.

'Yes, master.'

'The handle of the whip, like a dildo?'

'In and out of her.' His eyes burnt fiercely. The top edge of the napkin had slipped out of his trousers and Melinda was having trouble keeping his cock under it as she moved her hand up and down.

'*Aragosta griglia,*' the waiter announced as he arrived with a silver tray on which sat a chafing-dish containing two lobsters, grilled and split open.

'Don't take your hand away, *caro,*' the master said, feeling Melinda's fingers loosening their grip as another waiter wheeled a trolley up to the table. The first waiter set the chafing-dish down on it while a third brought a big white bowl of salad and set that on the serving trolley too. The team of three went to work laying the lobsters out on huge white plates, dressing the salad and dividing that between two smaller plates. None of this activity lessened the master's erection. Melinda felt it pulsing in her hand. She squeezed it tight.

The waiters placed the lobsters in front of their customers, together with the salad, and added little silver jugs of melted butter.

'*Grazie*,' the master responded calmly.

'*Prego*,' came the response.

The wine waiter appeared, showed the master the wine, uncorked it and poured a small amount into his glass to taste. As he leant forward to pick up his glass, the master's napkin slipped to the floor. The sommelier was standing at the master's shoulder and it was impossible for him not to see the master's erection sticking up from Melinda's fist.

'*Scusi, signor*,' he said immediately. He strode to the waiter's station four or five yards away, picked up a neatly-folded starched napkin, flapped it open and returned to lay it across the master's lap.

'*Grazie*,' the master said, smiling. He took a large banknote from a money clip and slipped it into the waiter's hand. He said something in Italian.

'*Naturale*,' the sommelier said. He poured the wine and bustled away.

He was not the only person to observe what was going on however. A woman in a bright yellow dress at the next table on the left-hand side had been looking at the master with, Melinda thought, more than a little interest. Her eyes widened as the napkin fell to the floor and she stared with her mouth wide open.

'And what else has happened to you?' the master asked. He poured melted butter over the flesh of his lobster, then leant across the table to butter Melinda's. 'Did you see that American friend of my wife's?' He pulled a large piece of lobster from its shell with the special fork and fed it into his mouth. Butter dripped from his chin. He used the napkin to dab it away, giving the woman at the next table another view of what lay beneath it in case she had not believed her eyes the first time.

'Yes, master. She wanted me to . . .' Again she was lost for the right word.

'What, girl?'

'To lick her, master. To lick her sex. Aldo whipped me, master, while I was doing it.' She felt his cock swell again. She looked over at the woman in yellow who was busy trying to attract the attention of a friend on the other side of her table, obviously wanting to tell her what was going on.

'Aldo was watching?'

'Yes, master. Then she wanted to use him, master.'

'Really?'

'Yes, master.' This was what he wanted. She could feel his cock pulsing as she moved her hand up and down again. He was turned on by her words and by the situation; by the fact that he was in a public place, using his slave so brazenly. 'He got on top of her. He put it inside her. She was moaning.' The master's cock jerked in her hand again. 'At the last minute, master, just as he was about to come, he pulled out of her.' She wasn't doing very well, she thought. She was trying desperately to please him, to excite him with her words, but she did not know how to do it or which words to use to best describe what he obviously wanted to hear.

'Just as he was about to spunk?' the master prompted.

'Yes, master.'

'And did he do it? Did he spunk?'

'Yes, master. All over her belly.'

'With you watching?'

'Yes, master.' She wished she could find a way to paint an exciting picture for him and describe exactly how it had made her feel but all she could find to say was, 'Big gobs of it, shooting out everywhere.'

Suddenly the look in the master's eyes changed. He caught Melinda by the wrist and pulled her hand up on to the top of the table.

'I think we'll leave that until later,' he said.

Melinda felt a wave of disappointment. She had failed. The woman in the yellow dress looked disappointed too. She turned back to her companions at her table.

The master saw Melinda's expression.

'You have done nothing wrong, *caro*. Quite the contrary. I find you very exciting.' He offered no further explanation as to why he had stopped her but the words lifted Melinda's spirits. 'Eat your lobster.'

Melinda attacked the fish with a vengeance, suddenly very hungry. She saw the master stuffing his shrinking erection back into his trousers and zipping up his fly.

'Giorgio!' A tall and very burly man in an ill-fitting suit approached the table.

'Luigi!' The master got to his feet and embraced the big man. 'Sit, sit, please.'

A passing waiter was summoned to bring a chair and the man sat at the table, talking in rapid-fire Italian. He stared at Melinda intensely as she ate her lobster and salad.

'She is one,' he said in English.

'Yes.'

'Hard to believe.' He was looking at Melinda's breasts under the white georgette. 'Hard to believe.' He was shaking his head slowly from side to side. 'And how is Bianca?'

The master replied in rapid Italian, lowering his voice and leaning towards the man. Melinda saw Luigi nod and smile. She wondered who Bianca might be. She had seen no one of that name at the villa.

The waiter arrived to clear away their plates. Melinda saw the master looking at his watch. He said something in Italian which obviously greatly surprised the man.

'*Realmente?*' he said.

'*Si, si.*'

'*Ora?*'

'*Si, ora.*' He looked at his watch again as if trying to calculate how long something would take.

The big man looked incredibly pleased. He got to his feet and shook the master's hand warmly.

'Go with him,' the master said to Melinda. The command came as a shock. The man stood waiting. It was not any desire to disobey that made Melinda hesitate but her disorientation. She had not expected this. From being so close to the master, and feeling the warmth of his pleasure, she was being sent away casually on a sudden whim. However much she felt uneasy at her initial response to the master, this was a cruel blow.

'Do it,' the master said, angry that she had not got up at once.

Melinda stood immediately. The man took her arm and led her through the restaurant. As she looked back at the master she saw him take out a small pocket telephone and punch in a number. By the time they got out on to the street the big black car was drawing up outside the entrance. The chauffeur climbed out and opened the rear door, saying something to the man in Italian, the only word of which Melinda recognised was '*telefono*'. Clearly the master had summoned the driver by phone.

Melinda climbed into the back seat, followed by Luigi. She settled into the grey leather as the driver got back behind the wheel. The car started away from the curb. Luigi turned to look at Melinda. He grinned, his flabby face creasing into rolls of fat.

'Down here,' he said, indicating the floor in front of his knees. Melinda slipped to her knees on the thick woollen rug that carpeted the car, noticing the driver angling the rear-view mirror downwards. Luigi leant forward and groped at her breasts with the fat sausage-like fingers of one hand, while the other struggled to unzip his fly. He fished out his flaccid, circumcised cock and pulled her head down on to it.

'Nice lunch,' he said. 'Now *dolce*.'

Melinda had no choice. She wrapped her lips around Luigi's cock. It began to swell immediately.

He dropped his hand to her lap and inched up her skirt until he could get his fingers between the top of her thighs. He tried to push them against her labia.

'I have one hour. A little present from, how do you say, your *maître*.' He stroked his hand against the lace welt of her stockings. 'Pull your blouse up.'

Without taking his cock from her mouth Melinda obeyed, tugging the white georgette out of the waist of the skirt and pulling it up over her breasts. The car had reached the bottom of the Via Veneto.

'*Bella*,' the man said, rubbing his hands over both breasts and pressing them back against her chest. 'And *calza*.' Her skirt was still ruckled up around her thighs and he was staring at the stocking tops. 'Very sexy, ah?' He drove his hand down between her thighs again, then worked it up towards her sex, dragging her skirt up further with his wrist. When the hairless crease of her labia came into view she felt his cock swell in her mouth, engorging rapidly now.

The big car turned left sharply with a squeal of tyres. It headed down the ramp of a multi-storey underground car park. The bright sunlight was replaced by dim intermittent lights from overhead lamps set in the ceiling. The tyres squealed loudly every time the car turned down a new ramp, winding its way ever deeper into the bowels of the building. Finally it reached a level completely devoid of cars. The driver headed for a corner and parked.

Luigi's cock was fully erect now. Melinda sucked on it hard. She could hear the driver turning around in his seat to watch.

'I should take you outside and fuck you,' Luigi said. He said something to the driver in Italian.

'*Si, si, tutto,*' the driver said. She guessed they were talking about her shaven labia.

The man's hand pressed into the folds of her sex then pulled away. He slumped back into the grey leather seat and allowed her freer access. She began moving her mouth up and down on his shaft as it poked out from his trousers and underpants. She wanted to do a good job because it was obviously her master's wish.

The man moaned. 'I think I fuck you now,' he said, but did not move. Almost before the words were out of his mouth and as Melinda drove her mouth down on his cock, she felt a sticky wetness in her mouth. It seeped out of him rather than jetted. He moaned. She swallowed all she could but a little escaped her mouth and dribbled on to his brightly-coloured boxer shorts.

'*Molto buono,*' he said, resting his head against the back of the seat and closing his eyes.

Melinda wasn't sure what to feel. Her first reaction was to feel used and abandoned by her master. Their illicit intimacy had been cast aside, the master clearly so unimpressed with her that he had thought nothing of discarding her as casually as a paper handkerchief.

But then she remembered what he had said about

finding her exciting. He had no reason to lie to her. She was his chattel, his property, and her feelings and emotions were of no account. He had no need to placate her. The only reason he had to say such a thing was because it was true. She also remembered Luigi had said he had been given her for an hour, which meant, she guessed, that she was to be returned to the master when the hour was up. That thought made her feel better.

'You can get up,' Luigi said. Melinda climbed back into the seat. She wriggled her skirt down and pulled her blouse back over her breasts. Luigi did not look at her again.

The driver started the car and began to drive back through the levels of the car park to the surface. He paid the toll at the exit and they were soon out of the busy streets of Rome after a diversion of no more than fifteen minutes. Luigi's excitement at his unexpected good fortune was obviously too great for him to contain.

They drove through the traffic with Luigi giving the driver instructions in Italian. After some minutes the car came to a halt outside a modern office building.

'*Ciao*,' he said, getting out, the remark addressed to the driver and not to Melinda.

'*Ciao*,' the driver responded as he drove off.

They drove in silence. The rear-view mirror was adjusted again and occasionally she saw the driver's head turn to look at her, but the black lenses of the sunglasses gave no clue as to what he was thinking.

She badly wanted to ask him where they were going but even if he had spoken English, she knew it was forbidden.

After twenty minutes of crawling through traffic the car swept through an imposing wrought iron gateway and into a cobbled courtyard in the middle of which was a bronze fountain in the shape of a dolphin, water spraying from its mouth. The building that fronted the courtyard was a beautifully-restored Renaissance period townhouse with large stone mullion windows with triangular entablature. The massive front door was made from wood that looked original.

The driver picked up the phone set into the central division between the two front seats and punched in a number. He spoke three or four words of Italian then put it down again. A couple of minutes later the wooden door of the house swung open and a woman, neatly dressed in a knee-length black skirt and a white blouse with a frilly collar, strode to the back of the car and opened the rear door. Her face was hard with an expression that looked as though she was permanently cross. She wore horn-rimmed glasses and had her auburn hair tied in a bun at the back.

'Out,' she said in a heavy Italian accent.

Melinda stepped from the car.

'Follow,' the woman said, turning on her heels and walking back into the house.

As Melinda obeyed, the car drove away. She stepped past the incredibly thick wooden door but instead of the palatial antique interior she was expecting from the outer appearance, she found herself instead in a large open-plan, modern office. There was a small reception area at the front, with ranks of desks at the rear all equipped with computer monitors, complex-looking telephones and other hi-tech devices. Men and women, all comparatively young, sat at the desks or buzzed around them in a whirlwind of chaotic activity, shouting loudly at each other, holding as many as three phones at the same time. Others punched the computer keyboards with studied concentration.

The woman led Melinda to a metal staircase, made from extruded sheet steel and steel cable, suspended from a side wall. It led to a gallery constructed from steel girders that had been set into the ancient stone walls where once, no doubt, oak beams had supported an upper floor. As they walked up the stairs Melinda could see that the outer wall of the gallery was made from plate glass, with a door at the top of the stairs in the same material. As they walked through the door she saw more desks and more frantic activity.

Dividing the gallery in two was another plate glass wall but this time in black. The woman led her through a door in this. It closed pneumatically, with a long hiss, shutting out the noise from outside completely. Melinda found herself in a large open space, furnished with a modern black leather sofa and a large coffee-table made entirely from green plate glass, each leg a series of foot-square sheets of glass piled on top of each other and glued together. The surface of the table was larger than a double bed. On the wall that was part of the original building, its stone blocks in stark contrast to the modern materials all around, was a Francis Bacon oil, its angular structures pointing at a twisted, barely recognisable human figure at the very centre of the bold, bright colours.

Opposite the stone wall was another wall of black plate glass.

'Here,' the woman said, making her distaste for Melinda perfectly obvious by her manner.

To the side of a door cut into the second plate glass wall was a hook, projecting from the glass. The woman stood under the hook and indicated that Melinda should stand in front of her. As soon as Melinda did so she grasped her bracelets and clicked the snake's tail into the snake's head, manacling Melinda's wrists together. There was a small metal stool by the door and the woman pushed it over to Melinda with her foot. Standing on it, she pulled Melinda's arms up above her head, shuffled her forward and positioned the bracelets over the hook, stretching Melinda's arms high above her head. Melinda's body pressed against the glass and her feet barely touched the floor. She took a small length of cord from the pocket of her skirt and used it to bind the bracelets to the hook. Dismounting from the stool, she pushed it away.

Callously, the woman yanked the front of Melinda's blouse up until it was around her throat. Melinda's breasts were immediately squashed against the black glass. She unzipped Melinda's skirt at the back and pulled it down her hips until it fell to her ankles, this time forcing Melinda's belly and thighs, clad in the white lacy-topped stockings, to be laid out on the glass.

Without a word the woman disappeared through the door into what was obviously an inner office behind the black plate glass wall.

Melinda's body was churning. The sudden and brutal bondage had its usual effect on her, a rush of excitement adding to the expectation that she had been brought here to see the master. Indeed, though the glass was completely opaque, she suspected that from the other side the glass was transparent and that the master was there beyond it, watching her, when he cared to, pinned like a butterfly against the glass. She confirmed her suspicion as to the qualities of the glass by looking over her shoulder at the outer wall. Sure enough, she could see the employees rushing about their duties, as clearly as if it was normal glass.

Eagerly, she pressed her body forward, wanting the master to see her, wanting him to be tempted by her. Perhaps because of its size the glass did not take on her body heat and remained cold, but oddly this proved exciting. It puckered her nipples of course, but if she pressed her thighs and belly against the glass she could make the fingers of cold penetrate through her labia to her clitoris, which felt hot and sticky in contrast.

She imagined how she must look from the other side of the glass, her naked breasts ballooned out against her chest, the hairless triangle of her mons perfectly framed by the black lace of the suspender belt, the long black suspenders running down the front of her thighs and the lacy white welts of the stockings. She squirmed against the glass obscenely, circling her breasts against it and angling her belly up so her sex was exposed. Despite her initial response to the master, and the odd chill he had made her feel, she wanted him to see she was anxious to continue from where they had left off. It was not for a slave to choose a master, it was not for her to decide which master she would like or dislike; it was up to her to serve whoever her master was. It was as simple as that. The distaste she had felt in the restaurant only heightened her awareness of her duties, which in turn increased her sexual temperature because it required a more fundamental display of obedience.

How long she waited she could not tell. The dull ache from her arms and shoulders began to turn to agonising cramp. There was pain from her legs too, her calf muscles protesting at being stretched taut, her feet barely in contact with her shoes. But the pain did not lessen Melinda's sense of excitement. She was in this position because it was what her master wanted and she knew he was looking at her through the glass.

In the outer office the workers began to drift away. Computer screens were turned off and the building emptied of people. The door in the black plate glass wall to which Melinda was bound opened and the bespectacled woman came out, a handbag on her arm and a cardigan over her shoulders. She walked through to the outer office without sparing Melinda a glance.

Almost immediately the door opened again. Melinda was already facing it and looked straight into the eyes of the master.

'A little uncomfortable I'm afraid,' he said. It was not a question. 'Is it?' he snapped as he came up behind her. She could see his reflection in the black glass. He had taken off his jacket, tie and waistcoat and was wearing only his trousers and shirt, the collar open. His hand smoothed across the rich curves of Melinda's pert, apple-shaped arse.

'Yes, master.'

'I've been watching you. Did you know that?'

'Yes, master.'

'You were performing for me, weren't you? Showing yourself to me through the glass?'

'Yes, master.'

'Very pretty. I was not sure when Sophia insisted on all the slaves being shaved but in your case it is *eccellente*.'

He rubbed his hand harder against her buttocks, the tips of his fingers working down towards her sex. She could feel them butting against her labia.

'You're wet, as I suspected,' he said.

In the black glass she saw his reflection step back slightly and unzip his fly. He extracted his cock from

107

his underpants then changed his mind, unbuckled the Gucci belt that held up his trousers and pulled them and his pants down over his legs until they were around his ankles. His cock was semi-erect. He took it in his hand and pulled back his foreskin.

'What did Luigi do with you, girl?' he asked.

'He . . . I . . .' Again she found it difficult. 'Had me take him in my mouth, master.' She watched him shuffle up behind her and press his cock into the cleft of her buttocks. She felt it swell immediately and she wriggled her bottom from side to side to encourage it further.

'He didn't fuck you?'

'No, master.'

He began to buck his hips, his cock sliding between the soft cheeks of her arse. It was engorging rapidly now. 'So he made you kneel,' he continued. 'Kneel in the car?' It was what he had done in the restaurant; using the description of what had happened to her as a means of exciting himself. Melinda just wished she was better at it.

'In the traffic?'

'No, master, in an underground car park.'

'Yes?' The master's cock was fully erect now. His hands were on Melinda's hips, holding them firmly, the gyrations of his body pushing her against the glass. She wished she was naked, that the woman had stripped off her blouse and jacket as well as her skirt, so the master could see all of her body.

'Then he made me kneel between his legs. He'd taken his cock out of his flies . . .' It all seemed terribly tame. She wished she could think of something to make it more exciting for him, wanting, above all, to please him. She wanted him to like her and be impressed by her and remember her. All the masters had

108

their favourite slaves. The favourites were seen regularly and given the largest quantity of what a slave craved most – attention. Less favoured girls might spend weeks never setting eyes on their master. She suddenly remembered the driver. 'The driver was watching, master. I know he was. He could see me taking the cock between my lips.'

'Was it hard?'

'Oh yes, master, and throbbing. He wanted to feel my sex, master. He put his hand down between my legs.' Melinda felt the master's cock ploughing the furrow of her arse. It was hot and hard. His hands slipped down to her thighs, stroking the top of the stockings, feeling the contrast between the coarseness of the lacy welts and the smoothness of her flesh. 'He kept touching my breasts too, master . . .'

The trouble was that it had all been over so quickly. There was little to tell. Melinda was hardly going to be able to impress her new master with the tale of Luigi's performance. Then it occurred to her, in a flash of inspiration, that she didn't have to tell the truth.

'His cock was pulsing in my mouth. I was sucking on it, licking it with my tongue, cramming it deep into my throat, master, really deep, so deep I wanted to gag on it. Then he said to the driver to get out and the driver came round to the back of the car. He opened the car door and pulled me out on to the concrete.' It was beginning to come easily now, an image of what the two men might have done to her forming in her head.

'Yes . . .' The master's voice was getting breathier.

She had already told him Luigi had only used her mouth and didn't want to contradict herself. 'The driver made me undo his trousers. He had this really big cock. He made me lick it all over, cover it with saliva. It was enormous. Then he turned me over and got me down on all fours. He came up behind me and rammed it up into me.'

'Were you wet?'

'Yes, master, I was. But he was so big, master. And he was so deep, driving it in and out of me. Then the other man got out of the car. He knelt in front of me, pulled my head up and forced his cock into my mouth. Two cocks, master. They were taking me together, one in my mouth and one in my sex.'

The effect of all this on the master was dramatic. His cock was pulsing wildly. His hands came up along the sides of her body, under her jacket and around between her flesh and the glass, to knead her breasts. He took her nipples in his fingers and pinched them hard.

'Go on,' he urged.

'I could feel the driver coming. His cock was so big I thought it would split me in two.'

'Did he put it in your arse?'

It was a clue, she knew, to what he wanted to hear. 'That was the worst, master. Just as I thought he was going to come he pulled out of me. I could feel his cock at my anus, master. It was soaking wet and I knew what he was going to do. I knew it was too big for me there. Much too big. I tried to beg for him to stop but the other man held my head on his cock and wouldn't let it out.'

The strange thing was that the story was turning Melinda on too. The tingling pleasure the master was creating in her breasts linked with a throbbing, urgent passion flooding out of her sex. She hoped the master would slip his cock down between her legs; that he might even put it in her sex.

'Then he pushed it hard, and it went straight into

110

me. Oh God, it was big, master. He pushed it right up me, so deep I didn't think I could stand it. I would have screamed but I couldn't, not with the cock in my mouth too.'

'You were coming weren't you, girl?' The master's voice was husky with excitement now.

'Oh yes, master,' Melinda said taking her cue again. 'The driver was using his finger on my clitoris, pushing it up and down. Then he started to push his fingers up into my sex, master, right up alongside his cock. Two fingers I think, or three. The thing was it felt like another cock, side by side in the depths of me.' That was a feeling Melinda remembered well. She had experienced it many times. 'My sex was throbbing, master. Two big cocks inside me and one in my mouth. I couldn't stop myself, master, I just couldn't.'

The master was bucking his hips against Melinda's arse. His hands on her breasts were pulling on her body, pulling her manacled wrists against the hook, waves of pain flooding over her from her tortured arms. But the pain was swamped by the intensity of her pleasure. Suddenly his cock slipped down between her legs. She felt it burrow into the folds of her labia, but it did not penetrate her vagina. Instead the crown of his glans butted hard against her clitoris, causing a shock of pleasure so extreme her whole body shuddered helplessly.

'It was, it was . . .' She struggled to concentrate, to put her own feelings aside. 'It was too big, master. And it was getting bigger. Both of them were. The one in my mouth and the one in my back passage. They were swelling up, I swear, and throbbing. It was making me come, master. I knew they were both going to spunk me, I could feel it.'

The master's cock sawed between her legs, each forward movement jolting it against her clitoris, taking her closer and closer to orgasm.

'I'm coming . . .' She was getting confused between what she was describing and what was actually happening to her. 'They were making me come. Their cocks were so hot, master. And so hard. They were coming together. Oh God, master, my whole body's alive. It hurt so much, there's so much pain, but it's like it makes the pleasure better.' That was a description of what she felt now. She tried to pull herself back to the story. 'Oh, he was ramming into my rear. Deeper and deeper. And the other man was holding my head, pushing his cock in and out of my mouth, right into my throat. I could feel him start to spunk first, the one in my mouth. Then there was this incredible feeling in my bottom, master, jerking and spasming and then this hot, gushing liquid, flooding me, master . . .'

The fantasy had become a reality. As she said the last words she felt the master's cock jerk violently against her labia. A jet of hot spunk seemed to hit her clitoris, while the rest of it spattered her legs. She squeezed her thighs together instinctively, trapping him there, feeling his cock throbbing as he came. She instantly came herself, her body consumed with excitement, the fact that she had made the master come a triumph that only seemed to reinforce the strength of the orgasm that rushed through her body. She pulled against the silver manacles, wanting, at the most profound level of her being, to remind herself of her bondage and knowing the feeling of helplessness it created would take her to yet another pitch of sensation – pure, raw feeling that was like nothing else.

She saw herself hanging from the steel hook, her

clothes rucked around her body, her breasts and sex exposed. She felt a trickle of wet running down the inside of her thigh and on to the welt of her stocking. She looked down and saw the black glass was spattered with sticky white liquid that had run, in streaks, down to the floor.

Five

The harness was tight and uncomfortable. It
stretched her arms and bit into her flesh but Melinda
had been strapped into much more hurtful bondage
devices by other masters, some of whom seemed to
have derived a fiendish delight in designing bondage
apparatus that would cramp and confine their slaves
in the most awkward way.

The evening after Melinda's experience with the
master, Aldo had collected her from the bedroom. He
took her down to the long, narrow, windowless room
where the old woman waited, just as she had the day
before. But this time Melinda was not to be dressed.
The woman in the same black dress applied a heavy
make-up, emphasising Melinda's eyes with mascara
and an eye-shadow that brought out their greenness.
She had replaced the varnish on her fingernails and
toenails too, with a deeper crimson red. Apart from
a pair of black high heels, Melinda had been left
naked.

It was only after these preparations that Aldo returned with the leather harness. As the old woman
left the room, her job completed, the overseer strapped a pair of leather cuffs around Melinda's arms,
just above her elbows, and another pair around her
wrists. Each cuff had a sturdy metal D-ring secured

to the leather. The overseer then took a short chain, threaded it through both D-rings at her elbows and secured it by means of a small padlock, cinching her elbows together but leaving a certain amount of slack. Taking a second and much longer length of chain he threaded this through the D-ring on the cuff at her left wrist. He pulled her lower arm up at right angles to her elbow so her hand was out in front of her body, then stretched the chain across her chest, just under her breasts. Positioning her right arm in the same manner, he threaded the chain through the D-ring on its cuff and tightened it until it was taut, thus taking up the slack in the chain that bound her elbows. He secured the second chain by means of another padlock. The key to the padlocks was hanging from a small silver chain which Aldo looped over Melinda's head and around her neck, the key dangling between her breasts.

Melinda looked down at her body. Had she cared to, it would have been possible for her to spread her fingers out over the fleshy curves of her breasts but otherwise the movement of her hands and arms was severely restricted.

She was surprised when Aldo produced a gag. She had not been gagged for a long time and could see no need for it, but the overseer held a big ball of rubber in his hands, through the centre of which was a metal rod. At each end of the rod was a ring and this, in turn, was attached to a leather strap. Aldo pushed the rubber between Melinda's lips and buckled the leather tightly at the back of her head, securing the gag in place. The rubber filled her mouth, making her cheeks bulge. The metal rod bit uncomfortably into the sides of her lips.

The overseer looked at his watch, then at Melinda's naked body.

'I'm looking forward to our next time together,' he said. His hand covered one of her breasts and pinched at her nipple. 'You've had it far too easy. What you need is a punishment. Just give me a reason.' He laughed. 'You may well have reason to be punished after where you're going tonight.' He laughed. 'I look forward to it.'

What that remark meant Melinda did not know. She tried to puzzle it out as he led her down the main staircase. For the second time in two days the black car was waiting for her outside the front door, engine running, the grey-uniformed driver at the wheel. Despite the fact that the sun was setting behind the hills at the other end of the valley he still wore his sunglasses. As before, the overseer shepherded her into the back seat of the car but this time did not get in himself, closing the rear door and walking back into the house.

To Melinda's surprise, a few minutes later the master strode out of the front door. He was casually dressed in a pair of beige corduroy trousers, a dark blue shirt open at the neck and a soft brown suede blouson jacket with a small double 'G' on the tongue of the zip. He walked around the back of the car and got in beside Melinda.

The driver started off the moment the master slammed the door. In the rapidly fading light, Melinda saw they were taking the opposite direction from the way they had headed yesterday on the drive to Rome.

'Comfortable, *caro*?' the master enquired, his tone of voice quite cold and mocking.

Melinda shook her head. It was quite obvious she was not. With her elbows held tightly, like chicken wings, behind her she could not sit back in the seat and was hunched forward. The weight of her body increased the pressure on the cuffs at her elbows which in turn pulled at the cuffs at her wrists.

'I want you to play with your nipples for me,' he said. 'You can do that, can't you?'

Melinda nodded, but she wasn't sure it was true. The blood supply to her fingers was so restricted they were numb. She groped her breasts and managed to trap her left nipple between her fingers but for some reason she could not do the same with her right hand. The master appeared satisfied however. He reached over and covered her right hand with his own, then pulled her hand away and pinched her nipple so hard that Melinda moaned through the gag.

Then he relaxed, sitting back in the seat and closing his eyes.

The car had been climbing steadily for the whole trip and it was nearly dark when it finally turned on to a steep, narrow road, wide enough for only a single vehicle, which twisted and turned around a precipitous hillside. As the road swung sharply to the right, Melinda could see the lights of what looked like an ultramodern house cantilevered out from the top of the hill. It was built from an odd-coloured yellow brick, a rectangular building with the lateral walls made entirely from glass with a large terrace projecting from the main house supported on triangular girders set underneath it and over a sheer drop. A ramp led down to a walled courtyard at the back of the house where a new convertible Jaguar XJ6 was parked next to a white Range Rover.

The driver pulled the car up to the rear door. A security floodlight rigged to a motion detector bathed the whole area in bright light. The sudden brightness wiped away Melinda's ability to see into the shadows of the hills all around.

117

'Out,' the master ordered, the first word he had spoken since he had touched her breast. He climbed out of the car himself as the driver got out and opened the rear door on Melinda's side.

Melinda struggled to obey, her bondage making it difficult. As soon as she had managed to wriggle out of her seat and scramble through the doorway, the driver slammed the car door, got back behind the wheel and drove off, the car's suspension rumbling on the cobblestones that covered the courtyard area.

It was colder up in the hills and Melinda felt her nipples stiffen. The air was very still and very clear. It was scented with the smell of conifers.

'Well, what have we here?' The rear door of the house opened and a woman stared out at Melinda. Her voice was hard and harsh and from her accent Melinda knew she was definitely English.

'You are to do everything she says without question,' the master said in Melinda's ear. 'Don't let me down.'

The master led Melinda forward by the arm and the woman stood aside so they could both enter the house. There was a long corridor beyond and he marched her down it. He opened the door at the far end and directed her into a big bedroom, one of its walls made entirely from the glass that Melinda had seen from the outside, and extending up to the floor above. It overlooked what would have been, in daylight, a spectacular view of the hills.

'So this is my present, is it?' the woman said, following them into the room.

'A present from Sophia,' the master said. He laughed and went up to the woman to kiss her on both cheeks. As she drew back she caught his face in her hand and kissed him again, this time on the mouth, darting her tongue between his lips.

The woman was large in every sense. She was tall, with the high-heeled boots she wore, even a little taller than the master. She had a broad back, round, wide buttocks and meaty thighs, and her bosom rose from her chest at a precipitous angle, a huge cushion of flesh. But though she was a formidable size she could not be described as fat. Her body was firm and supple, not flabby and flaccid, and the clothes she wore – tight black leggings, a leather bustier wrapped around her waist and laced at the front and a tight white blouse – showed it off. She looked like a warrior queen from another age.

This impression was confirmed by her hair, which was a striking flame red, scraped back severely into a pony-tail. Like her body, there was nothing small-scale about her face either. She had large eyes of emerald green and red eyebrows that, had they not been carefully plucked, would have been thick with hair. Her mouth was big with fleshy lips and very regular, very white teeth. Her cheeks and jaw were sharp and angular. On any other woman the size of her head would have been too large; on her it was perfectly in proportion to the size of her body.

Her stance – legs apart and arms akimbo – reflected her dominance. This was a woman who feared nothing, who exuded confidence and authority and who was used to getting her own way in everything. Her eyes roamed Melinda's harnessed and naked body.

'She's beautiful,' she said, after a careful examination.

'I told you. I bought her for you.'

'You bought her for Sophia,' the woman corrected tartly.

'Bianca, you know that is not true.'

119

Melinda remembered the name from the conversation in the restaurant, but had expected its owner to be Italian not English.

'It doesn't matter.' She walked around Melinda, looking closely at her buttocks. 'Has she been whipped?'

'Three strokes on the first day. Not since then.'

'Good. That will make her more responsive.' Bianca walked around to the front again and Melinda could see a glint in her eyes. She took the silver chain with the key in her fingers and lifted it over Melinda's head.

'Do you want me to stay?' the master asked. The tone of his voice indicated that he very much hoped she would say yes.

Bianca ignored the question. 'There's something about her, isn't there? Something wonderfully vulnerable. She's a natural submissive.'

'They're all natural submissives.'

'No, Giorgio, you're wrong. Some merely get sexual gratification from being submissive. With this girl it goes deeper than that, much deeper. Submission is at the well spring of her life.' Bianca's finger traced along the strap of the gag that bit into Melinda's cheek and over the rubber ball that projected from her mouth. 'Is that true?' she asked, looking directly into Melinda's equally green eyes for the first time.

Melinda nodded. An icicle of fear formed in the pit of her stomach. She had a feeling that this woman had a streak of cruelty in her that went as deep as her own need for submission.

Bianca twisted the key in the padlock of the chain under Melinda's breasts. The leather cuffs sprang apart the moment the padlock was freed. Melinda could not help gasping with relief. Bianca released the

120

padlock that held the elbow cuffs too, then carefully unbuckled the rest of the harness and threw it to the floor.

'You can stay,' she said decisively, looking at the master. 'Go and get ready. And you,' she said, turning to Melinda, 'kneel up on the bed for me, will you?'

The walls of the room were clad in pine and the double bed, very low to the floor, was made from the same wood as the bedside units that extended out from the headboard. One wall was largely taken up by built-in wardrobes, their sliding doors painted in a mottled beige, a similar shade to the carpet and the counterpane, which was pulled tightly over the bed. The drapes at the side of the wall of glass were in a much darker brown. There was a door on the far side of the room and the master opened it and went inside. Melinda glimpsed a bathroom before the door was closed again.

Melinda walked over to the bed and knelt on it as she had been instructed. She could feel her heart beginning to thump and her breathing becoming shallow.

The room was lit by two modern bedside lamps. Bianca operated a switch built into the headboard and dimmed them both until the light in the room was a pleasant glow. Then she slid open one of the wardrobe doors and reached inside. Melinda could see that part of it was lined with drawers. Bianca's hand came out with what looked like a thin black belt. On closer examination the 'belt' had no buckle and one end was sown into a loop clearly intended to fit around a hand. The leather itself was tapered from the width of a cigarette at its broadest to a very thin thread at its tip. Transferring the whip to her left hand Bianca delved in another drawer, this time coming out with a silver snake, exactly like the one Sophia had used on Melinda the first time they had been alone. The sight of it made Melinda's nipples pucker even tighter than they already were.

Bringing these two items over to the bed, Bianca stood directly in front of Melinda.

'Are you frightened?' she asked, reading the expression in Melinda's eyes.

Melinda nodded.

'I had him gag you,' she said, tracing her finger over Melinda's upper lip. 'It excites me. I like to know you can't scream, whatever I do to you.' She stroked the back of her hand against Melinda's cheek.

The master came out of the bathroom. He was wearing a short blue cotton robe.

'Sit down, Giorgio. And be quiet. I'll let you know when you're required. *If* you're required.'

Without a word, the master did as he was told, pulling a modern *chaise-longue* around to face the bed then slumping on to it.

'She's frightened of me,' Bianca told him.

'They're all frightened of you,' he said.

'Unlace my bustier, sweetness,' Bianca said to Melinda.

Melinda found the bow at the top of the lacing and unknotted it. Carefully she pulled the lacing from the dozen or so eyelets set into the leather on each side. When the laces were loose enough she pulled the garment down over Bianca's broad hips. It fell to the floor.

'Now my boots.'

Bianca put one foot up on the bed. The boots laced up the front too, in much the same way as the bustier. Melinda followed the same procedure, loosening the laces from the eyelets. It was difficult for her not to stare up Bianca's tightly-clad thighs to the plane of her sex. The leggings had been sucked up into the crease of her sex, dimpling the material. With the laces loosened, Melinda pulled the boot away from Bianca's foot. The second boot soon followed.

'Now my blouse, sweetness.'

Bianca sat on the bed. The blouse buttoned down the front. Melinda pulled the little white buttons from the button-holes. As it opened she saw the large wired cups of a white satin bra, struggling to control the mass of Bianca's breasts. The bra pushed the two mounds of flesh into a deep, dark cleavage, its straps biting into her shoulders under the weight they supported. Holding her arms out one by one, Bianca watched as Melinda unbuttoned her cuffs then stripped the blouse off.

'Pull my leggings down,' Bianca ordered, getting to her feet again. This time she turned her back on Melinda, her pear-shaped buttocks of Rodinesque proportions surprisingly firm. Melinda grasped the waistband of the leggings and wrestled them down the rich curves of Bianca's bottom. The cleft between her buttocks was as deep as the cleavage of her breasts and had tufts of wiry red hair sprouting at its base. A thin thong of white satin was its only covering. It emerged from deep in the cleft and was sewn into a tiny triangle of the same material. Thin bands of satin extended from the two top corners of the triangle and wrapped around Bianca's big hips. Melinda tugged the black leggings down Bianca's thighs. Then Bianca turned back towards her and put each foot in turn on the low mattress, just as she had done for the boots, allowing Melinda to peel the leggings away.

The white satin strips followed the line of Bianca's pelvis, holding a satin triangle in place over her mons. The pubic hair under the satin puffed it out so it looked as though it had been inflated. Stray hairs escaped on all sides and between her legs, where the panties tapered to a thong again. Melinda could see her sex was as thickly coated with hair as any animal.

Melinda waited, kneeling on the bed. Bianca had said nothing about taking off her panties. She could see Bianca's eyes examining her breasts again. It was difficult for her not to do the same with Bianca, fascinated by the shape and weight of her brassièred bosom.

'All right. That was very good, sweetness. Now I want you to lie on your back on the bed.' As she said it Bianca picked up the silver body of the snake. Melinda lay back in the middle of the bed and Bianca knelt beside her. 'Now ...' she said, opening the spring-loaded clip that formed the jaw of the snake's head. She positioned it over Melinda's nipple then allowed it to close, the cold metal biting into the tender, puckered flesh. Melinda moaned through the gag. Whether the clip on this version was tighter or the jaws were indented with serrations, she did not know, but the pain was far more intense than it had been before. So, of course, was the pleasure that followed the pain. It raced through her body with an intensity that took her by surprise. The second clip produced a similar result, Melinda's body overtaken by a throbbing bout of feverish sensation.

Though she saw clearly what Bianca was doing – pushing her right hand into the loop at one end of the whip and raising her arm while still kneeling at the side of Melinda's body – the passion that flooded out from her tortured nipples made it impossible for her to think straight. It was only at the moment when the whip began to fall that she realised Bianca's intention. The whip was aimed at her breasts.

'No!' she screamed. Fortunately, the gag prevented anything more than a muffled moan. Bianca's hand was gripping her left arm firmly so she could not roll away and the thin lash at the end of the whip whistled down on to Melinda's right breast, wrapping itself around the snake's head that held her nipple. There was a shock of sensation so intense that it could not be described as pain. Pain and pleasure always went together when Melinda had been whipped before but she had never experienced this. The two had fused to become another thing; a boiling heat that seared through Melinda's body, homing in on her clitoris as if guided by some invisible force.

Bianca raised the whip again. This time Melinda tensed but did not protest. The lash whistled down on her same breast, again knotting itself around the nipple clip and again causing a red weal of sensation that seared through her body to her sex. Again Melinda was overwhelmed by a feeling she had never experienced before. She felt a flood of wetness emanating from deep inside her. Looking down at her breasts she saw the red weals crossed each other on the soft flesh of her breast.

Bianca got to her feet. She walked around the bed, glancing casually at the master. A large erection tented the cotton robe.

'See how she loves it,' she said.

She knelt on Melinda's right side, held her arm and lashed the whip down twice in quick succession across her left breast. Each stroke made Melinda moan. Each stroke produced a bright red weal. Each stroke raised the temperature of Melinda's body and made her clitoris throb so hard she thought she might come. In her fevered state everything was a provocation. The gag, which she had hated and resented before, had suddenly become animated in her imagination. It began to feel like a cock. She sucked on it deliberately.

'So sensitive,' Bianca said. She raised the whip again, aiming it not at the nipples this time but at the meat beneath them. The lash seared across both breasts. Another stroke of the same type followed.

'Look at her,' she said to the master. 'You've never been whipped like this, have you, sweetness?'

Melinda shook her head. The movement made her breasts quiver and in their sensitised state this created another wave of feeling.

'Turn over, sweetness. On to your stomach.'

Melinda rolled over. Instantly a new sensation assailed her, the cool silk of the counterpane rubbing against the super-heated weals on her breasts. She gasped with pleasure, writhing herself against the mattress instinctively, forgetting the nipple clips. They soon reminded her as the chain that held them dragged against the bed, making the jaws dig deeper and producing a sting of pain. It served only to exacerbate her condition however, the engine of the orgasm that had begun to churn inside her turning everything to its purpose.

Bianca raised the whip, ready to create another layer in the complex conundrum of pleasure and torment Melinda was experiencing.

Thwack. Bianca brought the whip down much harder on the pert curves of Melinda's buttocks than she had on her breasts.

'No!' Melinda screamed into the gag. But she knew she meant yes. The whip burnt into her, the feelings moving straight to her sex, the distance they had to travel much shorter now.

'She's coming,' Bianca told the master, her voice cool and objective. 'Two more strokes is all it's going to take.'

The master leant forward, watching Melinda's writhing body intently. She had scissored open her legs and he could see her carefully shaven labia glistening with her own secretions. 'I think you're right,' he said.

Thwack. The whip was perfectly aimed, this time at the top of the thigh so its thin tip curled into Melinda's labia, stinging the sex itself and adding further provocation.

Bianca changed her position. The final stroke was to be the most telling. She aimed the whip down into the cleft of Melinda's arse so that the tapered end would lash against her anus and the bottom of her labia.

'Only a woman can whip you like this,' she said, as the whip whistled down.

Melinda was coming. She was completely out of control. She had never been whipped like this – so precisely, so intimately. There was layer upon layer of sensation in her body, every part of her sensitised, but her breasts and tortured nipples and her clitoris had become as one, the pleasure in all three indistinguishable. The hot, throbbing, almost sticky feeling in one instantly communicated to the others.

It was time for the test. Bianca smiled to herself. 'You must not come, sweetness. I forbid it.' Her voice was clear and calm.

'Oh no,' Melinda cried, though the words were no more than a muffled moan.

'You must not come until I allow it.'

'Please, please,' she begged into the gag. Her whole body was trembling on the brink of orgasm. To hold back was a torture beyond endurance. She wasn't even sure she could.

Bianca's cool hand stroked up her thigh. It smoothed against the weal just under the buttocks, then slid up on to the camber of the buttocks themselves, its coolness so soothing against the heat that the weals generated that it provoked another shock of pleasure in Melinda's body as Bianca knew it would.

'You must not come,' she reminded her cruelly, seeing Melinda barely managing to maintain control, a hairbreadth away from orgasm.

The hand fondled the red stripes the whip had produced with a touch so light it felt like silk.

'No, no, no,' Melinda moaned into the gag, burying her face in the counterpane. Every muscle in her body was rigid. She was on fire. Her clitoris felt so big it seemed to be bursting out of the confines of her labia. Her nipples too, felt enormous, swelling against the silver jaws of the snake's heads that held them so tightly.

'Do you want to come?' Bianca asked unnecessarily.

Melinda nodded violently, trying to scream the word 'yes' through the gag.

Bianca laughed, a harsh, strident noise that did not appear to come easily. 'I should keep you like this. I should be cruel, shouldn't I?'

Melinda shook her head.

'Be still. Absolutely still.'

With the greatest of difficulty Melinda obeyed. It felt as though an army of ants was crawling all over her body. Every inch of her flesh cried out to be scratched, but she managed to hold herself completely motionless.

128

She felt Bianca's hand leave her. For a moment that stretched for an eternity nothing happened. The room was silent and completely still. She dared not look around.

The silence was broken by one word.

'Come,' Bianca commanded. As she said it her finger pushed between Melinda's legs and pressed into her bloated clitoris. It was exactly as if she had pressed a button. The nerves and sinews Melinda had strained to hold back for so long were cut loose. She felt herself falling, her body quivering uncontrollably, the tip of Bianca's finger the epicentre of a quake that shook her to the core and gathered in all the sensations she had felt since she'd lain on the bed. Each layer and pleasure was separate and distinct, yet at the same time, all as one.

Bianca looked over to the master, who was watching intently.

'I told you she was special,' she said quietly, as Melinda's body quaked for a second time, the accumulation of sensation too great to be contained in a single orgasm.

Eventually the tremors in Melinda's body were stilled. She lay on the bed in a state of euphoria, her contact with reality removed. She felt Bianca's hand on her arm, rolling her over on to her back, and allowed herself to be turned, but found it hard to reconnect her body with the dreamy quality she was experiencing in her mind.

The removal of the gag began to bring her down to earth, however. Bianca raised Melinda's head and unbuckled the leather strap that held it in place, pulling the rubber ball from Melinda's mouth. The strap and metal rings at the side of the ball had left indentations in her face. Immediately, Bianca pinched Melinda's cheeks together with one hand so that her mouth was pursed into a perfect 'O', then kissed it, sucking Melinda's lips between her own.

She broke the kiss and scrambled off the bed. Melinda watched as she drew the tiny white satin panties over her large hips and down her big meaty thighs. She made no attempt to take off her bra. Her eyes were glinting with excitement.

'See what you've done to me,' she said. The thick red pubic hair between her legs was darkened with moisture and plastered down against her labia. She looped the whip around her hand again, raised her arm and aimed a blow across the top of Melinda's thigh. It instantly brought Melinda back down to earth.

Throwing the whip aside, Bianca pulled Melinda by the foot until her head was in the middle of the big bed, then climbed astride her shoulders. The great mass of her buttocks was poised above Melinda's face, her sex exposed and her crinkled scarlet labia thick like the gourds of some exotic plant. The entrance to her vagina was open and Melinda could see beyond it a cavern as dark as the deepest cave. Slowly Bianca spread her thighs further apart, lowering her sex to Melinda's mouth.

Melinda did not hesitate, raising her head from the bed and licking the whole plane of Bianca's sex, from her clitoris to her anus, using the whole width of her tongue and wanting to show her master's surrogate what a good slave she could be.

'Oh yes,' Bianca said, holding herself in that position to enable Melinda to continue. Melinda did just that. She pressed her tongue into the deckled labia as she stroked it back and forth, feeling the wetness that lay between them. She moved from the pink promontory of Bianca's clitoris to the puckered rosebud of her arse, tonguing her vagina in between. Then Melinda attacked each individually. First, she concentrated on Bianca's clitoris, pushing her tongue against it as hard as she could. Next, she pulled back to the other end of her sex and centred the tip of her tongue on the circle of her anus. She felt the ring of muscles resist reflexively before giving way, then she plunged her tongue inside. The exercises the countess had made her do meant that her tongue was strong and supple. She used its strength to wriggle around the tight passage, provoking the sensitive nerves and making Bianca moan. Finally she applied the third phase of her assault, plunging her tongue into the open maw of Bianca's vagina, straining it up as deep as it would go and lapping at her juices.

This produced a sharp contraction in Bianca's sex. Her body shuddered, the first tendrils of orgasm already beginning to coil around her nerves. Quickly Melinda moved her mouth back up to her clitoris, found it with her tongue, and began pushing it from side to side with absolute regularity. Bianca's body tensed. Melinda could see the big muscles in her thighs lock, their contours raised from the surrounding flesh. At the same time Bianca ground down on Melinda's mouth, forcing her head back against the mattress and increasing the pressure on her own clitoris.

'Yes, that's what I want,' she cried, as her orgasm broke over Melinda's adeptly trained tongue. She fell forward so she was on all fours, the white satin bra brushing Melinda's navel, her head hanging down between her arms, waiting for the climax to pass.

When it had, she looked up at the master. He had opened the folds of his robe and was holding his erection in his hand.

'You know what I need now,' she said, without moving the rest of her body.

He got to his feet without a word and discarded the robe, his big cock sticking out from his belly. A tear of fluid had formed at the slit of his urethra. He knelt on the bed behind Bianca and caressed the big cushions of her buttocks with both his hands.

'You're so sexy, Bianca,' he said. 'Just what I love.'

'And I'll be all yours soon, darling,' she said.

Melinda watched as the master's cock nudged into the thick folds of Bianca's labia immediately above her face. He butted his glans up against her clitoris, parting her labia like the bow wave of a ship. He moved it to and fro so it would batter the little nut of nerves.

But Bianca didn't want that. 'Put it inside me, for Christ's sake,' she said, wriggling away then pushing her sex back and impaling herself on his erection. She thrust back until Melinda saw the shaft disappear into her vagina, the wetness she had created making the penetration effortless.

At that moment Melinda felt her thighs being prised apart. Almost before she realised what was happening Bianca's mouth fell on to her sex, her tongue finding her clitoris and ironing it back against her pubic bone. Melinda gasped, Bianca's mouth as hot as her sex had been.

Above her face the master ploughed into Bianca's vagina. Melinda watched the engorged shaft emerge, slicked with the sap of Bianca's sex, then lunge forward again until his balls were knocking against her scarlet labia. This sight, and the pressure on her clitoris from Bianca's hot tongue, kicked Melinda's body into life again, an orgasm beginning to assert its own needs as strongly as if she had not already come. The breadth of the master's cock had spread Bianca's labia apart and at the top Melinda could see her clitoris, a lozenge of pink flesh, visibly pulsing with excitement.

Without being ordered to do so Melinda tilted her head back and raised her mouth so she could lick at Bianca's clit, sucking it up between her lips. The effect on Bianca was instantaneous. A hot breath of exclamation escaped her mouth and blasted against Melinda's sex.

With her head in this position the master's balls were banging against Melinda's chin as he pumped his cock forward. When he pulled back Melinda slid her mouth on to the fat tube of flesh on the underside of his shaft and pinched it with her lips. She heard him gasp. Delving back further she managed to capture the sac of his balls between her lips. She reeled it in, like a net containing two slippery fish, until both balls were in her mouth. She felt his cock jerk wildly as she sucked her prize.

The master rammed his cock into Bianca's vagina again but did not withdraw this time. As his cock kicked and bucked against the tight confines of Bianca's silky wet sex, Melinda knew he was about to come.

Melinda let his balls fall from her lips. She transferred her attentions back to Bianca's clitoris, tonguing it again from side to side with all the pressure her strong muscles could muster.

'Yes, yes, like that!' Bianca cried as a second orgasm exploded in her body.

Bianca's orgasm took Melinda over the edge too. As she came, the big woman instinctively squirmed her mouth down against Melinda's sex. The tiny weals the whip had left on the delicate flesh produced

133

a sting of sensation just as Melinda's orgasm exploded, driving it to a new intensity. For a moment, Bianca's mouth and Melinda's sex appeared indistinguishable, both sticky, wet and pulpy.

Then Melinda, though saturated with the sensations of orgasm, felt another provocation. The master's cock pressed deep into Bianca's sex, kicked once more then spasmed uncontrollably, jetting spunk into the dark cavern of her body, gob after gob of it spattering out from his throbbing phallus.

That was too much for Melinda. Her orgasm went from total rigidity in every muscle to complete relaxation, her sex melting over Bianca's mouth, this release of tension the only way her body could cope with the extra stimulation. She tried to keep her eyes open to watch as semen started to seep from Bianca's sex, but it was impossible. The currents of feeling were too strong and she could do nothing but wallow in them.

She wasn't sure where the voices were coming from at first. They had left her on the bed and she must have fallen asleep because she woke with a start, the sleep so deep that for a moment she could not remember where she was.

Sitting up, she winced as her arms brushed her nipples. She saw the silver snake lying on the bed next to her and it all came flooding back. Everything Bianca had done to her. As she examined the red weals that marked her breasts, she heard the master's voice.

'Bianca, you know it's only a matter of days now.'

Bianca's voice was less audible. 'We should have . . .' was all Melinda could make out of what she said. The rest was muffled. But she still could not understand where the voices were coming from. The bathroom door was open and she could see they were not in there. Then she realised the voices were coming from the huge wall of window. The ceiling was not connected to the glass that extended up to the room above, so there was a small gap between it and the glass. It was not more than an inch or two but it was obvious that the voices were coming from the upper room via this opening. Perhaps the master was standing next to the wall of window, staring out at the view, while Bianca was further away. Though it was completely dark now it was a cloudless night and the waning moon was still large enough to light the hills and valleys outside.

'I have to be careful.' The master's voice again. 'It's all her money. You know that. Everything belongs to Sophia. The house, the business, everything.'

'... why we've taken so long ... careful.' Bianca's voice was still less clear.

'Exactly. So there's no point in taking any risks now. It'll all be worthwhile. Together we'll be able to take everything. I can install you in the house where you belong.'

'Surrounded by obedient slaves. I look forward to that.' Melinda thought she heard a kiss. Bianca had obviously moved closer to the window to kiss the master and now Melinda could hear every word. 'This one in particular. How long before she has to go to another master?'

'She's only just arrived.'

'She's the best, Giorgio.'

'There's a specially constructed punishment room at the house. Sophia had it built. Lots of toys for you to play with.'

'Mmm. Sounds intriguing. I can't wait.'

135

'You won't have to wait long now.'

Bianca's voice faded again. Melinda only caught the words 'trace her'.

'No, it's quite impossible,' the master said in reply to what had obviously been a question. 'It can't be done. The girl downstairs was kidnapped by an ex-member of the O.I.M. He took several girls. But they couldn't trace *him*. There's no way any member of the organisation can be traced by any other. It's built into the system. That's the whole point.'

Melinda heard Bianca laugh, the same strident sound she had heard earlier. '. . . her family,' was all she heard after that.

'Sophia's family, you mean? What can they do? If the O.I.M. can't find him, they certainly won't be able to.'

'. . . body.' This was the last word in a long sentence.

'It doesn't matter. In Italian law they'll have to prove she's alive before they can do anything. Even if he doesn't kill her, he's not ever going to let her go. Either way I end up with everything. Her family will never be able to find her, dead or alive.'

Melinda thought she heard a kiss again. Her mind was racing. Even without being able to hear much of Bianca's side of the conversation it was clear they were talking about some sort of plot that involved Sophia.

'How do you know he'll be at the Seraglio?' Bianca asked, obviously standing by the master again.

'I had him followed the last time he came to Rome, and the time before that. He always goes there.'

'But how did you find him if the masters are all so completely anonymous?'

'Who? The Arab?'

'Yes.'

136

'Oh.' Now it was the master's turn to laugh. 'Pure chance. A chance that handed us our opportunity on a plate.'

'But how?'

'It was Leilah. Somehow she'd managed to hide a little trinket he'd given her – a gold locket. Completely against all the rules, of course. It had his name in Arabic. A rather unusual name, fortunately. I knew he was from Cairo. It was easy to trace from there.'

'Lucky for us.'

'I have already recommended to the O.I.M. that all slaves are searched thoroughly at the halfway houses.'

'Talking of slaves, I think it's time to resume our little tête-à-tête downstairs.'

'Good idea.'

Melinda heard footsteps coming down a staircase. She was desperately trying to remember everything she had heard. She wished she'd had a pen to write it all down. As the couple approached she lay flat on the bed, just as she had been when they'd left her. She pretended to be asleep in case they suddenly realised the conversation could be overheard from below.

'Oh, how sweet. She sleeps,' Bianca said, sitting on the edge of the bed. 'Wake up, sweetness.' She slapped her hand hard across the top of Melinda's thigh. Melinda pretended to start awake. 'Sit up,' Bianca ordered.

As Melinda obeyed she felt the sting of pain from her nipples again and gasped.

'Are you sore?' Bianca asked, the glint of cruelty Melinda had seen earlier clearly rekindled.

'Yes, mistress.'

'Not as sore as you're going to be,' Bianca said. She was wearing a white satin robe tied tightly around her waist. 'I was too kind to you. You have to be taught more control and more discipline, don't you?'

'Yes, mistress.'

The master was still wearing his cotton robe. He stood looking down at Melinda's body.

'This time we're going to set you a different task. And if you don't achieve it . . . well, that'll be too bad, won't it?'

'If you say so, mistress.'

'Oh I do, I do.'

Melinda's pulse was racing. From what she had heard, the master was planning to have this woman usurp Sophia at the villa. If they succeeded there was no doubt it was going to be very unpleasant for the slaves. The pleasure Bianca took in her cruelty was all too obvious.

Bianca slipped the satin robe from her shoulders. She was still wearing the white satin bra she had worn all through their previous encounter.

'You haven't seen my tits, have you?'

'No, mistress.'

'Oh, they're spectacular. They're very heavy and need a lot of support so I keep them restrained most of the time. Then I give your master a treat. He loves my tits. Sometimes . . .' Melinda saw her tongue playing coquettishly over her lips, '. . . I let him come over them.' She turned her back on Melinda. 'Undo the clasp, sweetness.'

Melinda reached up to the fastenings on the white satin strap that ran around Bianca's back. Her hands were shaking, not from excitement for once, but from fear of what she'd heard. She managed to open the clasp of the bra at the second attempt.

'Take it off me, sweetness.' Bianca turned to face Melinda again.

138

Melinda pulled the shoulder straps of the bra down over Bianca's arms, her hands still trembling.

'You're trembling,' Bianca snapped. 'Why is that?'

'I don't know, mistress.'

'See how she loves it, Giorgio. See how excited she is? You love it don't you? You love being punished.'

'Yes, mistress.' Melinda eased the huge cups of the bra away from Bianca's breasts. Two vast globes of flesh appeared. Though their weight was apparent they sagged remarkably little, standing firm on her chest like two big melons. Her nipples were equally large – at least the size of strawberries – and projected from the dome of her tits like the spikes on a floating mine.

'Here,' she said. She hooked her hand around Melinda's neck and pulled her into her bosom. She shook her shoulders from side to side, making her breasts slap into Melinda's face. She laughed. 'Now make me come, sweetness,' she said, lying back on the bed.

Melinda ran her hand down Bianca's round belly. Bianca's hand snatched it away immediately.

'Oh no. Just use your mouth, sweetness. And only on my tits. Make me come on my tits, or this time I'll show you what punishment really means.'

She laughed, that odd strident noise filling the room. It made her bosom turn to jelly, wobbling on her chest.

'Come here, Giorgio,' Bianca said.

The master knelt on the bed by her side. She reached up and opened the cotton robe, hooking her hand around his cock which had already started to unfurl. She pulled back his foreskin and turned her head to the side so that she could kiss his glans.

'Perhaps it'll be your turn then, Giorgio,' she said, smiling. 'Perhaps I'll let you have your wicked way.'

'You've always known what I like,' he said.

'Yes, I have, haven't I? Why don't you have a competition?'

'A competition?' Then he realised what she meant.

As Melinda sank her mouth on to Bianca's right nipple the master eagerly sucked on her left.

'Yes, that's good,' Bianca said, opening her legs and bending her knees.

Melinda tried to concentrate, nibbling at the puckered flesh with her teeth, but her mind was still full of the consequences and implications of what she had heard. The long thin whip lay next to the silver snake on the bed. She was sure she had not felt the last of the lash or the metal jaws clamped tightly around her tender nipples that night.

Six

Melinda had no idea of the time but both girls were asleep. She stood by the bedroom door waiting for Aldo's footsteps to recede down the corridor. He had been waiting by the front door when the car arrived back and had taken her straight up to the bedroom, as instructed by the master.

The house was so quiet Melinda could hear his footsteps tramping down the narrow staircase. As soon as she was satisfied he wasn't coming back, she ran over to the bed.

'Wake up.' She shook Amber by the shoulder. 'Wake up both of you.'

The girls groaned and started to sit up, the single sheet that covered them falling away from their naked breasts.

'What is it?' Leilah asked.

'What is this?' Amber was rubbing her eyes. 'God, it's the middle of the night.'

Moonlight flooded in around the curtains, lighting the room in a ghostly grey.

'What's the matter?' Leilah asked again.

'Have you been taken up to a house in the hills?' Melinda asked, not sure what to tell them first.

'In the hills?' Leilah repeated.

'She means Bianca. Right?' Amber said.

141

'Yes, Bianca. You've been there?'

'Sure. We've both been there. She's a complete bitch. Is that where you've been? Did she hurt you? Are you marked?'

'I think so.'

'She is a hard woman,' Leilah said.

'Does Sophia know about her?'

'Of course. She's a friend of Sophia's, I think.'

'And the master?'

'Sure, she's got the hots for him,' Amber said.

'Sophia knows that?' Melinda asked.

'She must do. It's always been the master who takes us up there. Sophia doesn't seem to care. I mean, they share everything, don't they? Why should she worry?'

'Master always says the same thing,' Leilah added. 'Got a present for you.'

'That's right,' Amber agreed. 'Always says that. She's got these fantastic tits, right? Like water melons. Makes you lick them and suck on her nipples till she comes. Then beats you for taking so long.'

'She is hard,' Leilah said again.

'She's an English bitch,' Amber said with feeling.

'Well, I think something else is going on,' Melinda told them.

'What do you mean?'

'I overheard this conversation. I don't think they realised I could hear. They were plotting something and it sounded serious.'

'Plotting?'

'To get rid of Sophia.'

'Get rid of her?' Leilah was puzzled.

'Bianca wants to take over. The master's got some sort of plan.'

'What plan?' Amber asked.

'I don't know. I didn't hear it all. It's something to

142

do with Leilah and her master though. Did you hide a locket?'

'Yes. My master gave it to me. I hide it in my body when I was moved. But Aldo found it when I got here. I thought he had given it to Sophia.'

'And it had your master's name on it?'

'Oh yes, in Arabic. He was so wonderful. I think I was his favourite. I know I shouldn't have kept it but . . .' Melinda knew how Leilah felt. All the slaves she had met had felt something special for their first master. She certainly felt that way about Walter Hammerton. 'But how can that make a difference?'

'I don't know. That's all I heard. That they found his name and traced him. And that he's coming to Rome.'

'He travel a lot, I remember.' Leilah said.

'How is that a plot?' Amber asked.

'I don't know. I only know what I heard. And it's going to happen soon. He kept telling her she wasn't going to have to wait long. Apparently everything – the house, the money – comes from Sophia.'

'Really?' Leilah looked surprised.

'Even the business belongs to her. I don't know how they're going to do it but if they can get rid of her everything will go to the master.'

'And to that bitch Bianca,' Amber said.

'Exactly.'

'So what do we do?'

'I have to tell Sophia,' Melinda said earnestly.

'You can't do that. What if you got it wrong. You remember what happened to Penny?'

'Penny, of course,' Leilah said.

'Of course what?' Amber queried.

'Don't you remember she was sent away the morning after she'd been with the master and Bianca. The very next morning.'

'Yes, that's true,' Amber agreed. 'We never saw her again when she got back.'

'Perhaps she found out something too,' Melinda suggested.

'If she did, Sophia clearly didn't believe her. You saw what happened to her.'

'Maybe she didn't hear what I heard.'

'Or the master realised she'd heard something and made sure she didn't get to tell Sophia. Remember how keen Aldo was to gag her in the punishment room,' Amber suggested.

'But it could have been only that she complained about the way Bianca treated her,' Leilah said, 'and nothing to do with a plot.'

'Could be,' Amber agreed. 'Truth is, if you say something there's a good chance you could go the way she went.'

Melinda shivered. That was the last thing she wanted. She was beginning to wonder if she had jumped to conclusions; if she had misinterpreted what she had heard.

'We better get some sleep,' Amber said.

Melinda climbed into the bed next to the American. 'I know I'm right,' she said, almost to herself.

'Sleep on it,' Amber advised.

'That's the best thing,' Leilah said.

They settled down on the bed, the new weals Bianca had added to those already engraved on Melinda's buttocks stinging as she rested on the sheet, reminding her of what had happened.

The two girls were soon asleep again but it was not until the first light of dawn crept through the gaps in the curtains that Melinda's mind finally allowed sleep to take over from her tormented speculations.

* * *

The day passed without incident and, more importantly, without a glimpse of Sophia or, for that matter, the master.

The next day too was passed normally, with domestic chores and exercise in the afternoon giving Melinda plenty of opportunity to agonise over what she should or should not say to Sophia the next time she was called to her room. She certainly had no intention of asking Aldo to take her to Sophia. She had the impression that the overseer was the master's man and would greet such an unusual request by taking her straight to the master, who would undoubtedly demand she told him why she needed to see his wife. Her only chance, *if* she was going to take it, was when Sophia called for her.

It had been over a week since they had been together and she hoped it would not be long before Sophia desired her again. Hoped was not an adequate description of what she felt. It was with considerable trepidation that she viewed the prospect.

Once again fate had dealt her a cruel blow. Once again she was going to have to break the rule of silence. Once again she was faced with the prospect of being accused of disobedience despite the fact that the situation was not of her making. Of course, there was a part of her that wanted to do nothing at all. Her obedience was to the master and to him alone. But she could not ignore what she had heard. The words 'dead or alive' echoed in her mind over and over again. She knew she had to do something.

Just as their evening meal was brought up to the bedroom that night they saw the large black car leaving the house, the master sitting in the back alone. Melinda had seen Sophia in the house earlier in the day and speculated that the master's departure might well mean she would be alone tonight and would summon one of the slaves. But it seemed she was wrong. The old woman returned for the empty tray but neither she nor Aldo arrived with any instructions by the time the lights were put out.

The girls settled down to sleep. It had been hotter that day than for the last week and the bedroom was sultry and humid. The sheet the girls covered themselves with was soon discarded and all three found it difficult to sleep.

How long they all lay there restlessly, their naked bodies tossing and turning against each other and the heat fuelling their ever-present sexual needs, Melinda had no idea. But apparently they weren't the only ones finding it difficult to sleep.

'You.' The lights came on and the door opened. Aldo was pointing at Melinda. He had obviously been roused from his bed as he wore only a thin cotton robe around his squat, muscular body. The girls all blinked against the sudden brightness. 'Come on, come on,' he shouted irritably, as Melinda failed to respond as quickly as he obviously thought she should.

Melinda scrambled to her feet. There was only one reason for her to be dragged out of bed like this. As they had seen the master leaving, and not heard the car return, she was quite obviously being taken to Sophia.

The overseer was holding a pair of white leather cuffs. 'Hands out,' he said as Melinda got to the door. He wrapped the cuffs around her wrists and buckled them tight. Hanging from the metal link that held the cuffs together was a short length of quite heavy chain. Aldo took hold of it and pulled Melinda after him out of the door and down the corridor.

Melinda's emotions were a mixture of excitement at being taken to Sophia and apprehension at the prospect of alerting Sophia to what she had heard. She was still not sure whether she would have the courage of her convictions.

They reached the bottom of the stairs and turned down the wide hallway that led to Sophia's bedroom. The overseer walked fast, pulling Melinda along almost at a trot, obviously anxious to get back to his bed. He reached the double doors at the end of the passage and opened one without knocking. The room, lit by a bedside lamp that had been dimmed to cast a pleasant glow, was deserted. Aldo pulled Melinda over to the foot of the four-poster bed. Its bedding was disturbed and had clearly been slept in.

'Get your hands up over your head,' he ordered gruffly.

Melinda raised her arms. Hanging from the centre of the canopy of the bed was a small metal hook, attached to a chain. The overseer stood on the edge of the bed, caught hold of the hook and slipped it into the last link of the chain attached to the leather cuffs around Melinda's wrists, pulling her forward so her body was at a 45 degree angle to the mattress. He jumped to the floor and disappeared behind her back, returning with a length of white rope. He tied one end of the rope around Melinda's left ankle and knotted it tightly. He pulled the rope over towards the left bedpost, looped it around the sturdy carved wood and tugged her left leg towards it too. Then he stretched the rope over to the right post, circled it around its base, then wound it around Melinda's right ankle pulling her legs apart then tying it securely.

'I'll get my turn with you again,' he hissed into her

ear, his hand slipping between her legs and momentarily grasping her labia, his fingers clawing into the tender flesh.

Then his hand was gone and Melinda heard footsteps padding across the carpet behind her. The bedroom door closed.

She looked down at her body; her naked breasts pendulous, her hairless sex open and vulnerable, the marks from Bianca's whip still apparent. As usual, her body responded to its bondage with a throb of excitement, rooted in her sex.

The door to the side of the bed opened and Sophia emerged from the bathroom, momentarily illuminated in a shaft of bright light. She had just stepped out of the shower and her naked body was glistening wet all over. Her hair on the other hand was dry, protected by a shower cap she had just taken off. She threw the cap aside and pulled the cord of the bathroom light switch, extinguishing the bright light.

'It's hot, isn't it?'

'Yes, mistress Sophia.'

'Were you asleep?'

'No, mistress Sophia.'

Sophia stood by the side of the bed, examining her helplessly suspended slave. 'The heat always makes me feel ... needy. I'm in a very strange mood,' she said, almost to herself.

Melinda judged this was not a good time to speak. It would be better afterwards, after Sophia had used her and she was relaxed.

Sophia lay on the bed, making no attempt to dry herself. Melinda could see the droplets of water running off the curves of her breasts. Sophia opened her legs wide and stroked her own hairless sex with one hand, as though gently petting an animal.

'I'm not sure what I need,' she said. She stretched over to the bedside chest and opened the top drawer. Melinda saw her pull out a large cream-coloured dildo. She brought it up to her mouth and licked it like an ice-cream cone. She reached up with her other hand and just managed to touch Melinda's nipple. 'I want to torture you,' she said. She reached into the drawer again. 'I want to torture you with pleasure.' This time the search produced a J-shaped tube of metal. Hanging from the base of the tube was a thin electrical cord which was connected to a rectangular box the size of a fairly hefty book. Sophia dumped the box on the bed. On top of it was a round gnarled knob and two rocker switches.

Getting up to her knees so that their faces were no more than inches apart, Sophia stared into Melinda's green eyes. 'You must not come until I allow it.' Strangely, they were exactly the words Bianca had used – the woman who was plotting to usurp Sophia's place in this very bed.

Sophia's hand ran over Melinda's belly and on to her hairless labia. Her fingers parted the nether lips and delved down into the opening of her vagina. Melinda was wet. Taking the oddly-shaped contraption, the brunette jammed the larger prong up against Melinda's clitoris. With her other hand she pushed one of the switches on the box and the whole thing began to vibrate. Melinda moaned as the vibrations engulfed her clit.

Sophia was eager for her response, feeding off it to stoke her own excitement. 'You are not allowed to come, do you understand?'

'Yes, mistress Sophia.'

Melinda felt the shaft sliding down the furrow of her sex. It nudged into the opening of her vagina, the

149

vibrations spreading upwards. At the same time she felt the other prong of the tube, the shorter end, press into the little crater of her anus.

'You want it, don't you?' Sophia said, seeing her excitement.

'Yes, mistress Sophia.'

She waited for a moment, teasingly, then pushed the double-headed tube home. The longer shaft plunged into Melinda's vagina while the shorter burst into her anus. Instantly her body was overwhelmed with sensation, the two passages contracting around the invaders, the presence and size of one enough to make her cry out with pleasure but the fact that there were two more than doubling everything she felt. The vibrations seized her, the thin membranes that separated the two phalluses inside her pulsing wildly.

'You have to hold it in there yourself,' Sophia told her.

'No,' Melinda said instinctively, before she could stop herself. Already the strange device felt as if it were part of her, the harmonies between its two prongs playing in her body and transmitting sensation from one to the other.

'Yes,' Sophia said, ignoring the disobedience. 'You must.'

Melinda saw her hand slip away. With a huge effort she used her muscles to try and hold the shafts inside her. The effort produced a shock of pleasure. The vibration against unstressed muscles was one thing, but as Melinda locked them to hold the shafts tight, the vibration seemed to be multiplied by the rigidity. Her clitoris spasmed and she moaned.

Sophia lay back on the bed. She opened her legs and unceremoniously pushed the other dildo deep into her sex, so far up that only an inch of it remained visible to Melinda. She writhed down on it, shaking her head from side to side as the tip of the phallus pressed against the neck of her womb.

Melinda needed to relax but she didn't dare. If she didn't relax the tension in her sex, the vibrations from the double shaft would be too great for her to resist. But if she relaxed, the shafts would slide from her body, slippery from the flood of juices she could not control. Desperately Melinda strived to hold off the orgasm that was creeping closer and closer. If only the vibrations would stop, if only her clitoris wasn't twitching against her labia, if only Sophia's slender body wasn't writhing under her so sensuously. The bondage that held her so tightly added to the provocation, the rope biting into her ankles, the feeling of being suspended from the hook above her head, pulling the sinews in her arms, driving her to fever pitch.

She wanted to beg for release but did not dare.

Sophia withdrew the dildo from her vagina. She pulled it up to her mouth and licked it, lapping up her own juices. Looking straight into Melinda's eyes she raised the dildo until its tip touched against Melinda's stone-hard nipple.

'No,' Melinda said without meaning to.

'That's the second time you've spoken without permission.'

Sophia raised her leg. She brought it up between Melinda's thighs and used the front of her calf to push hard against Melinda's labia, pushing the double shafts deeper into her body. But though this allowed Melinda to relax her muscles temporarily, it brought no relief. The vibrating heads of the shafts were thrust inward and the oscillations they produced were carried to new areas of sensitivity. Worse still, Sophia now moved her leg away slightly then pushed it back, giving Melinda the sensation of two cocks moving in unison, up and down. She continued this for some minutes, sawing the double shaft back and forth as she moved the other dildo on Melinda's breasts, from one nipple to the other, pressing them back into the spongy flesh.

'Torture, isn't it?' she said.

'Yes, mistress . . .' A wave of pleasure prevented Melinda from saying 'Sophia'.

'Mistress what?' Sophia snapped, thrusting her leg forward to push the double shafts into new depths.

'Mistress Sophia, mistress Sophia, oh please . . .'

'That's better. Now watch me.'

Sophia's left hand went down to her sex. Though her leg was still raised she found her clitoris easily and began strumming it as if it was the string of a musical instrument. There was no subtlety or finesse – just a flickering movement from side to side, so fast her hand was almost a blur. She moaned but did not take her eyes off Melinda's face.

'Hold it again,' she said, the movement of her hand lessening to a more gentle motion as she lowered her leg.

With an almost super-human effort Melinda tensed the muscles in both passages of her body. She felt the shafts slip slightly and thought for a minute they were going to fall out altogether, but she managed to hold them firm. The price she had to pay was another flood of exquisite sensation, the instinctive contraction of her sex not under her control.

Sophia smiled a hard, cruel smile, seeing Melinda's body racked by pleasure, clearly knowing that every nerve was stretched to the limit in the attempt to obey her command. 'Not yet. Not yet Melinda.'

Melinda could not remember Sophia using her name before.

Sophia stretched over to the left-hand post at the top of the bed. There, concealed in the carving, was a small button. She pressed it. Melinda heard the whirr of an electric motor and immediately felt herself falling forward, the chain to which the white leather cuffs were hooked descending rapidly. Sophia stopped the descent at the point where Melinda's wrists were suspended – about a foot off the bed – allowing most of her body to rest on it.

With her thighs on the bed Melinda could hold the shafts in place more easily, allowing her to relax slightly. But this relief was short-lived. Sophia slid herself under Melinda's arms and squirmed down until her sex was below Melinda's mouth. She hooked her legs around Melinda's tortured shoulders, crossing her ankles over her back.

'Make it good,' Sophia said with menace. She reached out to the rectangular box and turned the knob. The muffled hum of the vibrations in both shafts increased markedly and Melinda gasped. The vibrations were at their maximum, so strong now that Melinda responded instinctively, grinding her hips down against the bed, pushing the shafts deeper, unable to do anything but feel.

'Come on,' Sophia snapped.

Trying to fight her way out of the ecstasy that buzzed in every nerve of her sex, Melinda buried her mouth in Sophia's hairless labia. The position was awkward, having to push her head forward between her bound suspended arms, but she managed it. Sophia's legs were splayed so far apart that her clitoris was already exposed. Melinda circled it with her tongue, then nudged it from side to side. The psychological impact of serving her mistress in this way and the wonderful feeling she got from having her mouth pressed into her mistress's sex only compounded the physical feelings her body was prone to. She thought she had been close to orgasm before but now her whole body was trembling with the need for it. She lowered her mouth and plunged her tongue into Sophia's vagina, straining it upward as far as she could.

'Yes, yes,' Sophia gasped. Her hands clawed at the sheets, as if needing something to cling on to. She moved her hips up and down, establishing a rhythm as if being taken by some invisible lover and using Melinda's tongue as a substitute for a cock. Quickly, sensing how close she was to completion, Melinda brought her mouth up to her clitoris. Using the rhythm Sophia was dictating, Melinda's tongue drummed a tattoo against the little promontory of nerves, each beat making Sophia's body quake.

'God, oh God!' Sophia cried, her heels digging into Melinda's shoulder blades, dragging her down against her bonds. Melinda felt her body rock and suddenly her whole body was rigid, arching up off the bed. A noise, like the cry of a wild animal, echoed around the room. At the core of the steel-hard muscles, Sophia's sex seemed to melt, pliant and soft and incredibly wet like some ripe fruit turned to pulp, her clitoris spasming wildly against Melinda's tongue.

Exposed to this, the feeling of Sophia's orgasm transmitted perfectly to Melinda by the medium of her mouth, Melinda did not think she could hang on. Every nerve in her body screamed to be allowed to do what Sophia's had just done. Desperately she fought the waves of pleasure, physical and emotional, that swept over her. She pulled on the leather cuffs, hoping a jolt of pain would sober her. But the action had the reverse effect, the pain instantly translated into

154

passionate need. It reminded her too of her bondage, which added another kick of provocation.

Sophia came around from her shattering climax. She could feel Melinda's body trembling uncontrollably. It was striking one string of a harp and making all the others vibrate in harmony. There was not one part of her body that was not resonating to the two-pronged attack in the depths of her. It left her defenceless, the vibration arcing from the head of one shaft to the head of the other, her most delicate flesh trapped between the two.

Sophia could snatch the shafts away and leave her like this. She could haul her back up on the hook and make her watch as she used the double-headed monster on herself. She could whip her and fasten the nipple clips to her breasts again and use her in any one of a hundred ways she had used the slaves before – ways that would deny her an orgasm and keep her strung out.

But she didn't. She unwound her legs from Melinda's back.

'Come,' she said softly. 'I permit it.' And she watched as every muscle in Melinda's body shuddered and shook; as she reared up from the bed then ground down again; as her body went from total rigidity to absolute, over-ripe fluidity. The orgasm, held back for so long like the waters building up behind a dam, was all the more intense when it was finally allowed to break through.

Just as Melinda thought it was finally over, the double shafts of the metal tube slipped out of her body and their sudden expulsion created an aftershock almost as affecting as the original tremor. Melinda gasped, her bondage making impossible to do what came naturally and curl into a ball to harbour the exquisite sensation.

Sophia unbuckled the leather cuffs.

'Untie your legs,' she ordered. 'I'm not finished with you yet.'

Shakily Melinda stooped to the knots that bound her ankles, her hands trembling, her mind hardly recovered from the intensity of the orgasm that had assailed her. With difficulty she managed to free herself.

'Now,' Sophia said. She pulled Melinda on to the bed, kissing her full on the mouth, bowling her back on the sheets and falling on top of her like a man, using her thigh to push up between her legs and pressing her long slender body against her slave. Her black hair fell around Melinda's head, shrouding them both. Their stone-hard nipples were almost touching. She clearly wanted more – much, much more.

It was dawn. The birds were singing loudly. The sun crept over the horizon. There was a chill in the air which was pleasant after the heat of the night.

Sophia woke first. She sat up, looking at the beautiful blonde who lay on the bed beside her. Of course, she should have had the girl sent back to her quarters last night after she had finally slaked her appetites, but she had fallen asleep. The toys she had used lay littered on the sheets. Sophia scrambled off the bed and went into the bathroom.

The movement woke Melinda. She watched as Sophia disappeared through the bathroom door. When she came back, she knew she would be sent back to her room. It might be days before she saw Sophia again and the master had said the plan, whatever it was, would take place soon. This was her last chance. Her only chance.

She heard the toilet flush. Sophia came back into the bedroom, wrapping a pink silk robe around her naked body. She sat on the bed without looking at Melinda and picked up the phone on the bedside chest.

'No,' Melinda said, fighting all the conditioning she had received with the masters – not to speak without being asked a question first. She dived across the bed and put her finger on the bar that cradled the receiver.

'What the hell do you think you're doing?' Sophia cried.

'Sorry, mistress. I have to tell you something. I have to. Please listen.'

'Don't be so impertinent. How dare you!' Sophia tore Melinda's hand away from the phone.

'Please listen, mistress. This is important.'

Sophia must have seen something in Melinda's eyes, the desperation she felt at having to disobey only too apparent. She paused. She put the phone down.

'Go on,' she said, looking down at Melinda's naked body, which was highlighted in a shaft of early morning sun that slanted through a gap in the curtains.

'It was at Bianca's house, mistress.'

'Yes.' The name appeared to provoke no emotion in Sophia.

'I overheard a conversation . . .' Melinda had thought long and hard about whether she should tell her mistress but had not thought about the words she would use. She started again. 'I heard the master talking to Bianca. They didn't think I could hear. They're plotting against you, mistress Sophia.'

'Rubbish.'

'I think they are planning to do something to you.'

'What?'

'I couldn't hear it all. They're plotting to get rid of you, mistress.'

'That's enough. Stop this now. How dare you talk about your master this way. How dare you.'

'It's what I heard, mistress Sophia. I had to tell you.'

'After the way I've treated you. After the privileges I have allowed you. Now I know why you've had such a checkered history; why the countess let you go early. Perhaps the kidnapping story was exaggerated too.'

'Oh no, mistress.'

'How dare you.'

'You have to believe me. It involves Leilah's . . .'

'Don't say another word. Stop now.' Sophia's voice brooked no argument. She picked up the phone. Melinda made no attempt to stop her this time. She punched two numbers into the dial. 'Get up here,' she said when the ringing was answered, slamming the receiver down again.

'Bianca is a friend of mine, a good friend. She would never do anything to hurt me. It is I who suggested she should make use of the slaves. You are just trying to make trouble. Trouble has followed you wherever you've been, hasn't it?'

'No, mistress Sophia.'

'Don't argue with me.'

There was a loud knock at the bedroom door.

'Come in,' Sophia shouted. Aldo strode in purposefully.

'You will be punished, severely. It might be the end for you. The master is away. When he gets back he will have to decide what to do with you.'

Sophia's face was suffused with anger, her eyes dancing with fiery passion. There wasn't a sign that she had any doubt about Bianca or her husband. Melinda's story had clearly not struck a chord of already aroused suspicions. Her reaction was pure resentment that a slave had dared to behave in this way.

'Take her away,' she said to the overseer. 'You have my permission to make her very uncomfortable. She is not to see the other two girls. I don't want her spreading her poison.'

Aldo dragged Melinda off the bed. The white leather cuffs still dangled from the hook in the canopy of the bed. He picked them off it and quickly strapped them around Melinda's wrists, this time fastening them behind her back, the heavy chain from them dangling down into the cleft of her buttocks.

He grabbed her upper arm, his fingers like a steel claw in her soft flesh, and pulled her towards the door.

'Wait,' Sophia commanded. The overseer stopped.

Sophia marched forward until she was within inches of Melinda's face. She stared intently into her eyes as if trying to see what lay behind them. Melinda stared back, hoping she could see the strength of her convictions in what she had said.

'How could you?' Sophia said, the anger replaced by sadness.

Melinda said nothing. She hoped her eyes would tell Sophia she was telling the truth.

'Take her away,' Sophia said. She walked to the bathroom and slammed the door.

Aldo grinned, pulling Melinda across the bedroom.

'Well now,' he said. 'Looks like I'm going to be able to have my own way for a change.'

Melinda didn't care. She was not afraid of being punished. She had tried and failed. She deserved to be punished. She should have kept quiet and obeyed the rules.

Aldo took her down the back stairs. She thought they were going to the punishment room but just before they reached the outer door to the covered walkway he pulled her to the left, along a short passage which ended in a small door. He opened the door and Melinda saw a flight of stone steps. A smell of dank must rose from the depths. The overseer flicked on a light switch and led the way down.

Unlike the cellar under the punishment room and outbuildings, this one appeared little used. Cobwebs brushed Melinda's face as she tackled the steps, walking carefully to avoid toppling forward, unable to use her arms for balance. The cellar was huge and ran the whole length of the house, brick vaulted pillars supporting the floor above. It was lit by a string of naked lightbulbs hanging from the ceiling but there was not enough light to reach into the dark corners around the walls. No sunlight ever penetrated down here and the air was chilled and damp.

Aldo clamped his hand on her arm and pulled Melinda to the middle of the cellar, across its stone-flagged floor, her feet quickly filthy from the dirt and dust that caked it. There, in the centre of the crypt-like space, was a hole, lined with stone and about six feet deep with a wooden ladder perched on one side leading down into it. The pit was square and about eight or nine feet across. One side of it cast a long shadow so most of its floor was inky black.

'That's where you're going, child,' Aldo said with obvious relish. He unstrapped the leather cuffs. 'Climb down now. Don't make it worse for yourself.'

Melinda stepped on to the ladder and descended into the pit, every inch of her flesh covered with goosepimples. Aldo followed her down.

'Cosy, don't you think?' he said, the top of the pit

above both their heads. He dropped to his knees and groped around in the dark. Melinda heard a clink of a chain and felt something cold and metallic snap around her ankle.

'Sit,' he ordered. Melinda obeyed, the stone flags cold against her buttocks.

The overseer moved to the other side of the recess and found another chain. He caught hold of Melinda's wrist and pulled it out in front of her until he could snap a second manacle around it.

He satisfied himself that both manacles were securely fixed, then climbed out of the pit. He detached the wooden ladder from its mountings and hauled it up, throwing it on to the main cellar floor and causing a cloud of dust.

'I'll be back,' he said, as he turned on his heels and headed to the stairs. Melinda heard his footsteps echoing through the empty space as he mounted the stone steps.

It was a relief that he did not turn off the lights, though Melinda could see very little above the edge of the pit and nothing at all in the shadow it created over two-thirds of her new accommodation. Feeling around with her free hand she discovered the manacles that held her wrist and ankle were attached to very short chains which in turn were secured to rings bolted into the stone floor. The two rings were about four feet apart, making it impossible for Melinda to stand up. All she could do was sit on the cold, hard floor.

Her mind hadn't caught up with what had happened to her. Sophia had not given her any time to explain. She had dismissed her suspicions out of hand. Melinda had hoped she would have at least wanted to hear exactly what Bianca and the master had said. But clearly, for whatever reason, Sophia trusted Bianca – and her husband for that matter – implicitly. Given Sophia's penchant for lesbian sex, the bond had probably been forged in bed.

Sophia had been so firm in her convictions that Bianca would do no wrong that Melinda began to doubt herself. She had only heard part of the conversation. Was it possible she had completely misunderstood what was being said? She played the words over in her mind, over and over again, looking for other interpretations. But, in the end, she could come up with none and remained convinced there was no other explanation. Whatever Sophia thought, she was in danger.

To some extent these thoughts took Melinda's mind off her situation. But as the time passed she began to realise just how bad things were for her, both in terms of her physical discomfort and for her future.

She was very uncomfortable. The position of the manacles made it impossible to find a way of easing the hardness of the stone floor against her buttocks. Whichever way she sat, her muscles soon began to cramp, and she tossed and turned constantly. She was cold too, and the dampness all around her seemed to eat into her bones.

But that was not the worst. She had been in physically hard conditions before, her body bound and abused at the whim of one of her masters. She had learnt to cope with it, indeed, to revel in it. It was part of the price she had to pay for her absolute submission. She could not pick and choose, take one punishment and not another. That was not the way the system worked. She either accepted all of it and allowed her masters carte-blanche, or she rejected it all and left.

But now the question of her acceptance was academic. Her expulsion was inevitable. There was no way back and that was much more distressing than her bondage. As soon as Sophia told the master what had happened, he'd see Melinda was dispatched back home without delay; the gauze pads applied to the marks under her breasts and the old-fashioned black nylon panties drawn up her hips for the last time. She would beg and plead, as she had seen Penelope do, but it would make no difference.

She was sure now, now that she was in precisely the same position, that Penelope had been expelled for the same reasons. She had obviously not managed to tell Sophia of her suspicions. Melinda was sure that if she had heard the same thing from two slaves, even Sophia's rock-steady convictions about her friend's intentions would have been dented. The master must have realised that Penelope had been privy to something she should not have known. He had brought her back to the villa, had her confined overnight, probably in this very place, and told Sophia she had broken the rule of obedience. By the time she had been brought up to the punishment room the next day she would have been too concerned with saving her own skin – just as Melinda knew she would be – to throw accusations about Bianca in Sophia's face. Melinda remembered the overseer had stood ready with a gag, presumably on the master's instructions in case she said anything too near the knuckle. As it turned out, her own protestations had led Sophia to order her gagged in any event.

This also meant, as Melinda had always suspected, that Aldo knew all about the master's plans and might well have a part to play in them.

But there was nothing Melinda could do now to

prevent those plans from coming to fruition, nor to stop herself from being sent back home. The dank, dark cellar matched Melinda's mood perfectly. Her future prospects were bleak.

With no natural light to give her a clue, Melinda very quickly lost track of time. It might have been two hours or ten since she had been dumped in the pit. She tried to sleep but found it impossible to relax because she was so awkwardly bound and the floor was so hard. Eventually she must have fallen into a restless doze.

The footsteps on the stone steps roused her. She strained her head to see across the cellar floor but could see nothing until the figure of Aldo lumbered into view at the edge of the pit. He was naked apart from a pair of tight yellow briefs. In one hand he held a riding crop and in the other a fluorescent free-standing torch. He put both on the floor while he attached the wooden ladder to its mountings, then picked them up and climbed down to where Melinda was chained.

He set the fluorescent torch in the corner and pressed its control switch. Bright white light blinked on, blinding Melinda with its intensity after so long in the semi-dark.

The overseer stood in front of her. 'I can have my fun now,' he said. 'No limits anymore.'

The words chilled Melinda. If he was telling the truth, did that mean the master was back? If Aldo had been told he was allowed to do as he pleased with her, without the usual restrictions, that could only mean one thing. Her fate had already been sealed and she would never serve the master again, or any other master for that matter. She shuddered.

'Take my shorts down,' he said.

Whatever her position, Melinda was sure she did not want to antagonise the overseer. She knew what he was capable of. She reached up with her free hand and tugged at the waistband of the briefs. It was difficult without the use of both hands but she managed to drag them down to his thighs. His big circumcised cock began to erect.

Taking her head in both his hands he pushed her mouth over his cock. She sucked it in and felt it swell immediately. Using her tongue she rubbed against the ridge at the bottom of the glans. Her position was awkward, the manacle on her ankle making her stretch one leg out behind her and only being able to kneel with the other, while one hand was tethered to the floor. Trying desperately not to lose her balance, she began to pump the cock in and out of her mouth as it rapidly hardened to full erection.

'Got me nice and hard,' he said, stepping back, his cock popping from her mouth. He circled it with his hand. He walked around to the back of her. 'Thought you could spoil our little plan, didn't you? Thought you could put a spanner in the works.' He laughed. 'She isn't going to listen to you. She's too stupid.'

He raised the whip and slashed it down on the top of Melinda's outstretched thigh. The thwack of leather on flesh reverberated around the empty cellar. He aimed another blow, this one higher and falling across the meat of Melinda's buttocks.

'Pity, really,' he said. 'Bianca had taken a fancy to you. Still, she can't have everything, can she?'

He slashed the whip across Melinda's buttocks. The weals from the whipping Bianca had given her had partially faded but this stroke must have fallen on the same line because its intensity was much greater. Melinda struggled to cope with the overwhelming sensations that rushed through her body, the familiar pain of the whip translating instantaneously to a throbbing pleasure deep in her sex.

The overseer sank to his knees behind her, grabbed her hips and pulled her back towards him. Now it was her manacled arm that was stretched by her bondage, as he forced her to kneel on both knees. Melinda felt his grizzled, misshapen cock pulsing against her buttocks.

'Oh, let me suck it, master. I love to suck it.' She shouldn't have said it, but she was desperate. There was no point in obeying now and she wanted to stop him using her sex. In all the time she had been with the masters the overseers had only been allowed to have the full knowledge of slaves who were about to be cast out. It was the final indignity and it was one Melinda would do anything to avoid.

'Why not?' he said. She thought she could make him come in her mouth so he wouldn't use her sex.

He crawled round in front of her and she immediately gobbled his cock into her mouth again.

'Are you nice and warm?' He raised the whip and stroked it down over her back. Her buttocks wriggled under its lash.

Melinda concentrated. Her tongue flicked against the ridge of his glans, then she began sawing the whole shaft in and out of her mouth. She used her free hand to grope between his thighs for the sac of his balls. She reeled it in until it was nestled in her palm, squeezed it tight and pulled it down, feeling his cock jerk as a result.

But it was not enough. She was not getting the reaction she'd hoped for. He was excited, of course, but he was nowhere near coming. He was enjoying it, playing with her, in full control and clearly waiting until he decided it was time to use her sex.

166

Desperately, Melinda sucked hard, driving him so deep into her throat she had to control her reflex to gag. She wished she had the use of her other hand but she didn't. Letting go of his balls she ran her finger up between his buttocks to his anus. Almost before she touched it she felt his cock react with a spasm of expectation. Without losing the rhythm she had established as she pumped his cock in and out of her mouth, she pushed her finger forward, testing his sphincter. His initial resistance provoked another sharp kick from his cock. She pushed harder and suddenly felt the resistance disappear. Her finger slid inside him.

She didn't have time for subtlety. She knew she had found the key. His cock was throbbing violently. She drove her finger up into him, straining the tendons of her hand to get it as deep as it would go, then corkscrewing it around in him to get deeper still. She found what she was looking for – the little button she hoped would trigger a flood of sensation he would not be able to resist.

Immediately, as she scratched her finger against it, she felt his cock jerk and swell to an even greater size. She sucked him deep into her throat, tongued the thick tube on the underside of his cock where the spunk travelled from his balls and wriggled her finger against the gland at the very core of him.

'No!' he cried. She had caught him totally by surprise. Only minutes before he had been in control, toying with her, able to do whatever he wished. Even as she penetrated his anus he had imagined he could still pull away from her hot, wet mouth and use her sex. But as her finger probed and found the little gland it was as though she had thrown a switch that opened the floodgates to a force he could not control.

It was too late. His spunk spattered out of him and into her throat – a great long string of it, seeming to go on for ever.

It was a small victory for Melinda, but a victory nevertheless.

Seven

The old woman brought her food and a blanket. She brought her a bucket as a toilet which Melinda was forced to use while she watched. Perhaps that marked the end of a day. She was glad of the blanket and, after eating the food, managed to sleep fitfully.

In what Melinda took to be the morning the old woman returned again with the same accoutrements. She showed no emotion and said not a word, as if Melinda was some animal that had to be fed and watered but not one she cared for very much.

The arrival of the old woman was the only thing to break the monotony. To her relief, Aldo did not appear. It would be impossible this time to prevent him from exercising his newly-acquired rights over her. Once Aldo had taken her there was no way back.

Melinda hoped for a miracle but she did not realistically expect one. What she expected was, at any minute, to be dragged out of the pit and taken upstairs to the punishment room where Sophia would have her breasts taped up, then take the little gauze pads from their tin and press them against the two square purple 'M's that marked Melinda's membership of a very exclusive club. Aldo's last visit had confirmed that this was to be her fate.

What made it worse was that Aldo had also confirmed

that she had been right; that there was a plot and that he was involved in it. Unfortunately, by the time Sophia discovered the truth it would be too late. Too late for her and too late for Melinda.

The cold and damp of the cellar and the discomfort of the manacles matched Melinda's mood. She wanted to suffer. It was the last time she would be in this situation; the last time she would be punished at the behest of a master. Her freedom, her will, her ability to choose, which she had delegated to the masters, were about to be restored to her and the prospect gave her no pleasure at all.

She thought of her first master, Walter Hammerton. He would be told what had happened to her and she knew he would be sad. A girl's first master was always the most special and that had certainly been true in Melinda's case. He had been the progenitor of so much of what she had felt subsequently. She could imagine the expression in his eyes when he was told the news of her fate, and that was the most distressing thing of all.

Time went slowly. Melinda believed the old woman came twice a day, morning and evening, but she couldn't be sure. Her appearances might have been more frequent. She had lost track of time completely and couldn't even remember how many occasions she had heard the old woman's footsteps traipsing across the cellar floor. She could have been in the pit for a day, or for several days. It *felt* like several days.

But, though Melinda did not know how long the intervals were, she had the impression that the old woman's appearances were regular. So, when she heard footsteps coming down the stone steps at the far end of the cellar, she knew immediately it was too soon for it to be the old woman. Neither was it the overseer. His footfall was strong and loud while these steps were light and hesitant. Melinda strained against the manacles to see over the edge of the pit as the footsteps approached.

'Melinda? Melinda?' It was Amber's voice.

'Over here,' Melinda cried, her heart beating wildly.

'Where?'

'Right in the middle. There's a pit. Be careful.'

Amber followed the direction of Melinda's voice. Her face appeared over the edge. 'Oh my God,' she said.

'What are you doing here?' Melinda asked, her surprise clear in her voice.

'Are you all right? What have they done to you?'

'I'm cold, that's all.'

'What happened?'

'I tried to tell Sophia about Bianca. She had me brought straight down here.'

'That's what we thought had happened.'

'But how come you're here?'

'I think you were right. Something's going on. The house is practically deserted. The servants have been given the day off and Sophia's taken Leilah away. Aldo's gone with them. Leilah's going to perform at some private function for one of the master's most important clients. He likes to watch apparently and Sophia and Leilah are going to put on a show for him. I overheard them discussing it.'

'That must be it. The plot, I mean. It involves Leilah and her first master.'

'But how?'

'I don't know.'

'We've got to get you out of here.'

'There's no chance, Amber. I'm chained to the floor.'

'Is there a way down?'

'There's a ladder up there somewhere.'

Amber disappeared from Melinda's restricted view, then reappeared again, ladder in hand. She fitted it into the mountings and climbed down into the pit.

'See,' Melinda said, rattling the chain at her ankle and wrist.

'No problem,' Amber said, taking a hair pin from her long blonde hair. She flattened it out, inserted it into the lock on the manacle at Melinda's wrist and twisted it sharply. The manacle sprang open and dropped to the floor with a clatter that startled both girls.

'Where did you learn that?'

'I grew up in the Bronx. I learnt a lot from the local boys.'

Amber inserted the hair pin in the lock of the manacle on Melinda's ankle. With the same deft touch she freed that too.

'Come on,' she said.

'Where are we going?' Melinda was stunned at her sudden freedom.

'You'll think better when you're warm.'

They climbed the ladder and crossed the cellar floor to the stairs. At the bottom they listened for any activity above. Hearing nothing, they mounted the steps.

As Amber had said, the house was deserted. The old woman had a little room in one of the outbuildings and apart from a gardener working on the lawn, there was no one else to be seen.

They went back to their bedroom. Melinda was filthy and ran a bath, it also being the best way to rid herself of the cold that still chilled her to the bone.

As she lay in the bath, Amber sat on the toilet seat. 'You have to try and remember,' she said.

'Remember what?'

'They must have said something else.'

'They didn't.'

'Think.'

'He was telling her about how he'd found Leilah's master. About her locket. And he'd had him followed.'

'Followed? Why?'

'To find out ... hold on. I'd forgotten that. It was a place called the Seraglio. He had him followed there. He always goes there on his first night in Rome. That's what the master said.'

'The Seraglio Club,' Amber said at once.

'You know it?'

'It's a brothel. A very famous brothel. One of the most expensive in the world. Mostly for Arabs. It's a club. You have to be loaded to be a member. I heard one of my masters talking about it.'

Melinda got out of the bath. A light stubble had grown over her sex even in the short time it had not been shaved.

'A brothel. My God, that's it, don't you see?'

'See what?'

'The master's arranged for Sophia to perform with Leilah there. But it's not for one of his customers. It's for Leilah's first master.'

'And he'll think Sophia's been using her to make money at the brothel.'

'Which is absolutely forbidden.'

'Right. He'll go mad, especially as Leilah meant so much to him.'

'There's no telling what he'll do.'

'Dead or alive,' Melinda said, the words chilling her again. 'That's what they said. That's definitely the plan. They've worked it out perfectly. The Arab will

173

get hold of Sophia. Whatever he does to her she'll never be found again.'

'You were right all along.'

'We've got to stop her.'

'How? We don't even know where the Seraglio is.'

'We know it's in Rome.'

'And how do we get to Rome?'

'First, we need clothes. Come on ... we've got to hurry.'

Melinda led Amber down the back stairs to the first floor. They headed down the corridor towards Sophia's bedroom.

'What are we going to do?' Amber asked.

'Borrow some clothes,' Melinda replied.

They paused outside the double doors listening for the slightest sound, but there was nothing.

'Come on.' Opening the door to the mistress's bedroom without permission seemed a huge step to take. But Melinda had no choice. If her conjecture was right there was a slim chance she could save Sophia and in so doing save herself. There was no time to worry about disobedience, however strange it felt to be acting of her own accord after so long responding only to the direct commands of some other person.

Like everywhere else, Sophia's bedroom was deserted. Melinda led the way to the corner of the room where the wardrobes were set into a square niche. They rifled through the racks of clothes. There were drawers built inside the lower half of some of the cupboards and these were full of expensive lingerie, in a range of colours and materials, arranged drawer by drawer into bras, panties, basques, bodies and tights. There was an equally large selection of shoes.

All Sophia's clothes were from the best designers; chic and more than a little alluring. There was nothing practical or dull as they would have preferred for their adventure into the outside world. In the end Amber opted for a white silk teddy, its lacy bra cups much too big for her but otherwise a good fit, which she wore with a pair of glossy tan-coloured tights. Over these she pulled on a red silk blouse and a matching short red skirt.

Melinda chose a body too, in black, which was a better fit on her around the bosom, her breasts swelling against the black lace that most of the garment was made from. She found black tights and a short black dress.

Shoes were more of a problem. Amber climbed into a pair of tight black boots but they were too large for her. She stuffed nylon stockings into the toes to ease the problem though they were still uncomfortable. Melinda chose black boots too but found Sophia's feet were smaller than hers and the leather pinched and cramped her toes.

After so long naked or semi-naked it felt strange to be fully dressed again. Despite their rush they stared at themselves in the long mirror on the wall opposite the double doors, unable to believe what they saw and trying to convince themselves that the two elegantly-dressed women standing there in more or less normal clothes were actually them.

'Close it up,' Melinda said, 'in case someone comes back.'

They left the wardrobes as they had found them. Just as they were walking out Melinda stopped.

'Make-up, we've forgotten make-up. We've got to look normal out there.'

Quickly they found that all Sophia's make-up was on a dressing-table in her vast grey marble bathroom. They applied the basic cosmetics to themselves, the first time either of them had done this since they joined the O.I.M. Melinda found her hand was shaking as she tried to apply an eye-liner. It was going against everything she had been trained and conditioned to do. She told herself sharply that it was necessary, but that did not stop her hand shaking.

With their hair brushed and combed and make-up applied, they looked normal. An hour ago Melinda had been manacled and naked in a pit in the cellar; a helpless slave. Now she looked like a woman about to go out for cocktails. It was a thought that made her feel uncomfortable.

As they walked down the main staircase Melinda noticed the time on the grandfather clock that stood by the front door. It was six o'clock.

'Is it morning or evening?' she asked Amber.

'Evening.'

'My God, I thought it was morning. How long was I in the cellars?'

'Yesterday and today,' Amber replied.

'I lost track of time,' Melinda said, shaking her head. 'Come on.' Melinda led the way into the sitting-room.

'What are we looking for?' Amber asked.

'The master's study.'

'Why didn't you say so? He had me in there once. Bent me over the desk while he was working. Didn't do anything, just kept stroking my thigh.' Amber turned around and walked through into the dining-room. There was a smaller room to one side of it, the walls lined with books and a modern desk with a computer terminal in one corner.

'Come on, help me look,' Melinda said, rushing to the drawers of the desk.

'For what?'

'An address book. He has to have the Seraglio in it. We've got to find out where it is. I doubt it's in the phone book.'

They searched each of the drawers and found nothing.

'It might be in the computer,' Amber suggested.

'Yes.' Melinda sat down in front of the terminal and turned on the power. The screen lit up with the information that the user was requested to type in the security password. 'Damn,' she said, turning the machine off again. As she did so she spotted a spine of red leather. It was lying on the desk under the telephone. 'There.'

She snatched the book and opened the indexed pages at 'S'. The Seraglio Club was the last entry with an address on the Via Pandosa. Melinda replaced the book carefully from where it had come.

'Via Pandosa,' Amber said, looking blank.

'Let's go.' She hadn't the slightest idea how they were going to get to the Seraglio or what they were going to do when they got there but she knew that they had to do something even if they failed in the attempt.

They walked briskly back to the front door. Just as Amber was about to open it, Melinda held her back.

'Listen,' she said.

They listened. The unmistakable crunch of tyres on the gravel driveway announced the arrival of a car.

'What are we going to do?' Amber looked alarmed.

'In here, quick.'

There was a door under the stairs. Melinda opened it and discovered a cupboard lined with shelves. There were stores of lightbulbs, polish, candles and toilet paper. The two women crammed themselves into the small space and closed the door.

Though the sound was muffled they could hear the car pulling up outside the front door. Moments later they heard a key being inserted in the lock and the heavy door swinging open.

'Well.' It was a woman's voice. Melinda recognised it immediately. It was Bianca. 'Well, isn't this nice?' she continued. 'I think I'd like champagne Giorgio . . . out on the terrace.'

'I gave the servants the day off,' the master said.

'Good idea. Tomorrow I'll speak to them all, get them used to the idea of having a new mistress.'

'It won't be long now.'

'What time did they leave?' Bianca asked.

'An hour ago.'

'It's all set then?'

The master laughed. 'Oh yes, she suspects nothing.'

'Even after what the girl told her?'

'Aldo said she didn't believe a word of it. She thinks Achmed is a new customer with a huge amount of business and a penchant for watching women in bed together. She's going to perform with Leilah for him. It'll be quite a show I imagine.'

'And as soon as Achmed recognises his darling Leilah . . .' Her voice trailed off.

'Exactly. He'll be convinced Sophia has been using her full-time in the Seraglio to make money.'

'What time's he due?'

'Nine-thirty.'

'Wonderful. Come on, let's get the champagne. I'd like to swim too. Why don't you take my dress off? We can swim in the nude, can't we?'

'I can think of something else we can do in the pool.'

'Anything you want, master,' Bianca said mockingly. 'And tomorrow I'm going to start on this place. It's so drab. It needs completely redecorating.'

'Anything you want, mistress,' the master replied in the same tone.

Melinda heard their footsteps heading past the cupboard. Both girls held their breath until the couple had gone into the next room.

'Quick,' Melinda whispered. She poked her head around the door, checked everything was clear, then rushed to the front door which had been left open. With Melinda at her heels they dashed past Bianca's XJS convertible and headed for the shrubs that would hide them from view of the house.

'That was close,' Amber said, still whispering.

'Now all we've got to do is get to Rome.'

'And how are we going to do that?'

'What else can we do? We have to find a lift.'

'We could steal the Jag,' Amber suggested. 'I know how to hot-wire. I learnt that in the Bronx too.'

'No. That'll alert them immediately.'

'If they find I'm gone they'll be alerted soon enough.'

'That might not be for hours ... Come on.'

Keeping down behind the shrubs they reached the gates of the villa. As they walked through them Melinda felt her heart thumping.

'This is the real world,' she said to Amber.

'Scary, isn't it?' Amber said, clearly knowing exactly what Melinda was feeling. They had broken every rule they had been so carefully trained to obey but while they were still in the villa they had, somehow, still been in the world of the O.I.M. Outside, on the public road, that did not apply. This world was a very different place.

They walked quickly down the single track and on to the main road. There was very little traffic. A small truck passed with four pigs in the back, then a pick-up loaded with hay. Both drivers stared at the two girls as they went by but did not stop. A small, old, red Fiat driven by an old, red-faced woman hurtled by. She didn't even give them a second glance. That was the last of the traffic for ten minutes.

'What are we going to do?' Melinda asked. Time was not on their side.

'What can we do?'

They continued to walk along the road. It started to curve and descend steeply and they were both finding it hard to walk in the ill-fitting boots. There was nowhere to walk on the side of the tarmac so they had to use the surface of the road itself. At least the sun was low in the sky and it was not as hot as it had been earlier.

A large but rather battered maroon-coloured Lancia came speeding down the hill. Amber and Melinda both stood expectantly, their thumbs raised. The car raced past and turned the next sharp bend without braking, but as their hearts sank and they started walking again, they saw it had pulled up around the corner. They ran up to it as fast as they could, fearing it might pull away.

'*Signor*, *Roma*,' was all Melinda could think of saying as she bent down to speak to the driver. He was a small bald-headed man with thick-lensed black-rimmed spectacles. He was dressed in what had once been a very good suit but was now worn and shabby. His shirt was clean but frayed at the cuffs and collar and his colourful tie was stained with grease.

'*Inglese*?' he said. The driver's window was already wound down. 'I speak *inglese*,' he said proudly, with a smile that showed very white but very irregular teeth. 'You both *inglese*?'

'Yes,' Amber said. There was no time to split hairs.

'No,' he insisted at once. 'You *americano*. I know. I tell. Where you want?'

'Rome.'

'*Si, si*. In please. I take you Rome.' He reached back and unlocked the rear door. They climbed inside and before they had closed the door he set off again down the hill. 'Very pretty,' he said, looking at them in the rear-view mirror.

The dashboard on the car was inlaid with walnut and the seats were made of heavily worn black leather. There was a small clock at the side of the speedometer. Melinda was dismayed to see that the time was ten minutes to seven.

'We'll never make it,' she said. 'We don't even know which side of Rome it is.'

'You hurry?' the man asked.

'*Si, signor*. Do you know the Via Pandosa?'

'Via Pandosa?' The man wrinkled his forehead. He brightened. '*Scusi, scusi*. Me Ernesto.' He turned around and stuck out his right hand without taking his eyes off the road. They shook his hand one by one.

'Melinda.'

'Amber.'

'Ernesto,' he repeated, turning back to the wheel. 'Very pretty.'

'Do you know the Via Pandosa?' Amber repeated.

'You go there, Via Pandosa?' His eyes were studying them intently in the rear-view mirror.

'*Si*.'

'I not know,' he said flatly.

'Have you got a map of Rome?' Melinda asked.

'*Si, si*,' he said merrily, reaching over to the glove compartment. He opened the walnut panel and rummaged inside. 'Bologna, Firenze . . .' He threw maps

181

on to the front seat. 'Ah, Roma,' he said triumphantly, handing the map back to them.

The map was stained and old, its creases almost torn through. Melinda opened it carefully, found the Via Pandosa in the street finder printed on one panel then to her dismay found that it was located on the other side of the city to the north. Judging from the position of the sun, they were coming in from almost due south.

'Jesus, it's miles away,' Amber said, as Melinda's finger pointed it out on the map.

'*Problema*?' Ernesto said.

'*Si, si*,' Amber said. 'We have to get to the Via Pandosa by nine.'

'*Nove*?'

'*Si*.'

'Is possible. I drop you Piazzo del Cinquecento. Plenty taxis.'

'We've got no money.'

'Oh. Then *problema*.' His eyes stared into the mirror. Melinda had the feeling he wanted to say something but was not sure whether he dared. She decided to say it for him.

'We'll do anything,' she said.

'You do what?' he asked.

'Anything you want, if you'll take us to the Via Pandosa.'

'Anything?'

Both girls nodded. What choice did they have?

'You like each other?' he said.

'Yes . . .' Melinda did not understand.

'I mean, you show me you like each other. I like to see this. It . . . what you say . . . it turns me.'

'Like this,' Melinda said, catching on. She turned to Amber and kissed her on the cheek, then slid her

182

mouth on to the American's large fleshy mouth, pushing her tongue into it.

'*Si, si, bella.*' Ernesto bounced up and down in his seat, making the old springs creak. 'I like this.'

'Pull over then,' Melinda said, breaking the kiss.

'*Non comprendo.*'

'Park.' Melinda would have preferred for him to keep driving but the way his eyes had already veered off the road it was clearly too dangerous. 'Find somewhere quiet.'

'*Si, si,*' he said. After two or three miles he spotted a little rough track that led along the bottom of one of the more precipitous hills. He pulled the car off on to the track and parked after the first bend where it could not be seen from the road. '*Allora,*' he said, swinging his arm over the back seat and turning to look at his prize.

Amber took the lead this time. She hooked her arm around Melinda's neck and pulled her into a kiss, her other hand running down to Melinda's breast and kneading it through the black dress. Melinda responded by sliding her hand under the red skirt, flicking it up so that Ernesto could see Amber's long thighs sheathed in the sheer nylon.

Both women knew they had to be quick. The faster they gave the little man what he wanted the faster they could be on their way. Unfortunately, they had not planned for this. There were two layers covering Amber's sex – the gusset of the tights and the white teddy. Melinda, similarly, had tights and the crotch of the black teddy.

As quickly as they could they began to wrestle with their clothes. At first they started to undress each other, Melinda struggling to pull Amber's tights off as Amber reached for the zip of the black dress. The seat at the back of the car was a single bench but though it was quite wide there was not enough room for the manoeuvring required to divest them of their clothes.

They reached the same conclusion at the same time. Amber opened the car door and got out, giving Melinda room to pull off her boots, strip the dress over her head, unbutton the clasps in the crotch of the teddy and skim down her tights. Outside, Amber quickly tore off the blouse, unzipped her skirt and peeled off her boots and tights. She stripped the loose-fitting teddy down over her hips so she was completely naked. Leaving the clothes in a neat pile on the grass, she climbed back into the car.

Ernesto obviously couldn't decide which girl to look at. He stared from one to the other, shaking his head from side to side as if not believing what he saw.

'*Sfioramento*,' he said. 'What you say, shaved?' His eyes moved from Amber's mons to Melinda's.

'You like it?' Melinda asked. She stroked her own sex, then put her hand between Amber's thighs.

'*Si, si, meraviglioso.*'

'I like it too,' Melinda said. Glancing at the clock on the dashboard she kissed Amber on the mouth. It was five past seven. She pushed Amber back on the seat until she was lying flat on it, her head up against the window winder, her knees bent to allow one foot to press against the door on the other side while the other remained on the floor. Melinda was perched on the edge of the seat by Amber's thigh.

Awkwardly, Melinda turned her back to Amber's face and swung her left knee up over her body until it was slotted between the back of the seat and Amber's shoulder. Her right knee just had room on the outer edge of the leather. Immediately she pushed her sex down on to Amber's mouth and dipped her head between Amber's thighs.

Ernesto applauded, clapping his hands together excitedly as he watched Melinda's tongue delve between Amber's hairless labia. The silk of Melinda's teddy rubbed against Amber's naked breasts as the American raised her head slightly to enable her mouth to get a better position against Melinda's sex.

The first thrill was muted. Melinda tongued Amber's clitoris, pushing the little nut of flesh from side to side. She could feel the hardness of her own nipples pressed into Amber's navel and Amber's tongue searching out her own clit, but the awkwardness of their position and the worry of time made the movements seem mechanical.

At least they did to start with. As Melinda felt Amber succeed in teasing out her clitoris from her labia, she felt Amber's hand on her naked buttock. It was caressing the camber of her flesh and she felt it sliding down to her sex, her fingertips playing briefly with the labia at the opening of her vagina, then plunging inside – two fingers she thought, but there might have been three. Quite suddenly Melinda felt a rush of feeling that wiped away her other concerns. She renewed her attack on Amber's sex. There was no room to get her fingers under Amber's thighs and into her vagina but she managed to play her tongue around its entrance and felt Amber's body surge in response.

Despite the difficulties, a mutual passion began to assert itself. The nights of lying naked next to each other in bed, all the longing and need that it had produced and the pent-up frustration of being forbidden to do anything about it, was released. How many times had Melinda looked at Amber's long, lithe body and wanted to press herself against it like this, to sink her mouth into her sex and feel, in return, Amber's fleshy lips lapping at her own sex? Of course, it was wrong. It was disobedient. It was asserting her own will above the will of the masters. But briefly – she hoped very briefly – she was out of their bailiwick. She could justify what she felt, and the pleasure that coursed through her body, by telling herself it was necessary. It was the only way she was going to be able to save Sophia and ultimately, save herself. Amber, she was sure, felt the same.

Ernesto knelt on his seat to get a better view. Out of the corner of her eye Melinda could see him staring intently, his mouth open slightly, his tongue poised between his lips. She could see his arm working up and down as his hand rubbed the front of his trousers. He was moaning slightly, mewing almost, like an animal in need.

The penetration of Amber's fingers, straining forward to gain an extra inch, caused a sharp jolt of sensation in Melinda's body. Like her limbs, Amber had very long fingers and they seemed to be stroking the neck of Melinda's womb. Her tongue was increasing its pressure on Melinda's clitoris too. It was easy for her to find the right places, the tiny spots of ultra-sensitivity, because as her tongue slipped over them Melinda's body pulsed. The same was true for Melinda. As her tongue explored the little promontory of Amber's clit, she could feel the American's body tense and she would concentrate on that particular spot.

Both knew it had to be quick and could not be faked. If they short-changed Ernesto and did not give him the show he had bargained for, he, in turn, might not complete his side of the arrangement. And he was their only hope. It would have been wonderful to have time to explore, to kiss and suck at nipples, to lick and lap at each other's labia, to tease each other's vaginas and test the tenderness of the little buds of their anuses, but there was no time. The only thing they had time for was raw feeling. And that was what they were getting and giving in return.

The moment arrived rapidly. Locked together, their bodies sealed in a circle by the stickiness of their mouths, every action, every feeling in one was matched and equalled by a reaction in the other. As Melinda felt Amber's tongue pushing her clitoris to and fro, and she, in turn, did exactly the same thing to Amber, her orgasm began to break, forcing its way out from her other concerns to claim her mind as its own. Amber's orgasm broke too, built on exactly the same stimulations, the frustrations at last allowed to come to the surface and breathe. Clinging together as if for dear life, they felt each other's climax almost as acutely as they felt their own, the heat and passion that escaped their mouths indistinguishable from the heat and passion that exploded from their throbbing sexes. It was so sharp, so sudden and ultimately so needed that it was almost painful.

An odd noise filled the car. It was almost like the howl of a wolf. Neither woman could disentangle herself enough to see what it was though both knew it was the noise Ernesto made as he came. His cock spurted his semen into his trousers.

Slowly, Melinda picked herself off Amber's body, allowing her to sit up. Ernesto, still kneeling, watched as Amber got out of the car.

'Well?' Melinda asked.

'*Meraviglioso,*' he said quietly.

'So, now we go?'

'*Si*, straight now,' he said, as Amber got back into

the car with her clothes. To their great relief he reversed up the track and on to the road. 'Via Pandosa. You tell me from the map, yes?'

'Yes.'

They struggled into their clothes. As Melinda fumbled with the catches of the teddy she felt a surge of sensation. Her labia was wet and swollen and responded to her touch with an aftershock of orgasm that closed her eyes with its intensity.

A lorry was trailing the car. The driver got up close to the bumper as he realised there were two semi-naked women in the back. He hooted his horn as Melinda pulled the black dress back over her head. She managed to pull on her tights and the boots without any further display though Amber's struggle into her white teddy produced another round of enthusiastic honking.

Ernesto drove faster. The lorry tried to overtake but as the road flattened out and straightened, turning into a dual carriageway leading into the suburbs of Rome, he was lost in the other traffic. Both girls were respectable by then, with nothing for drivers overtaking on the outside lane to see.

As they got towards the centre of the city Melinda began to give Ernesto directions, which he took cheerfully and accompanied with a polite 'grazie'. The traffic was horrendous and the minutes ticked away.

The clock on the dashboard read 9.00 when the Lancia pulled into a broad avenue with a park along one side of the road and large houses, standing in their own grounds, on the other. A stone-carved slab on the corner of one of the high walls that surrounded most of the houses announced that they were in the Via Pandosa. They drove the length of the street and discovered that the house at the far end, its driveway fronted by large square-section pillars to which impressive wrought-iron gates were hinged, was number eleven, the address given for the Seraglio Club in the master's address book.

Ernesto parked on the other side of the street.

'*Allora*,' he said. 'It was been most ... entertainment.'

'Thank you,' Melinda said sincerely.

'We've got to rush,' Amber added, pulling Melinda by the hand as she got out of the car.

They watched as Ernesto drove away, Amber's fingers still laced between Melinda's, causing a little frisson of pleasure as she remembered what they had done in the car and wished they had had time to do more.

Eight

The Seraglio Club was in a large square building with wooden louvred shutters folded back against each side of its rectangular windows, spaced symmetrically on its façade. A high brick wall surrounded it on all sides and the large electronically-operated wrought-iron gates were firmly closed. A security video camera was mounted in front of the left-hand pillar to monitor anyone who approached.

There was clearly no way in through the front. As the house was on the corner of the street the two girls were able to walk down the intersecting road along the side of the wall. But the wall was featureless, high and unscalable. Eventually it butted directly into the lateral wall of the first building in the side street, with no possibility of a way through.

'What are we going to do?' Amber asked.

'God knows. There's no way we can climb in.'

They walked back to the front of the building, being careful to avoid the field of view of the security camera. A car, a large dark blue Mercedes, drove up to the gates. As it approached the gates swung open.

'Did you see that? We could sneak in behind a car as they open the gates. The camera's got a blind spot there,' Amber suggested.

'Great. Come on.'

190

They crossed the road to the park side to avoid the camera, then walked back on the other side of the road, hiding themselves behind the thick trunk of one of the many ancient trees that were spaced at regular intervals down the wide pavement. They waited, only too aware of time ticking by.

'I wish we'd stolen one of her watches,' Amber said, after what must have been ten minutes.

'This is no good.'

'Do you think he's in there already?'

'That Mercedes?'

'Might have been.'

'I've got an idea.' Melinda had suddenly had a brainwave.

'What?'

'It's a brothel, right? They need girls. Why don't we just ring the doorbell? They're bound to let us in or at least take a look at us.'

'Brilliant.'

They quickly checked each other's hair and straightened their clothes, then walked nonchalantly towards the house. They saw the security camera swivel on its mountings and the lens focus on them. There was an entry-phone set in the left-hand pillar under the camera. Melinda pressed the illuminated buzzer.

'*Si?*' The distorted voice from the small speaker was male.

Melinda had no idea what to say. 'Can we come in?' she asked weakly.

'We heard there's work,' Amber added.

The speaker went dead. There was a long pause. Both girls looked at each other apprehensively. Suddenly there was a metal click and one of the big wrought-iron gates opened inwards. It stopped after

191

a couple of feet. The two girls squeezed through. The gate clanged shut behind them.

Their feet crunched on the gravel drive. They walked up to the front door where three stone steps led to a porch, its roof supported under circular columns. There was a large old-fashioned doorbell pull set in the wall to the right of the panelled front door. Amber was just about to pull it when the front door opened.

A tall, rather skinny and gaunt-faced man stood in the doorway. He was dressed in a nineteenth-century footman's uniform with a ruffled shirt, frock coat, a striped white and yellow silk waistcoat and black silk knickerbockers tucked into white silk stockings. He wore big silver buckles on his black shoes.

'This way,' he said in a heavy Italian accent, standing aside to let them in.

If Melinda had been expecting a *fin de siècle* salon full of velvet upholstered button-backed love seats and *chaise-longues* with semi-naked girls in stockings and corsets she was disappointed. The front door opened directly on to a large room with a bar in one corner but the furniture was modern and drab and the room was deserted apart from the barman, who stood busily polishing glasses.

'Wait here,' the footman instructed.

Melinda and Amber sat side by side on one of the Dralon-covered sofas. Amber noticed a video camera at ceiling level in one corner of the room and nudged Melinda to indicate what she had seen. There was another camera mounted over the front door.

After a few minutes the footman appeared again. Ignoring them completely he marched to the front door and opened it before the doorbell sounded. He ushered in three relatively young Arabs, all talking excitedly to each other in rapid Arabic. They seemed to know their way around and walked straight over to the bar, ordering, in English, a bottle of Krug champagne.

As a bottle and three glasses were produced, the footman went to a door at the back of the room and opened it. After a few seconds a line of girls walked out in single file all clad in revealing outfits. There were tight slinky black satin basques, plain silk slips with spaghetti straps, a white frothily-trimmed bra and equally flounced French knickers with white silk stockings and garters, and a girl naked but for a black rubber girdle attached to latex stockings. Another girl wore only a leather G-string and there was a brunette in a leather harness strapped tightly around her body and complemented by a leather hood reminiscent of many of the restraints Melinda had seen in the houses of the masters.

Like their costumes the girls, ten in all, were of various shapes and sizes, one small and boyish, another plump and Rodinesque. There was a tall Amazonian woman with a shaved head and a virginal-looking blonde.

They each chose a seat among the numerous chairs and sofas and waited, crossing their legs and looking hopefully at the Arabs.

The three men quaffed their champagne. They had clearly already had a lot to drink. Melinda wondered if one of the three was Leilah's master, but doubted it somehow. All the masters she had met had a silent, quiet authority, an almost hypnotic quality that none of these three men exuded.

A second bottle was opened with the faintest of pops, the barman twisting the cork carefully in a linen cloth. The Arabs began wandering around the room, looking at the girls who greeted their gazes with some physical display such as slipping off their bras or opening their legs. The girl in the leather harness was asked to stand up by one of the men, who then walked around her, slowly examining her restraints. A second Arab sat next to the boyish-figured girl, who was dressed in a black fishnet leotard, and began fondling her. The third man walked over to Melinda and Amber, looking from one to the other as if trying to make up his mind.

Standing directly in front of them, he shouted something in Arabic across the room to the oldest man in the party, who clearly replied in the affirmative. Immediately the man took both Melinda and Amber's hands and brought them to their feet.

'Like this,' he said in broken English. 'Like both.'

He began leading them to the back of the room. Melinda glanced at Amber, who shrugged her shoulders. They had no choice but to go along with the man. It was their chance to get further into the building. The footman, who stood by the bar now, made no attempt to intervene and clearly neither did whoever was watching from the video cameras, as they were allowed to leave the salon without anyone arriving to stop them.

The Arab was in his thirties, with very black hair and a swarthy complexion. He wore an obviously handmade suit and shirt, a silk tie and highly polished brogues. A solid gold watch sparkled on his wrist, its rim encrusted with diamonds. He was not tall and was of quite a slight build.

There was a corridor at the back of the salon that led directly to an old gilded lift. The Arab opened the iron grille of the gate and the three squeezed inside. The lift rose two floors, clanking and groaning all the way, and they all tumbled out. The Arab knew the way. He took Melinda's wrist and guided her along a hallway decorated in rose-patterned wallpaper, with a light pink, rather worn, carpet. On the walls were cartoon sketches which looked as though they were caricatures of the *Kama Sutra*; line drawings of men with trunk-size erections trying to force them into the gargoyle-like labia of women in positions that defied the human anatomy.

He opened the third door down and led them into a pleasant, clean and functional bedroom that might have belonged to a three-star hotel. The furniture was all modern and cheap with a double bed that was neatly made, its top sheet and counterpane folded back in a diagonal, the pillows plumped and full. There were two other doors, one closed and one open. The open one revealed a small bathroom tiled in pink, its bath surrounded by a Perspex shower screen.

'You need?' he asked, pointing at the bathroom.

'Yes,' Amber said, going inside and shutting the door behind her.

The Arab took off his jacket and hung it on a wooden hanger in the wardrobe. He unbuttoned his shirt and hung that beside the jacket, taking his tie and laying it flat on the large chest of drawers opposite the bed. He was wearing a white T-shirt type vest. He sat on the bed and removed his socks and shoes, tucking the black silk socks into the brogues. Standing up again he undid the gold buckle of the black snakeskin belt and took down his trousers. Again he hung these over a hanger and made sure the creases were straight. He pulled the vest over his head and folded that over the back of a small armchair. His white boxer shorts were taken down and folded over his vest.

His body was scrawny and lacking muscle but he was not fat.

'You suck,' he said, pointing to his circumcised cock which was completely flaccid against a bed of thick black pubic hair. He lay on the bed and laced his fingers together behind his head.

'Yes, master,' Melinda said automatically, the order provoking her ritual response.

She knelt on the bed beside him.

'I like this,' he said. 'I like master.'

She took his cock in her hand and fed it into his mouth. As she began to suck on his shaft, she prised his thighs open with her hand and fingered his balls.

'Yes,' he said. His erection hardened rapidly, swelling in Melinda's mouth.

Amber came out of the bathroom. She had stripped off everything but the white teddy. The Arab looked at her approvingly and Melinda felt his cock throb.

'Now you,' he said.

Amber knelt on the other side of the man and replaced Melinda's mouth with her own. The Arab's cock was very smooth and quite long but thin and stick-like. Melinda got up and unzipped her black boots. She pulled them off then pulled the black dress over her head. She saw the Arab's eyes roaming the silk teddy as she unfastened the clasps between her thighs then drew the black tights down her legs.

'Is enough,' he said, obviously wanting her to keep the teddy on. He gestured with his hand, indicating that she should do the gusset up again. As soon as she had done so he patted the bed and she knelt at his side as she had done before. She noticed the gold watch and could see it was already 9.35.

'Nice,' he said, stroking the silk behind Melinda's

196

back, looking at the way the lace panels set into the teddy revealed Melinda's firm, very round breasts. His hand moved around and cupped each in turn, feeling their weight but not squeezing them. He ran his hand down to the apex of her thighs and pushed his fingers between her legs but did no more than rub his fingertips against the black silk that tightly covered her labia.

'Both now,' he said, nodding his head towards Amber.

Melinda leant forward and began kissing the man's thighs. As Amber pulled her mouth back to the top of his erection and her lips pursed around the ridge of his glans, Melinda edged forward to plant her mouth on the bottom of the shaft already wet from Amber's saliva. They felt the Arab's body shudder and he moaned.

With her eyes Melinda tried to draw Amber's attention to the Arab's watch, his hand lying on his stomach and the watch in plain view. Amber saw what she meant and read the time, raising her eyebrows in alarm. Immediately she started to pump her mouth up and down on the shaft, taking it deep in her throat and necessarily pushing Melinda's mouth aside.

'No,' the Arab said at once, angrily. 'Both.'

Melinda did not want to disturb Amber's rhythm. She pulled the man's legs further apart and worked down until she could get her mouth on to his balls.

'Yes,' the man said approvingly.

Carefully, Melinda managed to suck both his balls into her mouth, while Amber continued her onslaught on his cock. How many times had Melinda been used in this way, to service a master or the guest of a master, co-operating with another slave to bring

197

the greatest pleasure? That is what they had both been trained to do. It felt comfortable and familiar, despite the fact this man had probably never even heard of the O.I.M.

They both felt his cock beginning to pulse regularly. Amber pounded down on it, cramming it into her throat, then pulling out, giving his glans a pinch with her lips on the upward stroke.

'No,' he said. 'Stop.'

Had he been a master they would have stopped at once, taken their mouths away and knelt obediently with their hands on their knees, eyes cast down, waiting for their next instruction. But he was not. Melinda felt his spunk pumping through his urethra into his cock. She sucked a little harder to encourage it and, as Amber's lips descended and his cock was forced into the tight confines of her throat, it spasmed twice in quick succession and spattered out hot spunk, jerking vigorously. When the jets subsided Amber drew back a little, sucking on his glans and running her tongue on to the slit of his urethra to milk out every last drop. She swallowed it all bar a little dribble that escaped from the corner of her mouth.

Though he had ordered them to stop the man was not annoyed. As they straightened up he smiled at them. He got off the bed, collected all his clothes, then went into the bathroom, closing the door behind him. In minutes he came out again fully dressed and as immaculate as before. He took out an ostrich leather wallet, dropped two large denomination Italian notes on the chest of drawers and was gone.

'Did you see the time?' Melinda said as soon as the bedroom door closed behind him.

'Do you think we're too late?'

'I don't know. I just have a feeling he's not here yet.'

'Let's hope so.'

'Come on, we've got to try and find Sophia.'

Melinda looked at the money. Though she hoped they wouldn't need it, after their experience earlier she decided it might come in useful. She picked up her dress and stuffed the money into the little pocket at the side. Just as they both began to pick up the rest of their clothes the bedroom door opened again and another of the Arabs from the party of three stood in the doorway.

'Ladies,' he said. He closed the door firmly behind him. He was grinning from ear to ear.

Melinda looked at Amber. What could they do? If they refused to co-operate with the man he might cause a fuss, and the last thing they wanted at the moment was to draw attention to themselves and possibly be thrown out of the house. They had no choice but to go along with whatever he wanted, and hope they could dispatch him as quickly as the first.

Unlike his friend, this man was big and powerful. He had already discarded the jacket of his suit and his tie and was wearing only trousers and a white shirt. His chest was barrel-shaped and his arms bulged against his sleeves. His neck was almost the same width as his head.

'I show you what I have,' he said, his English no better than the first man's.

He took a key attached to a plastic tab, like the key to a hotel bedroom, and used it to unlock the door beside the bathroom.

'Is extra yes,' he said grinning. 'I pay extra for key.'

He shepherded them through the door.

The room beyond was small and its floor, ceiling

199

and walls were all lined with a peculiar black spongy material, the outer surface of which felt like rubber. The door, on a gravity hinge, swung closed with a clunk, it too covered on the inside with the same strange black sponge. The room was lit from a bright overhead light.

There was no furniture except for what looked like a small padded vaulting horse, a leather strap attached to each of its four feet, the padding on the top upholstered in green leather. Running across the centre of the ceiling was a sturdy RSJ to which were attached two pulleys. Running from the pulleys were chains, and secured to the ends of these, and no more than two feet apart, were two leather harnesses.

'You,' the Arab said, indicating Amber. He flicked the back of the white teddy. 'Take off,' he said.

Amber obeyed, skimming the teddy down her long legs as he watched, and revealing the smoothly shaven features of her sex.

The Arab went to a small panel set into the wall by the door. It had two stainless steel rotary knobs. He turned one and instantly the chain holding the leather harness descended, until it landed on the floor.

'Here,' he said, indicating by gesture – his English obviously not good enough to tell her by words – that he wanted her to sit on the floor by the side of the harness. The harness consisted of four extremely heavily-padded and very thick leather cuffs all attached by equally sturdy metal rings to a central ring which in turn was secured to the overhead chain. The Arab quickly picked up Amber's left wrist and strapped it tightly into one of the four cuffs. Her right was soon similarly bound. Reaching out to her ankles he pulled them up towards her wrists and fitted them one by one into the two remaining cuffs. He buckled them in tight, effectively binding her so she was bent double.

He went back to the rotary switch and turned it in the opposite direction. The chain began to ascend. It hauled up the harness and then Amber until she was hanging like a ripe fruit from a tree, her ankles and wrists uppermost, her breasts pressed into her knees. In this position her sex, pursed between her thighs was exposed and almost vertical.

Melinda could see how cleverly the harness had been designed. A man standing in front of the harness would adjust it to his height so his cock would slide straight into the bound victim's sex. What's more, he could push the harness away like a child's swing and have it fall back on him, impaling the sex on his erection every time. Similarly, with a second girl in the other harness, the man could move from one to the other with the greatest of ease. It was even possible for the two women to be swung together against each other. The impact would push aside the flesh of the buttocks so their sexes would touch and create a suction effect. The thought made Melinda shudder.

'You,' the Arab said, operating the other rotary switch and making the second harness descend to the floor.

Melinda felt a jolt of alarm. If she were bound into the harness like Amber there was no telling how long it would be while the Arab toyed and used them. They would have no control, no ability to do anything about it, and no chance, as they had had with his friend, of bringing about a rapid conclusion.

She had to think quickly, trying to fight her natural inclination merely to obey.

'No,' she said. She came up to him and put her arm around his shoulders. 'We have this very special service,' she whispered, nibbling on the lobe of his ear.

'Special?' he asked.

'Speciality.'

'Yes?' he said.

'Very sexy,' she said. 'Very pleasurable for a man. And exciting.'

'Is so?' he grinned, his hand groping her breast under the lacy teddy.

'You'll love it,'

'What I do?'

She broke away from him and knelt by the empty harness on the floor. 'Come here,' she said softly.

She saw his mind working behind his eyes, working out, no doubt, what it would be like if he allowed himself to be put in the second harness. Apparently he decided he liked the idea. He quickly pulled off his shirt, kicked off his shoes, pulled off his socks and took down his trousers and blue silk briefs. Unlike his friend he dropped the clothes on to the floor. His body was hairless apart from the curly pubic hair from which his cock sprouted and his muscles were obviously used to exercise, his thighs particularly broad. His cock itself, which was quite erect, was broad too, though his balls were rather small. Had he decided not to co-operate Melinda could have had little chance against his obvious strength.

Clearly, however, he had no intention of changing his mind. He sat on the floor by the harness so his feet were touching it. He moved his hands down to touch his toes and grinned up at Melinda, as if he had just performed a feat of which he should be proud.

'Like this,' he said.

Quickly Melinda strapped his wrists into the leather cuffs, buckling them as tightly as she could and double checking that they were secure. His ankles followed, then she took hold of his cock and balls and pulled them back through his thighs so they stuck out at the bottom of his buttocks. He would imagine, she hoped, that his cock would be swung into Amber's sex or perhaps alternate between that and her mouth. She walked over to the rotary switch and turned it as she had seen him do and the chain began to wind back up. The leather groaned as it took his weight and she held her breath, hoping it would not break. If it did her plan would be in tatters and they would be at the Arab's mercy. But, despite the alarming noises, it held.

Melinda immediately turned the other rotary knob and Amber began to descend. The sight made the Arab start to struggle.

'No!' he shouted angrily.

As soon as Amber was on the floor Melinda ran over to her and began unbuckling the cuffs.

'No ... stop ...' the Arab shouted, then started a stream of what was clearly abusive Arabic. He wrestled with the cuffs, making his body swing from side to side in the harness.

'The room must be soundproof,' Amber said as Melinda freed her wrists. 'That's what the padding's for.'

'Look at the time.'

The wafer-thin Patek Phillipe on the Arab's wrist told them it was ten o'clock.

Melinda freed the last buckle on Amber's ankle and they rushed back into the bedroom. The Arab was screaming at the top of his voice but as the door closed of its own accord and clunked against the jamb the sound stopped as effectively as if a radio had been switched off. They listened but could not hear a thing. Melinda turned the key in the lock and hid it under the mattress.

'Come on,' she urged.

They picked up their clothes and put them on, not bothering with the tights. Zipping up their boots they strode out into the hall, anxious not to get caught again.

'Which way?' Amber asked.

On the principle that they had seen nothing unusual on the way from the lift, Melinda turned in the opposite direction. They walked quickly, trying to make as little noise as possible.

At the end of the corridor was a staircase. They tripped down it to the first floor. The corridor here was identical to the one they had just left, the same rose-patterned wallpaper and pink carpet and the same spacing of what were obviously bedroom doors. Halfway to the lift the corridor was intersected by another.

Melinda led them in the new direction. The hall was much narrower and was decorated in plain cream paint. There were only two doors on one side of it, both identical and so small it would be necessary to stoop to enter them. Melinda tried the first door and found it locked. Amber tested the second, which opened with an alarming creak. As quietly as they could, they peered inside.

To their surprise they found the gallery of what was a perfect miniature of a theatre. Seeing no one, they crept inside for a closer look. The gallery comprised two rows of seats. Below, on what was obviously the ground floor of the house, were the stalls and the stage, complete with proscenium arch and dark red velvet curtains pulled back on either side of it. There were seven rows of seats in the stalls, normal theatre seats with a tip-up base, but more widely spaced than usual and generally more luxurious.

Sitting right in the centre of the stalls were four men, again all Arab. As Melinda carefully edged forward so she could see them more clearly she knew at once that the older of the four was Leilah's master. He was smartly dressed in an evening suit and black bow-tie, his olive-skinned face strong though heavily wrinkled. His once black hair was now almost entirely white as were the thick eyebrows over his large and very deep brown eyes. He exuded authority exactly as she had expected he would and, as she looked at his face, she felt herself succumb to an almost magnetic power, drawing her to him.

Only the crack of a whip broke the spell. She looked at the stage. Standing in the middle of the platform was a tall, muscular man, again from his black hair and olive skin, obviously an Arab. He was completely naked and his body had been oiled so that the contours of his muscles glistened under the very bright spotlights that lit the scene. On either side of him were two women, both blonde and very pale skinned. Though both of them were attractive they were distinctly different. One had very small almost non-existent breasts and a tight boy-like arse, while the other had a large pear-shaped bosom hanging down almost to her belly with buttocks of similar proportions. They were standing facing each other on either side of the stage, spread-eagled, their wrists tied by ropes that disappeared above their heads, their ankles secured to rings in large iron weights placed well apart so their legs were separated and their sexes exposed. Both women were completely naked and, like the man, had had their bodies oiled. The oil had plastered down their pubic hair and Melinda could clearly see their labia.

The whip cracked again. Several weals already criss-crossed the women's bodies and this latest lash provoked another one on the thigh of the woman on the right, the blonde with the large breasts. She gasped but it was quite obvious from the sound she made that her pain was mingled inextricably with pleasure. Her breasts quivered as the effect of the lash worked through her body.

It was a sight, Melinda thought, typical of many she had seen in the houses of the masters. Once again it felt odd that this was happening a long way from their jurisdiction and that she was not in some way involved. There was, of course, a master sitting watching the spectacle that had obviously been arranged for his benefit.

The women's tormentor had a massive erection. It too glistened with oil. Melinda thought she could see it pulsing under the lights, and there was certainly a tear of fluid at its tip.

With a flick of his wrist the massive Arab brought the short leather whip he held in his right hand down across the thigh of the blonde on the left, giving them equal treatment. She did not gasp but writhed against her bonds. Walking behind her the man delivered a much harder stroke to her small buttocks, then, in the spirit of equality, went over to the other woman to deliver a similar blow to her.

Coming back between them both he took the whip in his teeth and held out his arms. It was just possible for him to infiltrate his fingers between both their labia at the same time. Pushing his fingers against their clitorises he made both women moan loudly as he sawed his hands back and forth, rubbing each little nut of nerves.

Looking down into the stalls, he spat the whip out

and said something loudly in Arabic. Melinda watched the master respond. He raised a hand and pointed a finger at the blonde on the left, the one whose breasts were little more than raised extrusions on her chest.

Immediately the Arab circled around behind her. His hand reached round her body to knead what there was of her bosom, and Melinda saw his fingers pinch at her disproportionately large nipples. She, in response, pushed her small buttocks back against the man's erection. The Arab's hands slipped down to her hips as he sunk his mouth on to her neck, sucking on the corded sinews of her throat and making her throw her head back. He held her steady as he prepared to penetrate her, pulling his cock back and positioning it, Melinda could see quite clearly, not at the entrance to her vagina but at the higher orifice. The woman mouthed the word '*si*' over and over again.

The man bucked his hips forward, the sides of his buttocks dimpled by muscle, and drove his erection into her. The force of his plunge picked her off her feet, dragging her against her bonds. She moaned and Melinda saw her whole oiled body tense. Her eyes rolled up until Melinda could see only their whites and for a moment it appeared as though she might faint. But her body reasserted itself and began to move, grinding back on the phallus buried inside it. She moaned rhythmically as the man, his fingers digging into the soft flesh on her hips, began to move, pumping into her though not bringing his erection out very far before thrusting it back in.

The doors through which they had entered were on the right side of the gallery. From the corner of her eye Melinda saw that Amber had worked her way right across to the left-hand side and was gesturing for her to go over there too. Stealthily, she joined her.

'Look,' Amber whispered. From this position it was possible to see into the wings on the right side of the stage. There, in the shadows, stood Sophia. She was dressed from head to toe in black leather – black leather thigh boots with spiky high heels, skin-tight leather trousers and an equally tight leather top with a plunging neckline that revealed her ample cleavage. Her long hair was pinned to her head and she looked severe and unsmiling. Next to her was a bed, complete with a brass bedstead. The bed was on metal castors and its mattress was covered with a black silk sheet. Strapped across it, her wrists and ankles corded to each corner of the bedstead, was Leilah. She was naked, her long black hair draped carefully over the pillow. Lying between her legs was the vibrating ball Sophia had used on Melinda.

Sophia and Leilah were clearly the next act on the bill which the Seraglio Club had arranged to lay before the master.

Melinda indicated the door and Amber understood. They crept across the gallery, not wanting to attract the unwelcome attentions of the four men in the stalls.

'We were right,' Melinda said, the moment the door to the gallery closed. 'They're going to perform for him.'

'She obviously hasn't the slightest idea who he really is.'

'He'll go mad. You know what Arabs are like. It would be bad enough with a European master but with an Arab . . .'

'That's what Bianca's counting on.'

'Exactly. No wonder they said "dead or alive". We've got to stop it.'

'How can we?'

'I don't know but we've got to try.'

Melinda ran back to the stairs with Amber in hot pursuit. How long it would be before the big Arab ejaculated into the boyish blonde, or whether he was just using her first then would go on to the other woman, Melinda did not know. Even if the latter were the case there was not very much time, judging from his obvious state of excitement.

They ran down the stairs, no time to care about the noise they were making. Trying to work out the direction of the theatre Melinda careered down the passage at the bottom of the staircase and turned left when it reached a T-junction. There were two identically placed doors to the ones upstairs though they were a lot bigger. She opened one with the greatest of care, just wide enough to see the room beyond. She was right. It was the auditorium.

One of the Arabs in the stalls turned to glare at her but he looked back at the stage as she closed the door quickly.

There was a door at the end of the passage. They were on the right-hand side of the stalls so logically the door should lead into the wings where Sophia stood. With slightly less haste they walked to the door and turned its brass handle. It was locked.

'Damn,' Amber whispered.

They knew there must have been another way into the theatre but there was no time to look for it. Amber tried the handle again, rattling it slightly. It would not budge.

'What do we do now?' she said.

Melinda shrugged. They had come so far and were so near but it seemed they were doomed to failure. They turned to go back down the passage but as they did so there was a metal click from the door's lock and it opened. A small unkempt girl in dirty jeans and a dark sweatshirt stood with a clipboard in her hand. She held a finger to her lips to indicate the need for silence and beckoned them in.

Consulting her clipboard she pointed at a name on it and looked up at them, obviously believing they were on the list of performers. Melinda quickly nodded agreement, and the girl, apparently satisfied, nodded back.

A large black curtain separated the door from the rest of the wings. The girl went back through the curtain to a shelf that projected from the proscenium arch above which was a small lighting board to control the stage lights.

Melinda peeked through the drape to make sure Sophia could not see them, then pulled Amber through. On stage they were just in time to see the Arab extract himself from the first woman and stride up behind the second, to perform the same act on her. His hands sank into her fleshy breasts as he pressed his cock between her equally generous buttocks. Melinda heard her moan with pain then gasp with such extreme pleasure that Melinda found her own sex throbbing in empathy.

They were in time, just. But it was not the end of their problems. The moment Sophia saw them she was liable to go completely haywire and raise the alarm. Before they could tell her their story she would have them thrown out, especially if, as Melinda suspected, Aldo was lurking somewhere nearby.

There was another black drape hanging down between where they stood and where Sophia waited with Leilah. Melinda saw that to the side of the wings was a large room full of props and electrical equipment. Though the door was open it was thick and obviously intended to be partially soundproofed. If they could get her in there her initial reaction would at least be screened from the Arabs in the stalls.

Melinda whispered her plan into Amber's ear. She would come up behind Sophia and clasp her hand over her mouth while Amber grabbed her legs and they dragged her into the props room, leaving Leilah where she was for the time being.

On stage the woman's gasps had turned to little yelps of delight, like the barks of a tiny dog, each one provoked by the man's inward thrusts. They were mounting to a crescendo. There was no doubt the man was coming too, his body pumping savagely into the woman, ready to spunk at any moment. They didn't have much time.

Melinda and Amber readied themselves behind the curtain. Luckily, Sophia's back was turned towards them. Then they sprang. Melinda wrapped one arm around her body and her hand over her mouth. Amber swooped on to her legs, picking them off the floor. They carried her back into the props room, dumped her on top of a wicker costume hamper and Melinda slammed the soundproof door. Fortunately, Sophia was so taken by surprise she hardly struggled at all.

'*Mio Dio* . . .' Sophia said, gulping in air. They had knocked the breath out of her and she was having trouble getting it back. 'You!' she gasped, seeing Melinda.

'Please, you have to listen, we can explain,' Melinda said as she saw Sophia recognise Amber too.

'What have you done?' Sophia asked, regaining enough breath to form a sentence.

'I had to,' Melinda replied, hoping her sincerity would show in her face. 'You have to listen.'

'This is the end for you,' Sophia said angrily.

'Why do you think you're here?' Melinda persisted.

'That is none of your business, you impertinent slut.'

'Please, mistress Sophia.' It felt good to say those words again. 'Please, you must listen to me. You are in danger. You think you are here to entertain a client of your husband's.'

'Exactly,' Sophia snapped. 'What business is that of yours?'

'He is watching in the stalls?'

'Yes.'

'An Arab.'

'How did you know that. He's my husband's biggest client.'

'The Arab in the stalls is Leilah's master.'

'What!' Sophia's mouth fell open. Melinda could see her mind spinning as she tried to work out all the implications of that one simple statement. 'Why should I believe you?' she asked after a minute.

'Ask Leilah,' Melinda replied. 'If she doesn't confirm what we say you can do whatever you like with us. It's all a plot to get rid of you, mistress, it really is.'

'If he's her master and he'd recognised her ...' Sophia's voice trailed off, only too aware of what it would have meant.

She strode to the heavy door and opened it. They heard music. As all three women filed out into the wings they saw the red velvet curtain had been brought in and the stage manager was busy trying to free the two women from their bondage. The naked Arab passed by, his erection deflating rapidly. He let himself out of the passageway door without giving them a second glance.

Sophia rushed to Leilah. 'Help me untie her,' she said.

'What are you doing here?' Leilah asked, as she saw Melinda and Amber for the first time.

'No time to explain.'

'I want you to peek through the curtain. Tell me who you see in the stalls. Understand?' Sophia said crisply. They worked at the leather thongs that bound her to the bed but the knots were too tight. '*Scusi*,' Sophia whispered, walking up to the stage manager and plucking the knife she was using to saw at the ropes that bound the big-breasted blonde's ankle from her hand. '*Momento*.'

The stage manager hissed a sentence in Italian to which Sophia replied sharply. Obviously the girl was puzzled as to what was going on – the next act was supposed to be ready as soon as the two bound women were free. The two blondes appeared too exhausted to protest at the delay, hanging limply in their bondage, the oil on their bodies streaked with their perspiration.

Sophia returned to the bed, sliced through the thongs then pulled Leilah to her feet. She helped her over to the curtain, handed the knife back to the stage manager and opened a tiny chink in the red velvet. Leilah pulled it shut again after the merest glance.

'My master,' she said, her olive-skinned complexion whitened by surprise and fear.

'Right,' Sophia said at once. 'This way.' Melinda saw her face harden and her jaw set. There was now clearly no doubt in Sophia's mind that she had been betrayed by Bianca and her husband.

As they marched towards the passageway door the stage manager rushed towards them, speaking in rapid Italian again.

213

'*Si, si*,' Sophia said. '*Cinque minute.*' She fired off a string of sentences in Italian which appeared to placate the girl. Quickly they filed through the passageway door. 'I told her I have to get another girl, that there's been a mistake. We've got to get out before the Arabs get restless.'

They walked down the passage expecting at any second that the auditorium door would open and that Leilah would come face to face with her master. That, they all knew, would be just as disastrous as seeing her on stage. The very fact that she was in the Seraglio Club would be enough. But as they inched past the door it remained closed. Melinda thought she heard laughing coming from the stalls.

They headed along the passage into a much wider corridor which Melinda realised led straight to the lift. There were a couple of black plastic raincoats hanging on a hook in a little niche in the wall and Sophia grabbed one.

'Put this on,' she said to the naked Leilah.

They marched on past the lift and at the end of the corridor Melinda could see the salon where they had entered. But as they approached she suddenly saw Aldo, a drink in his hand, crossing the salon and selecting a chair right by the front door.

'Look,' she said at once, bringing the others to an abrupt halt. Fortunately, Aldo was busy looking at one of the girls sitting opposite him and had not noticed the activity in the corridor.

'He's in on it, yes?' Sophia asked. Melinda nodded. 'Waiting to see what happens, so he can report back. Report that I'm safely out of the way,' Sophia whispered with anger.

'I think so, mistress.'

They hurried back to the lift and hid behind it.

'That's the only way out,' Sophia said.

At that moment the lift began to descend, its mechanism clanging loudly as the big counterweight headed up and the little cubicle down. Through the grilles they saw the single occupant was a pretty short-haired redhead in a bright red basque, red stockings and red high heels. The basque had no bra and the girl's pert breasts were prominently displayed, as was her thick bush of red pubic hair.

She opened the inner door of the lift but caught her fingernail as she pulled back the outer grille. 'Blast,' she said in a very definite English accent.

Melinda suddenly remembered the money stuffed into the pocket of her dress. Without consulting Sophia she darted around the lift and caught hold of the girl's arm.

'Want to earn a little extra?' she asked, making sure she kept her back to the salon.

'Sure,' the girl said without enthusiasm. 'But I'm not into women.'

'Not with me. The man at the end there, with the shaven head.'

The redhead looked over Melinda's shoulder. 'Yes?'

Melinda took out the two notes. They must have been quite a lot of money because she saw the redhead's interest increase markedly. 'Keep him busy for ten minutes, will you?'

'What is this?'

'Just ten minutes. But don't bring him up here.' Melinda handed her the money.

'Sure, no problem.' The girl pushed the money down the front of the basque and strode off down the corridor while the four women cowered behind the iron cage. They watched as she went straight up to

Aldo. She shook her shoulders from side to side, making her breasts slap into each other, then climbed astride his lap and pushed them into his face, smothering him with them. Her hand delved down between their bodies and twisted into his lap.

Even from this distance Melinda could see the look of lust on his face. The girl got to her feet and stood with her hands on her hips, her legs open. Perhaps to encourage him further she turned her back on him, spread her legs wide apart and bent over, grasping her ankles with her wrists. Aldo stared straight into her open, red-haired sex as she wriggled her bottom. Convinced this was enticement enough, she straightened up and beckoned him to his feet with a single finger. Not waiting to see if he followed she headed down the corridor again and opened the first door she came to, disappearing inside but leaving the door open.

For a moment Aldo hesitated. He got up but stood where he was, obviously debating whether he could afford to abandon his post. Then, his decision made, he sprinted across the salon and through the open door.

'Well done,' Sophia said.

They raced out from behind the lift and down the corridor. The door through which Aldo had gone was ajar. The overseer was lying on a double bed with a pink candlewick bedspread and the redhead was sitting astride his face, her profusely-haired sex spread over his mouth as his tongue licked it eagerly. She waved at Melinda as she saw her pass by.

They got to the main salon which was full of girls and customers, all Arab. Looking at no one, Sophia walked to the front door and opened it. They all strode out into the balmy night air.

As they walked across the gravel driveway they heard footsteps running after them. Melinda hardly dared look back.

'*Signora, signora . . .*'

It was the liveried footman. Sophia stopped and he said something in Italian. She replied with a curt negative and he immediately turned and headed back into the house. Almost before the front door closed, the big wrought-iron gates began to open.

'He wanted to know if I needed a taxi,' Sophia explained. She led them around the corner of the house and Melinda saw a line of neatly parked cars among which was the master's. The keys were in its ignition. Sophia climbed behind the wheel and started the engine as the three slaves piled in, and in seconds the car swept through the gates, on to the street and away from danger.

Nine

Bianca stood at the open bedroom window. She was
dressed in a long, very tight black cocktail dress that
hugged the ample contours of her body. It was strapless, like the basque she wore underneath it, and the
huge cushions of her breasts were pressed together to
form a dark tunnel of cleavage which always drove
Giorgio, as it did most men, mad with desire. The
skirt of the dress was split almost to the hip, giving
glimpses of her thigh and the welt of the black stocking that sheathed it.

Around her neck she wore one of Sophia's silver
and diamond necklaces. She had pinned her red hair
up to show off to their best advantage the matching
diamond pendant ear-rings. Sophia's extensive range
of expensive jewellery was very much to Bianca's
taste. She had found an emerald ring that fitted her
perfectly and wore one of her watches, a solid gold
Cartier.

Unfortunately however, none of Sophia's clothes
would fit her much larger body. Nor would any of the
extensive collection of silk, satin and lace lingerie she
had discovered. Even the simplest pair of silk panties
were too small for the rolling curves of Bianca's hips.

It was a great shame, but tomorrow she would
have all the wardrobes cleared out and her own

clothes brought over. She would take Giorgio to the Via Condotti and get him to buy her outfits from Gucci, St Laurent and Valentino. She would have everything Sophia had and more.

Though it was dark there was enough moonlight to see the outlines of the garden and the wall beyond. This all belonged to her now. She had plotted and schemed for it ever since her friend Sophia had married Giorgio three years ago. Bianca had always preferred women to men but it had not been too difficult to seduce Giorgio. And, as luck would have it, she had discovered that he had an unexpected sexual secret that he had never chosen to reveal to his wife. Satisfying this need, it was not long before Bianca had him eating out of her hand, prepared to do anything for her. She had planted the seed, the idea of getting rid of Sophia, of taking her money and her house, and had watched it grow. It had surprised her how quickly he had taken the idea and made it his own.

Bianca smiled. She walked over to a small table where Giorgio had left a solid silver Georgian wine-cooler filled with a bottle of Dom Perignon champagne. She fingered the delicate filigree around its outer edge. It belonged to her now. Everything belonged to her. She refilled the tall crystal flute that stood by the cooler and sipped the delicious wine.

She was feeling in an expansive and generous mood. She would be kind to Giorgio tonight. She would allow him his pleasure. On other nights she would be less amenable. She had planned what she would do with the slaves too. There were not enough for her purposes. She would extend part of the house so more slaves could be accommodated. And she would change the regimen. The slaves would be kept separate and talking would very definitely not be allowed. They would learn to remember their three months at her establishment.

The thought made her smile. *Her establishment.*

She had toyed with the idea of going along to see the American, of giving her a taste of what was to come, or of going to see Melinda chained up in the cellars below but she had decided against it. There was plenty of time now. Tomorrow she would see them both and put them through their paces. And first thing tomorrow she would have to arrange for a replacement for Leilah, who like her erstwhile mistress would unfortunately never be seen again.

She finished her champagne, put the glass down and walked to the bedroom door. Leisurely, in no particular hurry, she strolled along the corridor admiring the pictures on the walls – her pictures – and the *objets d'art* – hers too – displayed on little stands or mahogany tables wherever there was an appropriate niche. She made mental notes of what she would keep and what she would change. The dress made a pleasant rustling sound as she moved, the silk of the skirt rubbing against the sheer black stockings.

At the bottom of the main staircase she could see her Jaguar parked outside. She turned and headed through to the back of the house, striding out into the covered walkway, its vine leaves floodlit by lamps set into the ground. When she reached the door of the punishment room she opened it quietly, not wanting him to know she had come back.

Giorgio had been stuffed into a tight leather helmet with no openings of any sort except for two small holes over his nostrils to allow him to breathe. He had been gagged with the largest ball gag Bianca could find before the helmet had been applied, and the skintight leather was distended by his bulging cheeks.

His wrists and elbows were tied tightly behind his back. His ankles were bound together by thick white rope and the binding hooked into the steel cable of an electric winch, which had been used to haul the neat package of his body up until it was dangling like a carcass of meat in a cold store, his head a foot from the floor.

Naturally, she had stripped him naked and his cock, still fully erect despite the fact that he had been in this position for over an hour, stood out at a right angle to his thighs. There was a little pool of moisture on the wooden floor underneath it where the sticky fluid it had produced had dripped to the floor; further testimony, had she needed it, that he found the treatment Bianca had subjected him to incredibly exciting. That, after all, was the secret she had discovered. He was born to be a slave not a master.

Being as quiet as she could Bianca picked up the leather whip she had left by the door. It was her favourite whip, a tapering snake of leather looped at one end. It was the whip she had used on the stupid slave who had tried to wreck her plans. She would have another taste of what it was like to be whipped by a woman in the morning and would soon discover that her first taste was only an appetiser compared to the main course.

Even on tip-toe Bianca could not avoid the sound of her footfalls on the wooden floor but the leather covering Giorgio's ears appeared to have prevented him hearing them. It was quite obvious, as she stood behind him, that he was quite unaware of her presence. That would not last long. She raised the whip and aimed it across his buttocks, already criss-crossed from the beating they had taken before she had left. In a fluid, practised stroke she brought the whip down, its thin lash cutting into his flesh, the shock of it making him rear up, his head jack-knifing up towards his feet. She heard him gasp, the noise effectively reduced to a slight murmur by the gag.

'Well Giorgio, have you missed me? Your cock's in quite a state, isn't it? Looks like it needs some attention.'

Giorgio's head nodded wildly. Bianca could see his erection pulsing vigorously. It looked red raw from being erect for so long with no possibility of relief.

'So, what shall I do?' she teased. 'Shall I leave you again?'

Giorgio shook his head with even more abandon, causing his whole body to swing from side to side. Bianca put out her hand to steady it then allowed her dress to brush against his flesh, letting him feel the silk, and pressed her big breasts into the back of his legs. His erection twitched.

'Tell me what you want,' she taunted. 'If you don't tell me I won't know, will I?'

He tried to say something, trying desperately to pronounce a word despite the enormous gag that filled his mouth, but could manage no more than a muffled groan.

Bianca raised the whip again, coming around to the front of his body and aiming at the top of his thighs. The stroke slashed down, narrowly missing his cock. Again Giorgio's head reared up in reaction.

'Answer me when I ask you a question,' Bianca snapped. Then she laughed. 'I'm going to take pity on you tonight,' she continued, in a different tone. She ran her long fingernails down his thigh, leaving a white trail in his flesh. 'Other nights I shall not be so lenient, Giorgio. Especially nights when you have annoyed me. You must learn to do exactly what I say at all times. Is that understood?'

Giorgio nodded his head.

'I am to be the master now. I will apply to the O.I.M. to replace you. And masters must be obeyed, mustn't they?'

Again he nodded.

'Good, that's very good.'

Bianca threw the whip aside. She reached behind her back and drew the long zip of the dress down. The black silk fell to the floor and she stepped out of it. The lacy black basque gripped her large body tightly and narrowed her waist, the cups of its wired bra pushing her huge bosom up and out. The equally large curves of her buttocks were unrestrained and uncovered as she wore no panties, her thick pubic hair fluffed up by the bath she had taken before getting dressed. The black suspenders strained over her thighs to hold the stockings in place.

She went to the button that operated the winch. With a whirr of motors she lowered Giorgio slightly until his shoulders and the back of his head were resting on the floor.

Bianca dropped to her knees. She found the lacing that held the leather helmet, unknotted it, then pulled the helmet off. Giorgio's face was red and wet with his perspiration. She pulled the ball gag out of his mouth and shuffled forward on her knees, opening her legs so his face was nestled between her thighs, her pubic hair against his mouth.

Carefully she folded the cups of the bra down under each massive breast, the shaft of his erection and the balls that hung upside-down over it pointing directly into her cleavage. She pressed her breasts forward then pushed them together with her hands from the sides until his whole cock was completely engulfed in the spongy, pliant flesh he loved so much.

'Well Giorgio, aren't you the lucky one?' she said as she pushed her sex down on his mouth.

They had come in two cars by the back road. Sophia and the three slaves in the first car, the four men Sophia's family had provided in the second. The men probably weren't necessary but it was possible Aldo had come back to the house and Sophia wanted to be absolutely sure she could cope with that eventuality.

They also wanted an element of surprise. The back road did not lead directly to the house but they could park the cars and take a footpath that skirted the orchard which adjoined the garden. There was a gate in the garden wall and though it was kept locked, it could be forced easily.

As soon as they were in the garden itself they saw the covered walkway was ablaze with light, as was the punishment room. Stealthily Sophia led the way across the lawns to the outbuildings with two burly men on either side of her, the other two accompanying Melinda, Leilah and Amber. They had all dressed in black to make it difficult to be seen, the women in Lycra bodies and leggings, the men in slacks and crew-necked sweaters. They had also covered their faces in black ski-masks.

Careful to avoid the large windows of the punishment room, Sophia followed the outer wall of the house until she reached the walkway. She stationed a man at the house door to prevent anyone who might be inside from getting out, then crept up to the door of the punishment room itself. Moving to her left and crouching down she stared through the small side window to survey the scene inside.

She straightened up with a broad smile on her face

which said that they could cope with the situation on their own.

'Wait here,' she whispered to the men. 'You three,' she said to the slaves, 'come with me.' She whispered instructions to them as to what they should do. 'Understand?'

They all nodded.

Sophia readied herself then pushed open the door and walked calmly into the room, followed by the other three. She tore off the ski-mask that covered her face, as did the three slaves behind her.

'Good evening, Bianca. It's a surprise to see you here.'

Giorgio's erection was still buried in her vast bosom. Her hands were grasping her breasts from the sides, forming a channel for his cock to move between as she pushed it up and down.

'He looks like he's having a good time.' Sophia said. Then she spoke in Italian, her tone of voice as cold as steel, the sentence obviously addressed to her husband.

In a flash she darted forward, caught Bianca by the shoulder and wrenched her back so she sprawled on the floor. With his face now exposed, his lips wet from Bianca's juices, Giorgio started to struggle wildly against his bonds, though he must have known there wasn't the slightest possibility of escape.

Melinda and Amber grabbed Bianca and pulled her to her feet. Before she could recover Leilah took a length of rope and bound her hands behind her back. She quickly tied her knees and ankles too, the rope wrinkling the smoothness of the black nylon stockings.

Sophia operated the switch of the electric winch, winding her husband up into the air again. She spoke to him in Italian and, from her tone of voice, was making it clear his future looked bleak. Then she turned to Bianca and moved to stand right in front of her. She pulled the diamond ear-rings from her ears and ripped the necklace from her throat.

'And I thought you were my friend,' she said, her eyes sparkling with anger. 'I was told what you were planning and I refused to believe it, do you know that?'

Leilah and Melinda were helping each other unfasten the zip that held the black basque so tightly around Bianca's body. Finally they managed to pull it all the way down and the corset fell away, releasing her quaking flesh. It pulled the stockings down with it until they were caught by the rope at her knees where it hung from the four black suspenders.

'Sophia, you've got to believe me . . .' Bianca tried desperately to think of something to say. 'It was all Giorgio's idea. I didn't know what he was going to do.'

'You bitch, it was your idea,' Giorgio shouted.

'Shut up, both of you,' Sophia commanded. 'At once.'

Bianca knew better than to continue. The lie was too obvious.

'That's better. I know the truth. And I know just what to do about it.' She looked straight into Bianca's eyes and smiled. 'You're going on a long holiday. You wanted to become part of the O.I.M. didn't you? That was your dream? Well, I'm going to grant you your wish. There's a new facility just opened and I'm going to send you there. It's for, shall we say, reluctant slaves, ones who aren't quite reconciled to spending the rest of their lives in servitude to their masters. By the end of your time there you'll beg to be allowed to come back here and serve me. And you will serve me Bianca. You will serve me long and hard, make no mistake about that.'

'You bitch,' Bianca spat, struggling against Melinda and Amber's grip.

'For that, I'm going to make sure the first thing they do when you get there is put you on a very severe diet. You'll be a shadow of your former self when you get back to me.'

Sophia stooped and picked up the leather helmet and gag that Giorgio had been wearing. Cramming the gag into Bianca's mouth before she could say another word, Sophia pulled the leather down over her head. Leilah laced it tightly at the back until the leather fitted her face like a second skin.

'Goodbye Bianca, see you in two months.'

One of the men was summoned. He heaved the bound body of Bianca over his shoulder, the basque still trailing from her knees, and carried her away.

Outside, two of the men had been dispatched to collect the cars from the back road. Bianca was bundled into the back of one of them and driven away. Giorgio, in the meantime, was dragged out of the punishment room, still bound tightly and gagged once again. He was carried to the boot of the second car. He was to be dumped in the countryside, cut off from everything he had once had, never to be allowed to see Sophia again.

Each slave was rewarded. Amber and Leilah were told that they could indulge the pent-up and mutual desire for each other that had accumulated over the many weeks they had slept together in the small bedroom. Sophia offered them complete freedom until the time they would be sent to a new master but they politely refused, preferring, they told her categorically, to

227

return to her service as her slaves. Their most profound desire would not be satisfied by freedom.

Melinda was given a different treat.

'Go and wait for me in my bedroom,' Sophia said to Melinda as the second car drove away. 'I have some phone calls to make.' One of the men had remained in case Aldo should try to return to the house. She gave him instructions in Italian and he nodded his understanding.

'Show him the way to the bedroom, Melinda,' Sophia said.

'Yes, mistress Sophia.' How good it was to be able to say those words again, she thought.

Melinda led the man up the stairs. Though it was late and an incredible amount had happened since Amber had rescued her from the cellars, she didn't feel in the least bit tired. She felt only the exhilaration of having saved herself from what was practically a fate worse than death. She had saved the honour of her first master too. Walter Hammerton, she hoped, would have reason to be proud of her.

They got to Sophia's bedroom. It looked normal enough except for a bottle of champagne in a silver cooler and one or two items of clothes carelessly thrown on the floor.

Melinda was allowed to strip off her clothes and shower in Sophia's bathroom. When she came back into the bedroom the man had taken out four leather cuffs from the top drawer of a cherrywood chest. Melinda's heart began to beat faster as he strapped each cuff around her wrists and ankles. Hanging from each was a length of chain at the end of which was a spring-loaded clip. Quickly he marched her over to the foot of the bed and attached the clips to four small steel rings, recessed cleverly into the elaborate carved bedposts so that they were all but invisible. Each post had two rings, one at the base and one well above shoulder height. With the clips attached Melinda was effectively spread-eagled between them, facing the mattress.

It was not what she had expected. Because of what had been granted to Leilah and Amber she imagined she would be sharing Sophia's bed more comfortably. But she welcomed it. After her freedom, after being forced to act for herself and make her own decisions and use her own voice, it was wonderful to feel restrained and restricted again; to be once more a submissive slave whose only duty was to obey. The bondage graphically illustrated that she was firmly back in the world of the O.I.M. To be done to not to do. The words echoed in her mind, thrilling her just as surely as the first time she had heard them.

Sophia knew her well. She knew that this was the best reward she could give her, to remind her that what she felt and thought were of no relevance and that once again all her decisions would be taken for her, even the decision as to what should be her reward.

The man left her alone. She heard the bedroom door close behind him. The house was utterly silent, the only noise she could hear the pounding of her own heart as her excitement mounted. Her legs were stretched apart but despite the fact that her labia were open and not pressed against her clitoris, Melinda felt it pulse. Her nipples were also throbbing, as puckered and stiff as they had ever been.

It was at least an hour before anything happened, an hour of feeling the familiar aches and cramps of bondage. Melinda welcomed them like old friends, so glad to be experiencing them again that even the strongest spasm of cramp brought with it a peculiar kind of joy. She was back in the O.I.M., back where she longed to be.

At some point she thought she heard a car draw up in a spray of gravel and angry voices raised but they were distant and definitely all Italian, and she could not make out what was being said. The car did not drive away again.

'A pretty picture.' Sophia's voice was calm and strong. She stood in the bedroom doorway surveying the scene, then closed the door and walked up to Melinda. Her hand stroked Melinda's back from the nape of her neck to the cleft of her buttocks. 'This *is* what you wanted, isn't it?'

'Oh yes, mistress Sophia,' Melinda said. She wanted to say more, to tell her exactly how she felt, but that was forbidden. She was a slave again, she had to remind herself.

Sophia was carrying the diamond necklace and earrings she had taken from Bianca. She put them down on her bedside chest.

'You might have heard a car arrive,' Sophia said. 'Aldo had decided to return to tell his master that we had all escaped.' She laughed. 'Fortunately, thanks to you, Giorgio knew that already, didn't he?'

'Yes, mistress Sophia.'

'I have heard there is a place where they train male slaves. Do you know if that's true?'

'Yes, mistress Sophia. The man who kidnapped me was sent there.'

'Oh good. I'm sure that seems like an appropriate punishment for Aldo, wouldn't you say?'

'Yes, mistress Sophia.'

'I shall arrange it in the morning. Meantime, I've left him in the punishment room with Leilah and Amber. They seem to know just what to do with him.'

Sophia walked into the bathroom. Melinda heard the shower running. A few minutes later Sophia returned, her long black hair wrapped in a towel turban-fashion, her slender body naked.

'You need a shave,' Sophia said, as she moved closer. As her hand felt the stubble on Melinda's mons, Melinda smelt the strong scent of the musky perfume she remembered from the first time she had seen Sophia. She inhaled it deeply, the aroma intoxicating. 'You like my perfume?'

'Yes, mistress Sophia.'

Sophia stroked her hand down Melinda's chest, squeezing the meat of her breasts then pinching her nipples. Melinda's response was out of all proportion to the stimulus. Her whole body jerked against her bonds.

'You are not to come, you understand that, don't you?'

'Yes, mistress Sophia.'

Melinda looked down at her own body, watching as Sophia's hand left the curves of her breast and slid over her belly to her labia. Her words had thrilled her almost as much as her actions. This is what she wanted, the chance to show she could be a perfect slave.

'Good.'

Sophia's finger pressed into her clitoris. It was already swollen, bursting out from between the open labia like a bud in bloom. Sophia pushed it from side to side, first with a heavy touch, then with the lightness like the touch of a butterfly's wing.

The hand left her sex. When Melinda opened her eyes again it was to see Sophia lying on the bed, stretching her hand out towards the bedside chest. She extracted the plastic vibrator from the top

231

drawer. Pulling the towel off her long black hair, which was still wet, she turned around and lay back so her head was right under Melinda's mons. Sophia spread her legs apart and ran the tip of the dildo into the lips of her hairless sex. She turned the gnarled knob at the end and the hum of vibration filled the air.

'So good,' she said. 'Feels so good against my clit.'

Slowly she slid the dildo down between her legs. Melinda saw most of it disappear into her vagina. She plunged it deep until only a little stub protruded, then closed her legs to hold it there. Reaching over her head she crooked her arms around the back of Melinda's thighs and levered her head back until her mouth was under Melinda's sex. She raised her lips and kissed Melinda's labia just as if she was kissing a mouth. Her tongue darted out and Melinda felt its heat and wetness against her clitoris.

Melinda moaned. The tongue manipulated her clitoris then descended lower, nudging against the entrance of her vagina, stretching it this way and that.

'Does that feel good?'

'Oh yes, mistress.'

'Mistress Sophia,' Sophia corrected immediately, the words making Melinda's labia tremble. Her tongue plunged into Melinda's vagina, lapping at the copious juices it found there, straining up to get as deep as it possibly could. It may have been a product of Melinda's fevered imagination but the vibrations inside Sophia's sex seemed to be so strong they were affecting her whole body, spreading outwards like the ripples on a pond. She could see Sophia's shapely breasts quivering and the hands that pressed into her buttocks carried the reverberations too. What's more, she knew Sophia had already begun the short journey to orgasm. As her lips worked tenderly at Melinda's sex, kissing it again, Melinda could see her belly undulating on the bed, moving up and down as if in response to some invisible lover.

In seconds every muscle in her body was rigid, arched off the bed like a bow, her thighs glued together, her breasts falling towards her chin.

'*Dio, Dio,*' she breathed, the words expelled against Melinda's sex.

The sight and sound made Melinda's body writhe, provoked by what she saw as much as the physical stimulation. But she did not dare come until she was given permission. This was her chance to prove herself. This was what she wanted. Though every nerve and sinew ached for release, though her bondage focused her whole world on the narrow compass of her sex and her aching clitoris that wound itself tighter and tighter in a helix of pleasure, she would not come. She would not.

Had she been allowed to speak, she would have thanked Sophia heartily. Her reward was perfect. She couldn't have asked for more. Bound tightly, she stood before the gates of heaven, waiting for the one word that would allow her through, with the exquisite delight of knowing it was not up to her whether it came at all. She was totally subjected to Sophia's whims.

Sophia's tongue, momentarily stilled by her orgasm, began again, pressing Melinda's clitoris back hard against the underlying bone, then sliding to her vagina, then licking up between the two, parting her labia and lapping at the sweet juices of Melinda's body.

It might, Melinda knew, be a very long time before her mistress finally breathed the one word that would release her from this delicious torment.

* * *

That was not her only reward. Nor was it the best, however perfect it had been. She had spent the night in Sophia's room but in the morning had been taken back to Amber and Leilah who looked as though they had barely been to sleep at all. As she bathed and the three shaved each other again, they told her of the tortures they had inflicted on Aldo before they had slaked their desire for each other.

The old woman brought breakfast as usual and it appeared that life would soon resume a normal routine. Which is what made Sophia's arrival that much more surprising.

'Put these on,' she said to Melinda. She handed her a pair of old-fashioned black nylon panties. They could only mean one thing. Melinda was being moved. 'I'm sorry to see you go. But it is a reward not a punishment. You will soon understand that.'

She was allowed time to say goodbye to the other two girls, then Sophia took her downstairs. On the first floor they walked along the corridor to the main staircase. Halfway down, Melinda could see a silver Rolls Royce parked outside the front door.

'I have to bind your hands,' Sophia said. She took a length of white cord from the pocket of the green suit she was wearing and made Melinda hold her wrists out in front of her. The cord bit deeply into her flesh, provoking a rush of feeling in Melinda's body that moistened her sex.

'Goodbye, Melinda,' Sophia said. 'I owe you everything. This is my way of saying thank you.'

She opened the front door. The chauffeur of the Rolls, in a grey suit and black boots, stood by the rear door. He opened it as soon as the front door opened, giving the near-naked Melinda not a glance. Melinda stooped to get in and it was then she saw him. Sitting in the dark blue leather upholstery of the back seat was Walter Hammerton.

'Master!' Melinda gasped in astonishment before she could stop herself.

'You're coming back home, my dear,' Walter said. 'It's all been arranged. You're coming back to me.' His eyes, the ice-blue eyes that she had seen so many times in her imagination, looked at her steadily. 'What do you say, child?'

'Oh thank you, thank you, master.' She was quite overwhelmed. She climbed into the car and looked out at Sophia, hoping her eyes expressed her true gratitude. This was her real reward and after all she had been through, she deserved it.

'Goodbye Melinda,' Sophia said again.

'You are allowed to say goodbye,' Hammerton told her.

'Goodbye, mistress Sophia,' she said, as the chauffeur got behind the wheel and the car slid, almost silently, away.

'You must stand absolutely still.' The woman's voice was full of authority, used to giving orders. She looked at Melinda as an object not as a person, just another of the many slaves that had passed through her hands. She wore a white nylon overall and her hair was tied up tightly under a white nylon cap. Her legs were sheathed in nylon leggings and she wore white rubber boots.

Two girls dressed in white one-piece swimsuits had taken Melinda into the showers and scrubbed her vigorously under a powerful jet of hot water. She had been meticulously dried and then brought to this strange room, its walls and floors completely white, lit extremely brightly by a bank of halogen lamps set in the ceiling, each angled in a different direction to eliminate even the slightest suggestion of shadow.

Made to sit on a small stool, the two girls had resumed their work on her. One had fitted her head into a tight white rubber cap, like a swimming cap but one which covered every trace of her hair. Its rubber was thick and when finally smoothed into place gave Melinda's head the appearance of having been completely shaved. Once this job was complete, the second girl carefully plucked Melinda's eyebrows until that part of her anatomy was also devoid of hair.

Both girls had worked on her face. They had applied a thick white make-up over every inch, the colour blending perfectly with the white of the cap. One had applied white mascara to her eyelashes, top and bottom, and the other a white lipstick of a consistency that would not be easily worn away.

It was only when they had left, taking the stool with them, that the older woman in the overalls had arrived. She had inspected Melinda minutely, making her open her legs so she could run her hand over her sex, and pulling up both breasts in turn to inspect her marks.

She wheeled in a spray gun, its flexible hoses attached to a powerful motor.

'Absolutely still,' she repeated as she began to spray Melinda's body, the normally tanned flesh turning instantly to white by the liquid that spread over it.

'This way, you must not be afraid.' It was the master's voice.

'But I am.' The voice was female and reflected the fear it spoke of.

'There is nothing to be afraid of. Look into my

236

eyes. Look deep into my eyes. All you see there is yourself. There is nothing to be afraid of. Nothing.'

'Nothing,' the girl said.

'There now. Open the door.'

The handle of the door moved and the door creaked slightly as it opened inward. The room was small with a single bright spotlight illuminating the dais. The dais was circular and about two feet high. On it Melinda knelt. Long white leather gloves had been drawn up her arms, almost up to her armpits. Then her arms had been pulled behind her back. There was a flap the entire length of each glove inset with white eyelets. White lacing had been threaded into the eyelets drawing Melinda's arms together from shoulder to wrist, thrusting her breasts forward. Her feet, in white six-inch high heels, were bound together by a white leather strap around her ankles and the lacing of the gloves had been tied off around this strap making it impossible for Melinda to stand, even had she wanted to.

But she didn't. She only wanted to serve, to be the perfect slave. The master, her master, had ordered her to be displayed in one of his sculpture rooms, to remain stock still, bound and painted as he required. It was in one of these rooms, perhaps this very room, that Melinda had first discovered the O.I.M. She had wondered how on earth the woman she had seen that day could stand being used in such a way. Now she understood. It was an honour. A privilege. A duty. Now she knew she only existed to serve her master's wishes.

'You see,' the master said.

The girl was young and beautiful. She wore a tight blue dress decorated with row upon row of tiny glass beads. It clung to her full breasts and her narrow waist and emphasised the flare of her hips. She had soft blonde hair and green eyes. Like Melinda, when she had first stumbled into the sculpture rooms, she was wide-eyed with astonishment. But Melinda could see her astonishment was already turning to another emotion; excitement was beginning to take hold.

'I call this sculpture "Submission",' the master said quietly. It was the perfect title. Kneeling as she was, Melinda portrayed the symbol of submission, what every slave must do before a master.

'She's . . . she's . . .' The girl could not think of what to say.

'She belongs to me, Andrea. She is my slave.'

'Slave.' Melinda could see the word sent a frisson of excitement through the blonde.

'Yes. That's what you want, isn't it?'

'Oh, Walter.'

'Look into my eyes.' He took the girl by the shoulders and turned her so she was looking straight into his deep, ice-blue eyes. Melinda knew their hypnotic power. 'I know you Andrea, I know what you want.'

'Yes, yes. I'm so excited Walter.'

'You must call me, master.'

'Master, oh master.' The word made her tremble.

'Very good.'

The girl looked back at Melinda as if to reassure herself it was not a dream.

'Now you must come with me,' the master said.

'Will I see her again?' she asked, her eyes locked on Melinda's white body.

'Oh yes, my dear, you will.'

They left the room. Melinda imagined the master taking her to his bedroom. She imagined how he would strip her and inspect her naked body for the first time, and decide how she would be bound. She

238

had seen in the girl's face how she would react, knew that the master had picked – like he had with her – a woman who would respond to the arcane world of the O.I.M. She would become a willing slave and would end up one day, as Melinda had, in the sculpture rooms, bound by more than the leather bondage that held her so tightly. She would become an object, to be done to not to do.

Melinda felt no jealousy or regret. She felt only, as she had so many times, a passionate yearning for her master to return, to give her once again the precious gift of his attention.

THE 1996 NEXUS CALENDAR

The 1996 Nexus calendar contains photographs of thirteen of the most delectable models who have graced the covers of Nexus books. And we've been able to select pictures that are just a bit more exciting than those we're allowed to use on book covers.

With its restrained design and beautifully reproduced duo-tone photographs, the Nexus calendar will appeal to lovers of sophisticated erotica.

And the Nexus calendar costs only £5.50 including postage and packing (in the traditional plain brown envelope!). Stocks are limited, so be sure of your copy by ordering today. The order form is overleaf.

Send your order to: Cash Sales Department
Nexus Books
332 Ladbroke Grove
London
W10 5AH

Please allow 28 days for delivery.

Please send me ____ copies of the 1996 Nexus calendar @ £5.50 (US$9.00) each including postage and packing.

Name: _____

Address: _____

_____

_____

□   I enclose a cheque or postal order made out to Nexus Books

□   Please debit my Visa/Access/Mastercard account (delete as applicable)

My credit card number is:

____ ____ ____ ____

Expiry date: _____

FILL OUT YOUR ORDER AND SEND IT TODAY!

NEW BOOKS

Coming up from Nexus and Black Lace

Demonia by Kendal Grahame
November 1995   Price: £4.99   ISBN: 0 352 33038 4

Hundreds of years ago, Demonia and her vampiric acolyte Sinitia struck terror into the hearts of young men and women all over the country, stalking the beautiful in order to drain them of their sexual energies. Now they have woken in the heart of modern London.

Melinda and Sophia by Susanna Hughes
November 1995   Price: £4.99   ISBN: 0 352 33045 7

In this, the fifth and final volume dedicated to the beautiful blonde submissive, Melinda enters a new domain where she is subjected to the whims of the Master's cruel, wife Sophia. Even more merciless is the courtesan Bianca, who takes an instant fancy to Melinda's youthful charms.

Serving Time by Sarah Veitch
December 1995   Price: £4.99   ISBN: 0 352 33046 5

Trapped in the House of Compulsion, Fern Terris discovers the depths and delights of discipline. The young temptress finds the touch of canes, belts and tawses opens up new realms of pleasure and the arrival of the mysterious Sonia brings her face to face with a whole new sexuality.

Lydia in the Harem by Philippa Masters
December 1995   Price: £4.99   ISBN: 0 352 33051 1

Bound for England with a complement of lusty mariners, Lydia finds herself and her all-female entourage stranded in Arabia. A charismatic local prince swiftly offers temporary shelter – in his harem – and Lydia, Tiliu, Felicity and Alice are determined to reward him for his generosity.

Rude Awakening by Pamela Kyle
November 1995   Price: £4.99   ISBN: 0 352 33036 8
When you are used to getting everything you want handed to you on a plate, abduction must come as something of a blow. So Alison and Belinda discover as they are stripped, bound, and forced to comply with the wishes of their cruel but intriguing captors.

Jewel of Xanadu by Roxanne Carr
November 1995   Price: £4.99 ISBN: 0 352 33037 6
Raised as a nomad in the Gobi desert, Cirina is used to meeting strangers. Antonio, on a quest for a Byzantine jewel, is special – but their blossoming relationship is cut short when Tartar warriors remove Cirina to the pleasure palace of the Kublai Khan.

Gold Fever by Louisa Francis
December 1995   Price: £4.99   ISBN: 0 352 33043 0
Trapped in a dull marriage in 1860s Australia, Ginny is determined nothing will stop her salacious fun. Enter her perfect match: Dan Berrigan, gold miner turned renegade. Together they strike gold – in more ways than one – but a scandal from her lewd past threatens everything.

Eye of the Storm by Georgina Brown
December 1995   Price: £4.99   ISBN 0 352 33044 9
Hired by handsome eccentric Philippe Salvatore to help aboard his private yacht, Antonia expects an easy life at sea. But it's far from smooth sailing – she must contend with a jealous wife, a dominant mother and bizarre sexual encounters, with the beautifully beguiling transsexual, Emira.

Nexus

NEXUS BACKLIST

All books are priced £4.99 unless another price is given. If a date is supplied, the book in question will not be available until that month in 1995.

CONTEMPORARY EROTICA

THE ACADEMY	Arabella Knight	
CONDUCT UNBECOMING	Arabella Knight	Jul
CONTOURS OF DARKNESS	Marco Vassi	
THE DEVIL'S ADVOCATE	Anonymous	
DIFFERENT STROKES	Sarah Veitch	Aug
THE DOMINO TATTOO	Cyrian Amberlake	
THE DOMINO ENIGMA	Cyrian Amberlake	
THE DOMINO QUEEN	Cyrian Amberlake	
ELAINE	Stephen Ferris	
EMMA'S SECRET WORLD	Hilary James	
EMMA ENSLAVED	Hilary James	
EMMA'S SECRET DIARIES	Hilary James	
FALLEN ANGELS	Kendal Grahame	
THE FANTASIES OF JOSEPHINE SCOTT	Josephine Scott	
THE GENTLE DEGENERATES	Marco Vassi	
HEART OF DESIRE	Maria del Rey	
HELEN – A MODERN ODALISQUE	Larry Stern	
HIS MISTRESS'S VOICE	G. C. Scott	
HOUSE OF ANGELS	Yvonne Strickland	May
THE HOUSE OF MALDONA	Yolanda Celbridge	
THE IMAGE	Jean de Berg	Jul
THE INSTITUTE	Maria del Rey	
SISTERHOOD OF THE INSTITUTE	Maria del Rey	

EROTIC SCIENCE FICTION

BLUE ANGEL SECRETS	Margarete von Falkensee	
CONFESSIONS OF AN ENGLISH MAID	Anonymous	
PLAISIR D'AMOUR	Anne-Marie Villefranche	
FOLIES D'AMOUR	Anne-Marie Villefranche	
JOIE D'AMOUR	Anne-Marie Villefranche	
MYSTERE D'AMOUR	Anne-Marie Villefranche	
SECRETS D'AMOUR	Anne-Marie Villefranche	
SOUVENIR D'AMOUR	Anne-Marie Villefranche	

SAMPLERS & COLLECTIONS

EROTICON 1	ed. J-P Spencer	
EROTICON 2	ed. J-P Spencer	
EROTICON 3	ed. J-P Spencer	
EROTICON 4	ed. J-P Spencer	
NEW EROTICA 1	ed. Esme Ombreux	
NEW EROTICA 2	ed. Esme Ombreux	
THE FIESTA LETTERS	ed. Chris Lloyd	£4.50

NON-FICTION

HOW TO DRIVE YOUR MAN WILD IN BED	Graham Masterton	
HOW TO DRIVE YOUR WOMAN WILD IN BED	Graham Masterton	
LETTERS TO LINZI	Linzi Drew	
LINZI DREW'S PLEASURE GUIDE	Linzi Drew	

Please send me the books I have ticked above.

Name ....

Address ....

....

....

.... Post code ....

Send to: **Cash Sales, Nexus Books, 332 Ladbroke Grove, London W10 5AH**.

Please enclose a cheque or postal order, made payable to **Nexus Books**, to the value of the books you have ordered plus postage and packing costs as follows:

UK and BFPO – £1.00 for the first book, 50p for each subsequent book.

Overseas (including Republic of Ireland) – £2.00 for the first book, £1.00 for the second book, and 50p for each subsequent book.

If you would prefer to pay by VISA or ACCESS/MASTER-CARD, please write your card number and expiry date here:

....

Please allow up to 28 days for delivery.

Signature ....